FALLING FOR THE PETTICOAT PHYSICIAN

Falling For The Petticoat Physician

By Clari Dees

Copyright © 2019 Clari Dees
Published by: Forget Me Not Romances, a division of Winged Publications
Cover Art: Cynthia Hickey

This book is a work of fiction. Names, characters, places, and incidents are the product of the author's imagination and are used fictitiously. Any resemblance to actual events, locales, or persons, living or dead, is coincidental.

All rights reserved.

ISBN-13: 978-1-959788-13-3

I

Dakota Territory
Spring, 1887

"Lady, you gonna get on my coach or not?"

Charley's gaze jerked from the mud-splattered stagecoach to the owner of the gruff voice.

Yesterday's coach driver had been a wizened old gentleman with sparse white whiskers and a gap-toothed smile, but the man checking the harnesses of the six-horse team was no more wizened than a full-grown oak. And the thick, reddish-brown beard covering the lower half of his face emphasized the annoyed scowl he leveled at her from beneath his battered Stetson.

Charley took an involuntary step backwards, but his attention shifted to the ticket agent who lugged a bulging canvas-and-leather bag out of the stage office.

"Here's the mail, Coop." The heavy pouch landed on the edge of the boardwalk with a thump, and the ticket agent jerked his head toward Charley. "And she's your last passenger."

The bearded man grunted acknowledgement and effortlessly swung the mailbag into the compartment beneath the high driver's seat, his worn leather slicker parting and giving Charley a glimpse of a pistol on his hip. "Make up your mind, ma'am. I've got a schedule to keep." He shot her a stony glance before walking around the coach to check the straps on the rear luggage compartment.

Although his broad frame and the weapon strapped to his side should've inspired confidence that he could handle any trouble that might lurk along the stage route, the impatient driver's appearance did nothing to assuage Charley's apprehension about the last part of her journey. She eyed the crowded interior of the coach again, her insides twisting. The problem that had initially caused her to hesitate hadn't resolved itself. The one remaining seat inside the wooden vehicle hadn't moved. It still faced the rear of the coach. The rattling, bumping motion of the train on the first part of her trip had been bad enough, but yesterday's stage ride from Buffalo Gap over dusty, rutted roads had nearly finished wringing out her poor stomach. And she'd been facing forwards. If she had to ride *backwards* for more than five minutes in that lurching, swaying, stomach-ache-on-wheels, a boxcar load of her mother's homemade peppermint candies wouldn't keep the contents of her stomach in their proper place.

And wouldn't that be a grand first impression to make upon her arrival in the territory she planned to call home.

Charley's nails bit into her palms. "I, uh, I don't think there's room. Maybe I'd better wait for the next one." She took another step backwards, proud that her voice didn't sound as shaky as her stomach.

"Suit yourself, Lady. Next stage is in two days." In a single, fluid movement, the brusque driver grasped the side of the vehicle and stepped onto the hub of the front wheel, heading for his seat.

The *forward-facing* driver's seat.

"Wait! May I ride with you?" The question burst out of her.

He paused, looking over his shoulder, his mouth tilted in a scowl.

If she hadn't grown immune to disapproving frowns years ago, his might've made her retreat, given the way he towered over her. But riding outside in the fresh air would be so much better than in the crowded coach that reeked of sweat and cigar smoke. And she'd actually be able to see the countryside of her new home.

She forced the tight muscles of her face into a hopeful smile and repeated the question. "May I? Ride up there beside you?"

His hat brim shaded his eyes, but she felt his gaze sweep over her from head to toe before he shook his head. "No."

Charley swallowed a scowl of her own, straightened to her full height, and stretched her smile into its most charming curve. "I promise I won't be a bother. You won't even know I'm there. I'll be quieter than a mouse."

Her stomach quivered again. Why had she said that word? It had to be the fatigue of traveling all the way from St. Louis to the Dakota Territory. On a normal day, she'd never have brought up the subject of that terrifying rodent.

"Please?" She fingered one of the small, paper-wrapped peppermints she'd tucked into her pocket before she'd left her hotel room.

Back home, her mother was rather famous for the homemade treat, and the potent herb that gave the candy its flavor also helped alleviate nausea. The hard sweets had been helpful on Charley's long journey, but she was growing heartily sick of their taste.

A flicker of irritation crossed the driver's expression, but he grunted and lowered himself to the ground then gestured for her to climb up.

"Thank you. Would you hold this please?" Charley handed him the smaller leather bag she'd refused to relinquish to the careless baggage handler earlier, earning her another frown from the curt man.

Too relieved to let it bother her, she lifted the hem of her skirt out of the way, grasped the handhold the driver had used, and stepped up on the wheel hub. Her second step onto the wheel rim was easier, but her full traveling skirt made it difficult to see the third step, and she had to hunt for the metal rung attached to the compartment below the driver's seat.

An impatient huff sounded behind her. "Lady, get movin' before I change my mind."

The warning propelled Charley upward, and she scrambled onto the hard seat and across to the left side, somehow managing to avoid the rifle stock protruding from the compartment below the bench and not fall off.

Her black leather bag landed in her lap with a thump, startling her, and she fumbled to stop it from tumbling to the ground while the driver sprang up beside her. The smooth way he settled in, scooped up the reins, and threaded them precisely through his gloved fingers contrasted sharply with her own clumsy efforts to get to her seat.

"See ya', Coop." An adolescent boy darted away from the head of the suddenly antsy team and lifted his hand in a wave.

"See ya'." The driver gave a curt nod and lengthened the reins. "Yaah!"

The horses jumped forward, taking the slack out of the harness, and the vehicle jerked into motion, slamming Charley backwards. Her feet flailed, searching for something more solid than air, and for one petrifying heartbeat, her body listed over the inadequate railing at the end of the bench. A muffled squeak squirted past her clenched teeth, and her free hand instinctively found the driver's forearm. She seized it in a desperate effort to regain her balance. She had not traveled nearly a thousand miles only to die a few miles from her destination.

The stage settled into a more predictable rocking, and Charley's feet finally landed against the footrest. She sagged against the top of the coach that created a short back rest, her panicked lungs gulping for air.

"You can let go now."

It took a second for the driver's terse words to make it past the thunder of her heartbeat. "What?"

Corded muscle flexed beneath her tightly curled fingers. "I said you can let go."

"Oh! Pardon me." She yanked her hand away and wrapped it firmly around the handle of her bag, but the imprint of his arm lingered on her palm.

A mix of nausea, fear, and humiliation at almost falling off the stagecoach coiled through her stomach, and she took several more calming breaths, inhaling deeply and deliberately.

Her heart rate gradually slowed, and her focus settled on her silent companion. His clothing bore the dusty traces of his job, but he didn't smell dirty. In fact, the only aromas her nose detected were the rather pleasant ones of leather, horse, sun-warmed earth, and maybe the faintest hint of soap.

She cleared her throat and offered a shaky smile of apology. "I'm sorry. I didn't mean to grab your arm. The abrupt start caught me off guard."

The surly man grunted but offered no other reply, and his gaze remained on the road ahead.

Suddenly remembering her earlier promise, Charley sealed her lips. If she didn't want the man to stop the coach and banish her to that cramped, smelly, rear-facing seat, she'd better prove she could be quieter than a...certain detestable rodent.

~

Cooper frowned. Why was he having so much difficulty keeping his eyes on the road? The horses knew this stretch as well as he did, but that was no reason to allow himself to be distracted. He was paid to transport his passengers, their luggage, the mail, and any additional freight safely to its destination, not to ogle the female passenger who perched nervously beside him. Not even if she was remarkably pretty and hadn't shrieked her head off when he'd urged the horses away from the stage office with more force than necessary. The ticket agent would no doubt tease him on his next trip for trying to impress the pretty lady passenger. He'd have to make it clear he had only been making up for the minutes lost while she'd dillydallied about getting aboard.

Cooper ruthlessly forced his full attention onto his job, and drumming hooves and jingling trace chains were the only sounds for several miles. If it weren't for a faint, sweet fragrance and a pair of slender, high-button boots propped near his, he could almost forget the woman sitting next to him.

The horses neared a creek, and Cooper slowed them, eying the crossing for any changes since he'd forded it earlier in the day. Everything looked all right, and he eased slack into the reins. The team surged ahead, eager to put the hurdle behind them.

His attention returned to his distracting passenger. The crossing could be a bit bumpy, and the least he could do was warn her. "Hang on."

She glanced at him as if he'd startled her before eyeing the crossing warily and bracing herself.

The team hit the shallow water with a satisfying splash, sending thousands of drops of moisture flying skyward from the coach's bumpy journey across the rocky creek bottom. The slender hand didn't return to his arm, though. Maybe he shouldn't have been so hasty to bring it to her notice earlier. Her touch hadn't been unpleasant, and it wasn't her fault he was in a rotten mood at having to deliver the newest quack to town. Indeed, a little conversation with a pretty woman might distract him from the passenger below who was bringing false hope and potential heartache to Puma Ridge.

The coach cleared the crossing, and Cooper darted a look toward the surprisingly silent woman. Water beaded the fabric of her elegant outfit, and a large drop rolled off the end of her neat, refined nose.

He hid a grin at the incongruous picture and waited for the complaints to start. She probably wouldn't believe he hadn't splattered her on purpose, but he was so used to water crossings he never gave the inevitable splashing a thought.

The older woman down in the coach set up a fuss about being sprayed through her window, her high-pitched voice carrying over the jingle of harness chains and pounding horse hooves. Cooper's dainty seat companion continued to remain silent, however. Producing a flimsy piece of lace-edged cloth from inside her sleeve cuff, she patted her face dry then dabbed at the wet spots on her skirt before catching him watching her.

He nodded toward the damp handkerchief in her hands. "Sorry 'bout that."

She shook her head. "It's all right. I appreciate the warning to hold on, though. I don't think I would have enjoyed taking a swim." Her lips stretched into a wide smile before she turned her gaze forward.

Cooper felt slightly dazed. He'd been fooling himself that she was merely pretty. That description was too shallow to describe her sparkling green eyes and laughing grin. He wanted to say something to make her look back at him so he could see that dazzling combination again, but his tongue had gone mute.

What was a fancy lady like her doing in these parts? She belonged on the arm of some wealthy easterner or one of those English bluebloods the newspapers wrote about visiting America from time to time. If he hadn't been in such a hurry to leave and been a mite friendlier, maybe she'd have been amenable to carrying on a conversation now. After all, it wasn't often a feller got the chance to drive a woman like her anywhere. Her clothing proclaimed her above the reach of a simple stagecoach driver, and it was unlikely she'd hang around this rough country long, but it couldn't hurt to talk to her.

He eyed her from beneath his hat brim while she studied the countryside. No. He'd probably trip over his tongue. It'd be wiser to simply enjoy having her beside him for a while and give her the smoothest ride she'd ever get on a stagecoach. He knew this road backwards and forwards and could avoid all but two or three of the worst of the bumps.

The miles flew by swifter than normal and quieter than he'd expected from a female. Other women—his own sister included—would be talking his ear off, but this one proved she was more than capable of holding her tongue.

The way station came into view, and Cooper slowed the tiring team, turning them toward the station house and halting them in front of it.

The horses stretched their necks, blowing and snorting, and Hank stepped off the porch to open the coach door. "Facilities are around back if you want 'em. Better hurry. Soon as a fresh team is hitched, Coop'll be on his way. He don't wait for laggards."

The warning was effective, and the passengers disembarked hastily, groaning and stretching limbs that had been cramped inside the jostling coach for nearly fourteen miles.

Cooper jumped to the ground and turned to assist the lady.

She sat eying the collection of buildings that had grown up around the stage stop in the last few years. "Is this Puma Ridge?"

"No. Puma Ridge is another thirteen miles down the road. This is the swing station."

She glanced down at him. "Swing station?"

"We change teams here but no meals are provided to the passengers."

The lady acknowledged his explanation with a single nod then slid over and twisted on the seat, tentatively reaching a foot over the side and feeling around for the first step.

"Hold up." If she came down that way, she'd get tangled up in all that skirt fabric and land flat on her face. "I'll lift you down." And maybe atone for some of his earlier brusqueness.

She shook her head. "No, thank you. I can do it." Her foot found the step, and she wrapped her hand around the brake handle and started down.

It shifted, throwing her off balance and forward.

Cooper caught her mid-fall, and she landed against his chest with a surprised puff of air. Her feminine form and her floral scent mixed with something minty that had teased his nose for the past two-and-a-half hours did nothing to slow the pulse that had leapt to a gallop when she took a header, and he held her a few seconds longer than necessary.

Dropping his hands from her slender waist, he cleared his tight windpipe. "Next time a stage driver tells you to wait, you wait."

A wide, unblinking, emerald-eyed stare was her only response, and he stomped to the pump to wet his parched gullet. A female like that should come with a keeper. Someone to stop her from getting into trouble or to at least warn an unsuspecting fellow to be on his guard. If Hank hadn't already unhitched the team and led them away before she'd disengaged the brake… Gut churning at the possible consequences of that move, Cooper returned to help Hank hitch the fresh team to the coach.

"You're runnin' behind today, Coop. Got somethin' on your mind?" Hank broke the silence while they finished up the task.

Cooper ignored the grizzled hostler's sly grin. "Two minutes is not late." He fed the end of a leather strap through a buckle then walked around the six-hitch team, running his hand along the backs of the horses. The lighter front leaders had to be the bravest because they were the first over, under, or past obstacles and real—or imagined—dangers. The middle swing horses were a little heavier to help with the pulling, but the heaviest of the horses were the rear wheelers. They had to muscle the unwieldy coach through turns along with pulling its weight. But all the horses worked hard and did it with an eagerness that would put some people to shame. The least he could do was make sure the leather straps and collars didn't rub sore spots into their sleek hides.

"You're never more than a minute late. I could set my watch by your runs. That fancy piece over there wouldn't be your 'delay', would it?" Hank's bony elbow landed in Cooper's ribs.

Cooper stepped out of range and followed the man's equally pointed gaze. His pretty seat companion appeared around the side of the station house, chatting with the other female passenger. The older woman wore a sensible bonnet and a plain wool dress covered by a man's overcoat to ward off the spring chill. The younger woman wore an elaborate get-up more suited to a sophisticated social gathering than a stagecoach ride, and her tiny, flower-decorated hat was worthless to protect its wearer from rain or sun. She made an attractive picture, but her whole getup shouted highfalutin and fragile. A fellow who worked sunup to sundown, day in and day out, scrimping and saving to get a ranch up and running would do well to heed the warning and swing wide of the velvet-lined trap.

Hank whistled long and low. "I ain't seen nothin' that purty in a coon's age."

The forthright appreciation in the older man's tone nettled Cooper. "Don't be boorish. That's a lady, and on my coach, she'll be treated with respect."

The hostler cocked a sparse gray eyebrow at Cooper. "Quit talkin' like a dictionary. I ain't bein' whatever it is you said. I stated the honest truth, and that ain't disrespectful." He stalked to the head of the team.

If it were possible to kick oneself in the seat of the pants, Cooper would do it. He had no interest in the woman besides appreciating her for the pretty passenger she was, so why hadn't he kept his mouth shut? Hank would likely be pricklier than a porcupine for the next week. Between the novel experience of a stylish woman riding on the driver's box with him and fuming about the new sawbones, Cooper's insides were twisted up six ways to Sunday. Which just proved city women were trouble.

He pulled his hat off and ran his hand through his hair before jamming it back on. Time to go. The sooner he finished this run, the sooner he could hightail it to the quiet hills of his ranch, far away from beautiful strangers and the town's welcome of the new doctor. Puma Ridge townsfolk had talked of little else since that freight wagon had delivered its load of trunks and crates of supplies to be held for the man's arrival. It galled Cooper no end that he had to be the one to deliver the charlatan. If it weren't for the lady, he'd make the next stretch of road the worst ride the sawbones had ever experienced.

"All aboard!" Renewed irritation fueled his bellow, but he got no satisfaction from the way the passengers scrambled toward the coach.

The bowler-hatted fellow who'd spent the rest stop puffing on a stubby cigar gestured for the pretty lady to enter the coach ahead of him. "There's an extra seat inside, ma'am. It'll be a pleasure to have your charming company with us. You'll relieve the monotony of this trip."

She backed up, eyeing the interior of the coach with barely concealed aversion. Then her eyes darted toward Cooper as if embarrassed that there had been an available seat inside all along. As if he hadn't known exactly how many seats there were and the ticket agent hadn't informed him exactly how many passengers he was to carry.

"Once you've picked your seat, I don't allow switching around. The lady's riding in the same place she started out. Now put out that cigar and get aboard. You're holding up my schedule." He hustled the slick dandy into the coach and latched the door with a firm click, ignoring the snort from Hank at his spur-of-the-moment switching-around rule.

If Cooper was a betting man, he'd put money on the fact the cigar smoker was the new doctor.

Interrupting the lady's attempt to juggle her cumbersome skirt and the handholds on the side of the stage, Cooper wrapped his hands around her waist and boosted her up. She wasn't tiny, but he regularly toted loads a lot heavier, and getting to grasp that willowy waist again was no hardship.

When she'd gained the seat and slid over, he sprang up after her. She'd relinquished her small leather satchel into the front boot before dismounting earlier and now grasped the seat rail beside her.

Hank stepped away from his position at the head of the team. Cooper tightened the reins until he felt the horses' mouths then lessened the tension and made a clicking sound between his tongue and teeth. The team stepped into their harnesses with much less of a jolt than the previous departure. He caught the lady's quick glance of surprise out of the corner of his eye when he swung the horses toward the road. Instead of commenting, though, she pinched her lips together and looked away.

Her restraint tweaked his growing curiosity, and when they reached the main road, he spoke. "Go on. You proved you won't talk my ear off, what is it?"

She exhaled. "I wanted to thank you for letting me ride up here again. I was dreading sitting down there in that awful, stuffy space." She pressed a gloved hand to her mouth, but it didn't hold back the words. "I'm sorry. That sounded rude. Your stagecoach is perfectly nice." Her apology spilled out like someone had pulled the plug from the bottom of a full water barrel. "I just—"

"I don't like riding down there, either." Cooper interrupted her apology.

Her hand dropped to her lap, uncovering a reassured smile that was directed straight at him. After several seconds, he managed to drag his gaze back to his team and the road, but his focus remained stubbornly fixed on his pretty passenger.

II

"It's beautiful here." Charley tried to absorb every inch of scenery the stagecoach rolled through. "I grew up on the edge of the Ozark Mountains, but they looked nothing like these mountains. And they're even more striking after the miles of flat, open plains the train crossed to bring me here. It's so good to see trees again. I've been missing them. A lot of them appear different from what I'm used to, though. What are the ones with the white bark?"

"Birch and aspen." The driver's forward focus didn't waver, but Charley suspected his sharp eyes didn't miss a single detail of either the passing scenery or his talkative passenger.

The thought was a bit disconcerting, and she returned her attention to the mountain range surrounding them. "What are the darker green trees?"

"Pine and spruce."

The man's answers were short and to the point, and he might be sorry he'd ever given her permission to talk, but despite her continuing chatter and barrage of questions, or maybe because of it, his gruffness softened. The only question he didn't answer was why the new team hadn't left the swing station like they'd been shot out of a canon, but that was probably because he spotted an elk in the distance at that moment and pointed it out to keep her from missing it.

Charley breathed in a deep lungful of the fresh, clean air, untainted by the smoke and cinders of the train. The light breeze on her face and the beauty of her surroundings was proving a better tonic than a whole handful of peppermint candies. Although it was cooler than it had been when she'd left St. Louis, the bright sunshine made the spring day mild and pleasant. And the high, tree-covered hills interspersed with exposed granite outcroppings seemed to block the stiff prairie winds that had buffeted the train, fought the pins for Charley's hat, and tugged her skirt at every station stop.

The closer they got to Puma Ridge, though, the more her nerves jangled. She might currently sound like a magpie, but channeling her energy into learning whatever she could about her new home quelled some of her mounting anxiety. There was a chance that her new home would reject her and send her packing, but she didn't intend to go without a fight. Thus, it would be smart to stop wasting her time on the flora and fauna around her and learn about the human inhabitants of the area, starting with the man beside her. If they were all as taciturn as him, she'd have her work cut out for her.

She shifted her attention to him. The parts of his face that she could see were pleasant in spite of their stern cast, but his hat and beard made it difficult to guess his age. He was taller than she by almost a head, which made him over six feet tall, and the shoulders that stretched his duster were broad and powerful. In the past, when someone assumed she couldn't handle the duties of her chosen profession, she'd wished she'd been blessed with a taller, sturdier frame, but that didn't mean she was feather light. Yet the man had lifted her up to the high seat like she weighed nothing. And he'd easily caught her when she'd fallen while trying to climb down. He also handled the six big horses as effortlessly as if he controlled nothing more substantial than a frisky puppy.

Responding willingly to his quiet encouragement, the team topped a long rise, and Charley got a bird's eye view of a small town.

"Is that Puma Ridge?" Her heart beat a little faster.

"Yep." Setting his foot against the brake lever, the driver slowed their descent, but the coach still rocked and bucked down the rutted slope to Charley's new home.

Tucked against the base of a long rocky ridge that had probably given the town its name, Puma Ridge looked miniscule compared to

St. Louis, but according to what she'd learned from her correspondence with the mayor, the little western town was growing rapidly due to the lumber, mining, and ranching prospects in the area. The town even boasted its own newspaper.

Charley sucked in a deep breath and straightened her spine as much as possible on the jostling seat. Standing on the threshold of obtaining her dream was no place to give into fear. God had given her the strength and a way through or around every obstacle in her path so far. There was a great need in the west, and if Puma Ridge didn't want her then she would find somewhere else to put her skills and training to use in the ever-expanding west.

"The next stage back to the train station doesn't leave until day after tomorrow, but a stage leaves in the morning for points west and north."

Charley's flurry of nerves eased as a spurt of humor shot through her. She'd asked so many questions the reticent stage driver had started offering unsolicited information. "Thank you, but I'll be staying in Puma Ridge." The statement earned her a brief sideways glance she couldn't read.

Two shaggy, ill-mannered dogs ran out to snap and bark at the wheels when the coach rumbled down what looked to be the town's main street. Weathered wooden buildings stood shoulder to shoulder with newer structures along several crisscrossing streets, and Charley realized the town was larger than she'd first thought.

A white two-story building with a scrolled-letter sign declaring it to be the Puma Ridge Hotel came into view, and the driver guided the horses to a stop in front of it. Almost before Charley could blink, a small crowd gathered on the boardwalk below her, between the stage and the hotel entrance.

A portly, middle-aged man in a bowler hat, round spectacles, and gray coat stepped to the front of the gathering. He hooked his thumbs in the pockets of his flashy red vest and squinted up at the driver. "Did you bring our new doc, Coop?"

Charley stilled, unwilling to betray by so much as a blink the way her insides jangled and jounced like the stagecoach over rocky roads.

The driver looped the reins around the brake handle. "I assume he's inside the coach, Mayor."

Charley wouldn't have thought it possible to stomp down the

side of the tall vehicle, but the driver accomplished it.

He frowned up at her when he reached the ground. "You'd better come off on my side again. It'll be easier than trying to get through that crazy mob." He jerked his head toward the crowd on the left side of the coach.

Charley slid across the seat. It *would* appear more dignified to announce her arrival after her feet were firmly planted on solid ground.

He reached up for her, and she leaned down and put her hands on his shoulders to let him help her to the hard-packed dirt street. The dismount was considerably more graceful than her last, and she felt surprisingly safe when the work-stained, unshaven man encircled her waist with his large hands and gently lifted her down.

She retreated from the unsettling sensation and cleared her throat. "Thank you for your assistance." It was only her continuing attack of nerves that suddenly made her not want to leave his gruff company.

"Coop, get over here!" The mayor didn't try to disguise his irritation.

The driver's scowl deepened, but he touched the brim of his hat politely. "Your baggage will be unloaded shortly. Let someone in the office know where you want it delivered." Turning on his heel, he stalked around the groom standing at the head of the team.

Charley brushed off her skirt—and the sensation of abandonment—and straightened the fitted jacket of the travel ensemble she'd chosen to arrive in. She'd chosen it in the hopes it produced the right combination of elegance and competence. Clothes didn't actually make the man—or woman—but they often unlocked the door of opportunity, and she'd take every advantage she could get.

Pulling off a glove, her bare fingers checked the placement of her hat and smoothed the stray hairs that had slipped from their confining chignon. A mirror would be nice, but since that didn't appear to be standard equipment on the side of stagecoaches, she'd have to go like she was.

Heavenly Father, thank you for bringing me this far. Help me through the next few minutes, please. And don't let this opportunity slam shut simply because I wear a skirt rather than trousers.

Licking her lips, she swallowed hard, drew her glove back over her hand, and followed in the driver's steps, nodding to the young man who held the team steady while another man unloaded the baggage.

The mayor peered into the interior of the vehicle. "Where is Dr. Adams, Coop? Your passengers say he wasn't on the coach with them."

"If a passenger has a ticket, they ride. I don't ask for names." Cooper stepped onto the wheel hub, reached into the boot, and tossed the mailbag to the ground with a hard thump.

The men at the front of the small gathering jerked backward to keep their feet from being in the line of anything else the surly driver decided to toss down.

"Cooper Knight, you *know* how vital a doctor is to the future of our town. You should have ensured he was on board before you left!" The mayor's face matched his scarlet vest while he scolded the unheeding driver who jumped to the boardwalk holding Charley's bag in his free hand. "You'll just have to go back and get him."

Pinning her imperturbable, smiling armor in place, Charley planted her feet on the boardwalk and used the tone that had routinely carried over the noisy, ribald jokes and insults of her fellow medical students. "That won't be necessary, Mayor Hennessey."

The murmuring crowd hushed and eyed her curiously.

Cooper Knight didn't move, but Charley felt his gaze boring into her.

Mayor Hennessey snatched the hat off his balding head. "Good afternoon, ma'am. You have the advantage of me. And you might be?"

Charley inclined her head. *Here goes nothing. And everything.* "I am Dr. Adams."

The words splashed into the silent pool of people like a rock. Ripples of surprise spread through them, bounced off the edges, and returned to the center in an increasing confusion of startled stares, gasps, and whispers.

Shock twisted the mayor's face into a comical expression, but Charley didn't feel like laughing. Her eyes darted to Cooper. He hadn't reacted with the rest of the crowd, but his motionless silence was somehow more ominous. Whatever friendliness had grown between them over the last few hours had disappeared, and now he radiated hostility. With the pistol peeking from beneath his duster and his hands curled into tight fists at his sides, he looked like the town's watchdog. Waiting and watching for the slightest signal to dispense with the unwanted intruder.

Charley stiffened her spine. She'd faced down an entire medical school full of contemptuous men. If she couldn't handle one grumpy stagecoach driver and a small, curious crowd, it was time to turn in her medical license. But why should she care about his opinion? He was merely the stagecoach driver. Any future dealings with him would occur only if she gave up and ran home to her parents. Something she had absolutely no intention of doing.

"But you're a...a...woman!"

She jerked her attention back to the stuttering mayor.

"You always did have a knack for stating the obvious, Hennessey." A smartly dressed gentleman to the right of the mayor spoke up. He pulled off his hat, uncovering a thick shock of salt-and-pepper hair, and another ripple spread across the crowd when the other men belatedly pulled off their own headgear. With the exception of Cooper Knight whose hat remained firmly untouched.

"I'm Ned Farnsworth, owner and editor of the Puma Ridge Gazette. I'm afraid there's been some mistake." His words were polite but held a hint of bemusement. "The doctor we sent for is Dr. *Charlie* Adams. A man."

Charley slid her hand into the pocket of her skirt and pulled out three folded papers. "I am Dr. Charley Adams of St. Louis. Here is your last letter to me, a letter of introduction from Dr. Tidd, my mentor and a well-respected St. Louis physician, and my diploma from medical school which allows me to legally practice medicine here according to the law passed by the Dakota Territorial legislature in 1885." She handed the documents to the mayor.

"Who names a woman *Charley*?" A gravelly voice in the crowd mumbled.

The speaker might not have expected an answer but she gave it anyway, keeping her imperturbable smile firm. "My full name is Charlotte, but I've been called Charley since I was a little girl."

"Why didn't you explain in your correspondence that you were a woman?" Mr. Farnsworth ignored the papers the mayor studied.

"Being male or female has no bearing on whether or not a person is a capable physician. If it did, you would have asked for that information along with my qualifications." She heard a few scattered chuckles from the women present. "Now, if you'll show me the building you said would be available for my use, I'd like to set up my office as soon as possible. I know you've been without a regular doctor for nearly a year, and I'm sure there are people who need my services without further delay."

Given the fact it was a free country and they couldn't actually toss her back on the stage, she shouldn't be having trouble maintaining her calm façade. It wasn't like this was the first time she'd ever had to be prepared for all arguments and stand her ground. But for a motionless statue, Mr. Knight was doing an amazing job of unnerving her, looming large and tight-lipped in her peripheral vision.

The mayor grimaced like he had a bad case of indigestion and returned her diploma and the two letters. "There's, uh, been some difficulty with that. We don't have a suitable place for you after all."

"Where did the previous physician house his practice?" Charley calmly folded the papers and returned them to her pocket, sweetening her question with a smile. Despite his noisy bluster when he'd thought the new doctor hadn't arrived, her unexpected revelation had badly flustered Mayor Hennessey.

"Uh, well, you see…" He sputtered to a stop.

Mr. Farnsworth broke in smoothly. "We were in the process of purchasing a newer building, but the sale fell through last week. The way the town is growing, buildings are at a premium, and we've been unable to procure anything else." His explanation was apologetic, but he offered no solution to the problem.

"I don't need a new building. I'll be happy with whatever the previous doctor used, if it's available."

"Well, it *is* empty, but—"

"That building is rundown and filthy." Mayor Hennessey interrupted. "Maybe it would be better if you moved on over to Wyoming. They let women vote and probably won't have a problem with a woman doctor." There was no malice in his tone, but the way he eyed her suggested he preferred a male physician for his town.

Charley didn't flinch. "That *is* unfortunate. If Puma Ridge is growing like you say, then you need a doctor." If they thought she'd quit without a fight, they had a second thought coming. Besides, they hadn't hired her, so they couldn't dismiss her. They'd simply advertised in eastern papers for a well-educated physician willing to locate to a growing western town. If worse came to worst, she'd pitch a tent.

After she purchased one.

Acting on a half-formed idea, she turned. "Mr. Knight, I'm sure you meet a lot of people in your profession. Do you know of an empty building suitable for a doctor's office?"

"No." In less time than it had taken to utter his terse refusal, he scaled the side of the coach and unwrapped the reins from the brake handle. Without another word or glance her direction, he clucked to the team, and empty coach and driver disappeared around the corner of the hotel.

Charley clenched her teeth. The man hadn't exactly been a friendly face, but she'd grown comfortable with him on the trip and now he'd left her in unfriendly territory without even a farewell. But it was probably better that way. Depending only on herself and God made her stronger. And that way she wasn't hurt when people she thought were friends—or something even closer—turned tail and fled.

"Well then, gentleman. Terrible shape or not, sounds like it'll have to be the former doctor's office until something better becomes available." She looped her arm through Mayor Hennessey's elbow and feigned a bright smile. "Shall we go check it out?"

~

Cooper led his horse onto the main street after turning over the stage and team to the company's hostlers and eyed the curiosity seekers milling around the front of the old doc's place. If he wasn't still reeling over the fact the lady he'd hauled beside him for twenty-seven miles was the new sawbones, Mayor Hennessey's consternation would be laughable. Cooper'd warned the man he risked bringing another charlatan to town, but the mayor and his cronies had persisted with their advertising. And now look what they had. A female masquerading as a physician.

That dainty, overdressed piece of femininity didn't appear tough enough to withstand a stiff breeze, and she thought she could be a doctor? What medical school allowed women to attend anyway? Especially one who looked like she'd stepped off the pages of the Godey's Lady's Book Hannah enjoyed looking through.

But maybe the woman hadn't attended a school. Maybe one of those new mail-order catalogs now sold diplomas to anyone with ready cash—they seemed to sell almost everything else.

Miss Adams walked around the side of the rundown building, her hand looped through Hennessey's arm, leading the man around like a bottle-fed, orphaned calf. Cooper's teeth collided in a grinding scrape. How many faces did this woman with a man's name have? She was silent on the first half of the trip, a bright, cheerful chatterbox on the last half, a refined but distant ice maiden when announcing her unheard of profession, and now she charmed the town council like a snake oil salesman, blinding them with flattering smiles and promises of health.

And he, Cooper Knight, had been the one to deliver the conniving female. Made a man want to do something to atone for such a foolish act. Like bang his head against a rock.

Dr. Adams might bamboozle the town council with her papers and captivate them with her beauty, but he doubted any of them would actually *use* her services. Oh, a few women might try her—if she lasted that long. But one glimpse inside that filthy abode the previous doctor had called an office, and she'd hightail it out on the next stage. If he had the misfortune to drive her again, she'd sit *inside* the coach and enjoy the worst ride she'd ever experienced.

Cooper vaulted into his saddle without the aid of the stirrup and turned his mount toward home. He'd known a new doc was a bad idea. He just hadn't realized *how* bad.

If Ma Jankins decided to call herself a doctor, nobody'd think anything of it. That woman had delivered so many babies and nursed so many sick folks, she was more of a physician than old Engstad had ever been. And she didn't cut somebody open every time they had an ache or a pain.

He jammed his hat tighter on his head. What was it about physicians that made them eager to pull out a scalpel and slice people open to see what was wrong? And why did people trust sawbones simply because they had a piece of paper saying they'd graduated some unknown school somewhere? He had nothing against women doing a man's work, some of them were downright tough and could outwork a man seven days of the week. But doctors in general, and that female in particular... He didn't trust any of them any further than he could spit.

Cooper urged his horse into a gallop. With one full day before his next stage run and enough work waiting to fill a week, he was more than ready to put the town and doctors, male *or* female, far behind him.

III

Charley hefted the heavy bucket with a groan she didn't attempt to stifle. There wasn't anyone around to hear, after all. The town may have advertised for a doctor, but they sure didn't seem to actually *want* one. She hadn't had a single patient or even a curious visitor since her arrival. She'd won her first victory, though. It had taken every ounce of charm she owned to sweet talk the mayor into *letting* her rent the filthy building she now called hers, and they were clearly unhappy about her gender, but she had her foot in the door. And enough sheer determination to force it the rest of the way open. *After* she finished cleaning the rubbish bin she'd rented. The town council should pay *her* for voluntarily tackling the mess.

From the outside, the six-room house looked solid, but a broken window in the back had allowed small critters free access, and cobwebs, dirt, and droppings of things she didn't want to identify had greeted her open entry. The building's rundown interior had been a convenient tool for the skeptical town council to use to discourage her from staying, but she'd won the minor skirmish. Once clean, the building would be perfect for her needs. It had plenty of space for a tiny office or waiting room, an examination room—that, wonder of wonders, had an indoor pump and sink—a room for any patients that might need overnight care, and private quarters for herself of a bedroom, kitchen, and small parlor. And until the place was scrubbed, repaired, and in order, she had a room in the hotel to retreat to each evening.

A weary chuckle huffed out. She'd trained to be a doctor and studied and worked to become a good one, yet all her efforts had led to this. A glorified scrubwoman. She'd naively supposed the biggest hurdle she'd have to face would be overcoming the distrust of a female physician. Instead, survival had become her main goal.

Throwing the dirty mop water off the side of the front steps, she gingerly stretched her aching back. If there was a single inch on her person that didn't hurt after four days of non-stop scrubbing, she hadn't found it yet. Yesterday morning, she'd almost pulled the covers over her head when a nearby rooster had started crowing, but her arms were too sore to go to the effort. Scouring away the layers of grime that hinted the previous physician was a poor housekeeper, chasing down spiders, driving out the birds who'd taken up roost inside the house, and cleaning up after a persistent rodent that kept leaving droppings on her cleaned floors was worse than the aloof stares and whispered conversations she encountered when she'd ventured to the mercantile for supplies. She'd grown used to unkind opinions concerning her gender and profession, but dealing with mice? She'd rather dissect a week-old cadaver. Thankfully, she hadn't actually seen one of the nasty rodents during her cleaning campaign, merely the evidence they left behind. When she got to heaven, she fully intended to ask God why He'd seen the need to create mice and rats. Personally, she saw absolutely no reason for their existence.

The jingle of chains and thud of hooves signaled the stage's arrival down at the hotel, and Charley leaned against the doorjamb to watch the passengers disembark. Monday, Wednesday, and Friday, the stagecoach left town at six in the morning and returned at five in the evening. She'd been exhausted after her day and a half of stage travel from Buffalo Gap to Puma Ridge, but Cooper Knight spent around eleven hours on that hard, unforgiving seat every other day. No wonder he'd been irritated at her for holding up his departure. He'd already had a long day before she'd met him.

Charley inhaled deeply, pushed away from the doorframe, and slowly walked inside. She'd had a long day, too, but she had a few more things she wanted to accomplish before she returned to the hotel for the night.

A flapping sound came from her freshly mopped parlor, and she entered the room in time to see a bird fly out of the fireplace with a poof of soot dust. Dropping the empty scrub bucket to the damp floor, she glared at the feathered intruder who landed on the mantle like it owned the place. She'd had the broken window repaired, but she hadn't realized the top of the chimney wasn't bird-proof.

"Enjoy it while you can, you persistent pest. Your boarding house closes today."

She opened the two windows in the sitting room and propped open the front and back doors to encourage the bird to take its leave before hurrying outside to her barn. She'd noticed a ladder inside the small outbuilding when she'd first explored her plot of ground. It was somewhat weather beaten but appeared sturdy enough to hold her, and Charley dragged it to the house and propped it against the eave.

After finding a piece of scrap lumber and a good-sized rock, she gathered up her apron into a makeshift pocket and tucked the items inside before gripping the hem between her teeth and carefully climbing to the roof. Once both feet were on the sloping surface, she gingerly made her way to the chimney and put the narrow brick structure between herself and the edge of the roof. Then she laid the board over the opening, and set the rock on top to hold it in place. She released the hem of her apron from her teeth and grinned in satisfaction. The board was wide enough to cover the hole, and until she got it properly capped and needed to use the fireplace—which wouldn't be soon since there was a separate stove in the kitchen with its own metal pipe out the back wall—it should protect her house from any more unwelcome visitors.

Taking her time, Charley eased back down the roof. A mischievous giggle made her pause, and she watched in disbelief as the top of her ladder slid sideways and disappeared from view. "Hey! My ladder!"

More snickers followed the thud of it hitting the ground, and Charley shuffled down the slope as fast as she dared. "Who's there?"

Sinking to her heels near the edge, she peered down. There was no one in sight, and her ladder lay flat and useless on the ground. She hadn't imagined the giggles, though. Had someone knocked it over on purpose?

Charley plopped onto her bottom. Wouldn't the townspeople love to see this predicament? The female doctor trapped on her own roof like a foolish kitten. She eyed the distance to the ground. It was far enough down she didn't want to attempt the drop unless absolutely necessary. At the moment, no one could see her because she'd climbed up on the back side of the house, but she'd have to get somebody's attention if she didn't want to risk breaking an ankle.

Then again, a broken bone would give her a break from scrubbing windows, walls, and floors.

~

Cooper shoved his hat brim up, not believing his eyes. What was that crazy female doing to her chimney? If she lost her balance, she'd fall and possibly break her neck. There might even be rotten places in the roof she could fall through. Who knew the last time anybody had checked it over thoroughly?

The woman disappeared below the peak, and he shook his head. It wasn't his problem, and he needed to get home. She'd gotten up there by herself, and he was starving and wanted his supper.

Three half-grown boys exploded around the corner of the doctor's house, glancing over their shoulders as they sprinted away.

Cooper groaned under his breath and started across the street when he recognized one of them. Benji had obviously overheard his tirade to Hannah about the new sawbones and decided to participate in some mischief against her. Doctor or not, though, Cooper couldn't handle someone else getting hurt if there was anything he could do to prevent it. He'd make sure the woman made it down safely, and then after he'd had a discussion with his scamp of a nephew, he'd be able to seek his supper with a mostly clear conscience.

He rounded the rear corner of the woman's house, and every last drop of spit disappeared from his mouth. A dilapidated excuse of a ladder lay on the ground, and Miss Adams scooted her backside ever closer to the edge of the roof, her heels inching past the eave.

"Stop!" His sharp command halted the woman's movements.

"Mr. Knight." Miss Adams straightened her skirt over her knees then folded her hands primly across her lap and eyed him politely. For all the world like she sat in church instead of perched on her housetop like some outlandish bird, her feet dangling over thin air.

"How nice to see you again."

"Lady," Cooper swallowed the urge to bellow and lowered his voice. "Are you trying to break your fool neck?" He crept closer, silently willing her to stay still until he was close enough to catch her if she slipped.

"The name is Dr. Adams, if you please." A cool smile graced her face.

He frowned. The dispassionate, regal woman who'd introduced herself to the town council was back in full force.

She shifted her weight.

Cooper flinched and threw up his hands. "Sit still! What are you doing up there anyway?"

"Would you retrieve my ladder, please? Our conversation will be more comfortable when you don't have to strain your neck looking up at me."

He eyed the trim, booted ankles peeping beneath the damp hem of her faded brown skirt. The roof wasn't terribly steep, and when she wasn't wiggling around, she didn't look to be in immediate danger of falling. "I'll get it after you promise not to climb up there again."

She tilted her head. "But what if something else needs fixing?"

"Get a *man* to tend to it." He growled impatiently.

Her brow lowered, and he caught the barest hint of a scowl before a worrisome gleam popped into her eyes. "A man?"

What kind of dumb question was that? "Yes."

"Like you?" Her face and tone were bland. Like she had simply inquired the time of day.

"Yes." This was the strangest conversation he'd ever had. And the most neck wrenching.

"All right, Mr. Knight. I promise to stay off the roof, if you'll fix what I can't."

"Now, hold on a minute."

"Don't worry. I'm not expecting you to do it for free. I'll pay for your services." Her smile reappeared, but it didn't reach her eyes. "Since that's settled, would you retrieve my ladder, please? I need to make sure the bird is out of my house before I go to supper."

"Bird? Never mind. Don't move. I don't want you slipping and falling while I'm out of reach." Keeping his eye on the confusing woman, he picked up the ladder and set it against the roof in self-defense. Miss Adams could change topics quicker than a man could blink, and if he didn't get her down, there was no telling what she might bamboozle him into next.

Lord, I don't need another person to keep an eye on no matter how much she might need a keeper. I've already failed too many times.

The splintery wood of the ladder pricked at his fingers, and he glanced up to warn the woman about its weak condition, but the sight of a slender, stocking-clad calf and lace-edged petticoat dried up the words. He yanked his gaze down, and stepped to the side, trying to erase the distracting image from his mind.

Miss Adams descended slowly, chattering about the unwelcome guests using her chimney to gain entrance and seemingly unaware of his consternation. He kept a steadying hand on the rickety frame and nearly sighed in relief when she reached the last rung, but the emotion snagged in his throat when the crosspiece creaked and split in two with a nerve-pinching crack.

His hands flew out to catch the woman, but she caught her balance quicker than a cat and scooted out of his reach before his fingers did more than graze the fabric at her waist.

"I'm glad you decided to put that end at the bottom." She calmly wiped her hands on her apron, eying the broken piece with amused annoyance.

Cooper sucked in air. Did the fool woman not know how close she'd come to breaking her neck?

Without a word—he couldn't have gotten it through his clenched teeth anyway—he carried the ladder to the property's weathered outbuilding. Wedging the end between it and a sturdy, rooted stump that had been used for a chopping block, Cooper gave the dangerous ladder a vicious jerk. The dry wood splintered with sickening ease, and he tossed the broken halves onto the remaining woodpile.

"Why did you do that?" A baffled expression replaced Miss Adams' reserved smile, but at least the new expression looked genuine.

"I'm keeping someone else from risking their fool neck." He dusted off his hands, glancing down when a sharp sting shot through his palm.

The blunt end of a thick splinter protruded from the heel of his right hand.

He scraped at it with his thumbnail, but the one piece of unrotten wood on the whole ladder had driven deep into the calloused skin of his hand and refused to budge. Thoroughly annoyed, he reached for his knife to dig it out.

Slender fingers caught his wrist, stopping him. Stepping closer, Miss Adams probed at the splinter with a soft touch that froze him in place. A sensation as unlike the sting of the splinter as velvet from barbed wire ran up his arm, and he stared at the handkerchief-covered head bent over his hand. Blonde wisps escaped the white, confining cloth and fluttered in the breeze, caressing her neck and ears.

A sharp prick brought him to his senses. "Ouch!"

A stronger grasp than he would have expected from a forearm half the thickness of his own kept his hand firmly in place. "Hold on. Let me make sure I got it all."

She poked and prodded and inspected it for several more seconds before finally releasing his hand and looking up with a smile. "All done." She held up a pair of sharp tweezers that grasped a sliver of wood. "I have some ointment inside that will help prevent infection." She blew the splinter away and returned the tweezers to her apron pocket before looking up at him with an inviting smile.

Cooper couldn't remember seeing a combination of green eyes and blonde hair before meeting the disturbing woman, but it sure was beautiful. She was beautiful.

And dangerous to his peace of mind.

He shoved his hands into the safety of his pockets and stepped around her. "No. I need to go. Stay off roofs from now on."

Her fingers brushed his sleeve. "If you'll step inside, it'll only take a second."

And have her claim he was her first patient? Absolutely not. He lengthened his stride and didn't look back.

"At least go wash your hands with soap and water, please."

Her resigned plea spurred on his swift escape, and he didn't relax until he reached the safety of his ranch. His beliefs hadn't changed. In fact, they'd been reconfirmed. Doctors were dangerous. *Especially* when they wore petticoats.

~

The pastor's greeting was warm and kind when Charley reached the open double doors of the white clapboard church building Sunday morning. But when she stepped inside, the instant silence, and wide-eyed attention of the other worshipers displayed the townsfolks persistent uncertainty over how to treat the female physician in their midst.

Charley pinned an unperturbed smile into place and headed for an open pew, drawing up short when a feisty, gray-haired woman whirled into her path two steps later.

"Good morning! I'm Mrs. Jankins. But you can call me Ma. I've been eager to meet you, but I'm the local midwife, and a couple of stubborn babies have kept me hustling between farms on opposite sides of town, waiting for their appearance." The woman's wide grin held no hint of censure or reserve about Charley's profession. "I want to have a good long chat with you, but I see Pastor Schwartz is heading for the front so it'll have to wait, but come sit with me." Without waiting for an answer, the woman shepherded Charley to a pew.

"Thank you." Feeling welcome for the first time since her arrival in Puma Ridge, Charley slid into place and looked around while the congregation sang the opening hymn.

The cozy building wasn't large or handsomely appointed like the one she'd attended in St. Louis, but the enthusiastic voices raised in song reminded her of Sundays back home. Her throat tightened, preventing her from adding her voice to the familiar tune. She'd overslept and missed last week's service, exhausted from her cleaning frenzy, and the intervening days had been spent working through the stacks of various-sized crates she'd shipped ahead of her to furnish and supply her office and living quarters. All while waiting in vain for patients.

She'd introduced herself to all the business owners in town, letting them know she was available for service. The newspaper had even included a notice about the arrival of the new female doctor in town, but whether Editor Farnsworth was being helpful or warning people away remained to be seen. It would take a while for folks in the community to grow accustomed to the idea of a woman doctor, but the reality of waiting was beginning to wear thin, and she needed activity to stave off her growing homesickness. She didn't wish illness or injury on anyone, but accidents, sickness, and disease were an inevitable part of life, and she simply wanted to be the one helping those afflicted by them.

The singing ended, and Charley opened her Bible to follow along with the pastor's sermon on the eighth chapter of Romans. He was a good speaker and easy to listen to, but when he reached the twenty-fifth verse, the words seemed to leap off the page at her, and she lingered, reading them over several times.

But if we hope for that we see not, then do we with patience wait for it.

By the time Pastor Schwartz closed his message with prayer, peace had replaced Charley's impatient frustration of the last week, and she added her own silent petition. *Lord, thank you for encouraging me today. Help me to practice patience while I wait for...patients.*

A real smile reached her lips. God had lightened her heart, and she was refreshed and ready to face the new week. Whatever it held. Or didn't.

"Would you join me for lunch?" Mrs. Jankins laid her hand on Charley's arm, stopping her exit from the pew. "I want to know what made you decide to become a doctor and where you went to school."

"I would love to, Mrs. Jankins. Thank you."

"I told you to call me Ma, young lady. Everybody does, including this strapping fellow." The woman smiled at someone behind Charley.

She turned and found a tall man eyeing her with solemn, almost wary, gray eyes. He wore charcoal trousers, a white shirt and black string tie, and shaggy, reddish-brown hair had been swept back from his broad forehead like he'd run a hand through it more than once since its initial combing.

"Dr. Adams, have you met Cooper Knight?"

Charley blinked. *That's* why the beard looked familiar. She wasn't used to seeing the man without the accompanying sweat-stained hat pulled low over his face. "I have. He drove the stage I arrived on." And if he'd seen her glancing out her front door or window to watch it arrive and depart multiple times this week while taking a quick break from her labors, he'd not acknowledged her.

There was something intriguing about the gruff man. She'd always loved solving puzzles, it was one of the reasons she was drawn to medicine, and the man was definitely a puzzle. Did he not like people in general, or was it her specifically? He was pricklier than an old scrub brush, yet he'd not teased her about being stuck on the roof, simply demanded she not do it again before helping her down and smashing the ladder.

That had caught her by surprise, but she was glad he'd done it. When the rung had snapped under her foot, her heart had nearly stopped, and all the different consequences of that happening at the top of the ladder had filled her dreams that night. She would have found a way to dismantle it herself after he left to keep anybody else from using it again and being injured.

"I didn't get a chance to thank you for your assistance the other day. Is your hand healing all right?"

He stuffed his hands into his pockets and stepped to the side, denying Charley even a glimpse of the tiny injury. "It's fine."

Mrs. Jankins followed Charley into the middle aisle. "What happened to your hand, Coop?"

"Nothing worth mentioning."

The older woman chuckled and patted her fingers on the big man's arm. "I think you'd have to have a leg amputated before you'd consider an injury big enough to mention."

Gray eyes hardened to flint and rasped over Charley in a hard glance. "A sawbones will never get that close to me with anything sharp." The words sounded oddly menacing, but his voice gentled a little when he looked at Mrs. Jankins. "But it was only a splinter and not worth anyone's attention."

Charley was surprised at how much his dismissal stung. Yes, it was only a splinter, but splinters could become infected, and he'd have had difficulty digging it out with his left hand.

Mrs. Jankins swatted his arm affectionately. "Well, your hair has my attention, young man."

"What's wrong with my hair?" He offered Mrs. Jankins the arm she'd swatted and led her toward the entryway where the pastor stood.

"It's time you got it cut, that's what's wrong. And while you're at it, trim up that wild beard. Winter's over, and you don't need the protection from the cold anymore. It's a wonder you don't scare your passengers away."

"They're more concerned with how I drive than what I look like." He stepped aside and let the woman proceed past him to speak to the preacher, then gestured for Charley to do the same.

She hid her sudden amusement behind the guise of thanking Pastor Schwartz for the sermon. The broad-shouldered stage driver was rather intimidating, but watching Mrs. Jankins scold him was like watching an old hen torment an easygoing sheep dog. The man might be big and gruff, but his protective gentleness with the spirited, gray-haired woman betrayed a softer side.

He shook the preacher's hand then snagged a black hat from the rack by the door and offered Mrs. Jankins his arm again.

The older woman took it and let him assist her down the front steps. "Where were Hannah and Benji this morning? I didn't see them."

"Benji got sick in the night, and Hannah looked worn out by breakfast time, so I told them to stay home and get some rest."

Charley's ears pricked up. She hadn't realized Cooper was married—not that she was interested. But she *was* interested in helping. "I'd be happy to go check on them and see if I can be of any help."

The broad back in front of her visibly stiffened. "No. They're fine. Hannah says it was something Benji ate."

Charley clenched her jaw to keep from showing a reaction. She'd experienced refusals and rebuffs before, but his curt rejection still hurt.

Mrs. Jankins patted the man's arm as if he were the one who'd been snubbed and gave Charley a placating smile. "I'm sure Benji will be fine. You know how boys are. Always overeating and getting a bellyache." She turned her attention up to Cooper. "I invited Dr. Adams to join me for lunch. Since Hannah is resting, would you care to join us? I'll send you home with a couple of plates of food for her and that scamp."

"No, thank you." Cooper set the newer-looking black hat on his head. It showed more of his face than the drooping, weathered tan one he wore when driving the coach. "I need to go check on them."

Mrs. Jankins nodded. "All right. Tell Hannah to send for me if she needs me. Meanwhile, I'm going to mine this doctor's brain for everything she'll share with me." She grinned. "I'm thinkin' she's purely what we need around here."

The grimace that crossed Cooper Knight's face before he strode toward a tall horse dozing at the hitching rail told Charley he didn't agree with Ma's chipper statement. "Take care, Ma." What should have been nothing more than a simple farewell had a confusing hint of warning threading through it.

Charley's brow wrinkled as she watched him ride away. What was his problem?

"That man." Mrs. Jankins shook her head then grinned at Charley. "Well, I don't know about you, but I'm hungry. What do you say we go find some food?"

IV

Charley picked up her fork after Ma finished praying over the midday meal. "Well, now that I've told you how I became a doctor, tell me how you became the local midwife out here."

While Ma had mixed up a batch of biscuits and a pan of gravy to go with the meal, Charley had set the table and talked about her training at the St. Louis medical school and her two years additional years of training working with Dr. Tidd in the poorer sections of St. Louis. But the fragrant smells of roast, potatoes, and carrots had been making her mouth water since she'd stepped inside the older woman's kitchen nearly half an hour earlier, and now she savored her first bite of gravy-soaked roast. All that talking had made her hungry.

"My husband died two years after we settled here. Don't forget to have some biscuits." Mrs. Jankins handed a small cloth-lined basket to Charley. "William never did find a big strike, but he left me well-provided for with this cabin and enough land for a garden, some chickens, and a cow."

Charley buttered a fat buttermilk biscuit and bit into its flaky deliciousness, happy to eat and let the other woman talk for a while.

"At that time, there were few women here but also no doctor for miles. I had learned healing and midwifing skills from my momma back in Kentucky, so I stayed on here to help after my William passed. We never could have any little blessings of our own, but I love helping bring them into the world." The lines creasing the older woman's face spoke of hardships faced and overcome, but her smile radiated the zest for life of someone who'd never experienced heartache.

Charley returned the smile, hoping she could be as resilient in the days and months to come. While she'd been the lone female in her class at medical school, at least she hadn't been the first female to attend the school or the first to graduate. But in Puma Ridge, she was the first and only female physician they'd ever had. And if she failed, possibly the last one they'd ever have.

Ma Jankins sipped at her coffee. "I'm more pleased than a hen with a new brood of chicks that there's a real doctor in town now, though. There are always things cropping up beyond my ability to fix or help with, and with all your medical schoolin' and experience working with a big city doctor, you're going be a real blessing!"

"Thank you." Charley's heart warmed at the woman's easy acceptance.

Mrs. Jankins broke a biscuit in half and dabbed it in the gravy on her plate. "I'll warn you right now, though. Getting established in this town will take time and a thick skin."

Charley's lips twisted in a wry grin. "I didn't become a physician because it was easy. Getting through a male-dominated medical school was an education in developing a tough hide."

The other woman chuckled but shook her head slightly. "This is the west. Women frequently have to do a man's work in order to survive here. A female doctor is unusual, yes, but that's not the obstacle I'm talking about. The last doctor we had in Puma Ridge made a better undertaker. Therefore, people around here aren't going to be very trusting of your skills until you prove yourself."

"That's rather hard to do without patients." The corner of Charley's mouth twisted downward. So, she'd not only have to overcome the distrust of her gender but the general distrust of physicians, too? "If what you say is true, why was the mayor so eager to bring another doctor to town?"

"Because having one makes this town look more attractive to new settlers, and your eastern medical college credentials made you look good to the mayor."

Charley huffed a humorless laugh. "Until I showed up in a skirt."

The skin around Mrs. Jankins eyes crinkled with her merry chuckle. "I wish I could've been there to see Hennessey's face when you announced who you were. I can just picture him puckerin' up like he'd bit into a green persimmon."

Charley grinned. The mayor *had* looked rather sour at that.

"But don't you worry. I've nursed a lot of people around here who wouldn't go see old Doc Engstad for a stubbed toe, much less anything serious. I'll introduce you around and recommend people start taking their problems to you. It may take a while, but eventually need will outweigh reluctance."

Charley tilted her head. "How do you know I'm worth your recommendation?"

"Because I've seen the results of your work to clean up old Doc Engstad's place. That man was as careless with the art cleanliness as he was with the art of healing people. And I've always believed that cleanliness is next to Godliness."

"But I might eventually take patients from you." Charley warned.

The gray-haired woman laughed delightedly. "Oh, honey. I hope you do. There's more than enough work to go around, and I'm gettin' old."

Charley joined in the laughter. "I have to disagree. I don't think you'll ever be old. You're too full of life."

The older woman's cheeks pinked in pleasure. "Pish! Quit trying to flatter your elders and finish your dinner so we can have some of my famous apple cobbler."

Charley grinned, did what she was told, and discovered the desert lived up to its reputation.

And Mrs. Jankins lived up to her promise when she arrived at Charley's house Monday morning in a buckboard. "Grab your hat, honey. We're goin' for a ride. And don't forget your doctoring bag."

"Yes, ma'am." Leaving a note on the door that she would be out for a while—an act of faith that someone would actually seek out her services—Charley secured her hat with a long pin and slid her bag under the seat before climbing into the buckboard. "Where are we going?" She settled beside the older woman, tucking her skirt out of the way of the tall wheel by her right foot.

"Mrs. Whipple is having trouble with a colicky baby, and I want to check on Mr. Porter. He suffers with rheumatism. Figured I'd introduce you, and if you have any better suggestions or treatments, we'll administer it together and let the results speak for themselves." She flicked the reins over the back of a sturdy strawberry roan.

"I appreciate the confidence. There's no pressure at all, is there?"

Ma Jankins grinned and patted Charley's knee. "No pressure at all, honey."

Their first stop was at the Porter farm. The senior Mr. Porter looked every one of his eighty-two years and eyed the female doctor with suspicion, but his plump, pink-cheeked daughter-in-law welcomed Charley and Ma with a bright smile and promised to try Charley's recommendations to make her father-in-law's old joints more comfortable.

After accepting payment for the house call in thick slices of buttered bread, coffee, and gingersnaps, Ma drove Charley to their next stop, where a weary-eyed mother of a colicky month-old boy and two stair-step toddlers welcomed them into her home. Lifting the fussy baby out of his mother's arms, Ma passed him to Charley before sending the tired woman to take a nap while she distracted the little brother and sister duo with cookie making.

Charley examined the fussy but otherwise healthy infant and administered a few drops of an herbal tincture to soothe its painful stomach, then she sat down in the sitting-room rocking chair and began to rock and hum softly. Within a few minutes, his whimpers quieted, and his nearly translucent eyelids closed when his tiny fist found his sweet pink mouth. She snuggled him closer and rocked slower. It felt good to hold a little one in her arms, but wistful longing tugged painfully at her heart. Maybe she wouldn't have been able to juggle her profession with having a family, but Leonard hadn't even given her the opportunity to find out. His ultimatum had been clear. There was room for only one doctor in their relationship. And it wasn't her. In the end, it had been easier to give up Leonard than her life-long desire to practice medicine, but after two years, the ache lingered. Especially when she cradled someone else's little one and realized anew the cost of her calling. No husband. And no children of her own.

Charley touched her lips to the baby's velvety cheek before quietly carrying him to his mother's bedroom and laying him in the bedside cradle. It was time to put maudlin thoughts aside. She was doing what she'd been put on this earth to do. Help people. And putting her hands and feet in motion would cure her sudden case of discontentment. Staying busy seemed to have worked for Ma Jankins after losing her husband.

Returning to the kitchen, Charley found the older woman entertaining the other two children with stories and bits of pie dough while preparing food for the family's evening meal. After Mrs. Whipple rose from her nap, Charley gave her the bottle of tincture along with instructions for its use, and after a few investigative questions, she also advised the young mother to abstain from coffee and onions until the baby was a few months older. When Charley and Ma took their leave, tears filled the mother's eyes while she thanked them for the much-needed rest.

The next couple of weeks passed in similar fashion. Ma incorporated Charley into her rounds, and Charley discovered that the midwife was as much a dispenser of comfort as medical aid. The busy lady delivered soup, looked after children, sent mothers for naps, and distributed local news. Occasionally, thanks to Ma's gentle bullying, Charley was even allowed to offer advice or treat minor ailments. It felt good to get a small foothold in the community, but although she was slowly meeting people around the outlying area, no patients darkened her office door in town.

Her frustration spilled out over breakfast a month after her arrival. "Lord, I'm grateful for Ma's willingness to help me establish a practice, but people are still going to her rather than coming to see me. Please soften hearts toward me and give me something to do. I don't want you to make people sick; I simply want to help the ones who already are."

Her restless spirit settled while she read a couple of chapters in the book of Psalms, but by the time she finished cleaning up from her meal, the silent house and the empty day ahead of her brought her homesickness and frustration to a simmer again. She wrote a long letter to her parents—not that she had anything new to tell since the last one—and then wrote one to her married brother. Then she rearranged her office, examination room, and medical supplies for the hundredth time, trying to keep her mind off her boredom and her eyes off the clock while its hands crawled toward noon. When a furious knock pounded against the outer door, it nearly jolted her off her feet.

Charley hurried to open it, straightening her work apron.

The young man on the other side gripped a hat in his hands. "Are you the doc?"

Hope ignited within her. "Yes. Can I help you?" She remembered seeing the young man's fiery red hair and freckled face around town a few times. If he was past nineteen or twenty, it couldn't be by much.

"A friend has had an accident and needs a doc real bad."

Charley's pulse leapt with excitement, and she fired questions at the young man while she packed her bag with all the supplies it would hold. Hopefully, she'd have everything she might need. In his agitation, the rattled young man had trouble describing his friend's injury, and she wasn't sure whether it was a straightforward flesh wound or something more serious.

After hanging her neatly lettered "The Doctor is out" sign on the door and locking it, she followed the young man to the two saddled horses waiting at her hitching post.

"Can you ride?" The freckled young man plunked his hat on his head and swung into the saddle of a big bay gelding.

Immediately grateful for the times she'd ridden astride in a skirt on her parents' farm, Charley nodded and mounted the smaller chestnut mare, looping the handle of her bag over the saddle horn.

With a whoop, the redheaded young man touched spurs to his mount's sides, and the animal shot down the street. Charley followed in his wake, and nearly an hour later, her guide pulled his mount up in front of a tiny, rundown building.

He leaned over and took Charley's reins. "My friend's inside the line shack. You go ahead. I'll water the horses before I come in."

Charley dismounted and retrieved her bag before hurrying to the shack. It looked like a stiff breeze would knock it down, but the door stuck when she tried to open it. She shoved harder, and it gave way with a noisy creak, catching her off balance. Stumbling forward, she quick-stepped to stay on her feet, and then straightened. Right into the path of an enormous winged creature.

She ducked, yelping when a huge wing thwacked her across the shoulder. Feathers rustled, beating the air around her when the large bird swooped over her head and out the open door. Heart thudding in her ears, Charley whirled and escaped outside in time to see the owl flee into the branches of a tall pine on the hillside.

A loud whoop made her jump.

Bent over his saddle horn, the rusty-haired man cackled hysterically.

Shaking off her momentary fright, Charley willed her pulse to settle and turned to eye the interior of the dusty, deserted shack. Instant understanding bloomed. She'd been tricked.

Charley yanked the door shut with a satisfying bang. "It would seem the patient is no longer in need of my services."

"You scared him away." Her tormentor laughed harder. "If that's the way all your patients react, you're not going to be very successful around here, Miss Adams." With a short sideways tug of his reins, he spun his horse and galloped out of the clearing, Charley's borrowed mare in tow.

"Hey!" Charley ran after him, but the rascal ignored her protest and quickly disappeared from view.

She slowed to a stop and blew out a breath, irritated at her tormentor and mad at herself. She'd fallen for the simple prank like the greenest medical student in class. The young man's answers to the nature of the injury had been suspiciously vague, but she'd been so excited about a real emergency, a real patient, she'd dismissed it as worry for his friend. And now she faced a long walk back to Puma Ridge.

"Lord, this is *not* what I meant when I said I wanted something to do."

"Hoo Hoo!"

"Don't blame me, Mr. Owl." She frowned at the bird who glared at her from across the clearing. "I had no intention of disturbing your sleep today. Or any day for that matter."

Large yellow eyes blinked at her twice before the disgruntled creature spread its great wings and silently swooped deeper into the woods.

If only *she* had wings to transport her to Puma Ridge. Charley gripped her bag in her fist and let the irritation surging through her veins fuel her march back up the faint trail. Sitting around pouting wouldn't get the job done any faster. Her long, swinging stride swished through the grass, but her ire faded when she began to take in the view. In her urgency to reach her non-existent patient, she'd not paid much attention to it on the way out, but now she had time to admire the beauty around her. The grasses bordering the trail were thick and green from the recent rains, and the evergreens on the hillsides scented the air with a delightfully invigorating fragrance. A cool breeze tempered the sun's warmth, birdsong trilled through the air, and delicate flowers added splashes of color. By the time she reached the road that lead back to town, though, her stride had shortened, and thirst made her throat sticky.

Charley kept plodding forward. The scenery was pretty, but she wasn't eager to spend the night out in it. Catching her toe in a deep rut, she stumbled, and the stinging on her heels turned into dull throbs. If she'd know she was going to spend the afternoon traipsing around the countryside on foot, she'd have pulled on a thicker pair of stockings.

She hobbled to a flat boulder off the side of the road and sat down her heavy medical bag before lowering herself beside it with a long groan. Stripping off her boots and stockings, she winced at the oozing blisters. If she had water, she could cool down the hot, painful sores. Where was a cool creek when a woman needed it?

A wry grin curled her dry lips. If she had water, she'd drink it, not waste it on her feet.

Charley took a small tin of salve and some bandages from her bag. At least she was well prepared for medical problems, if not thirst problems. Smearing ointment on a bandage, she wrapped it around the worst heel and replaced her stocking before treating her other foot.

A faint sound brought her head up, and she identified it a mere second before the stagecoach rounded a bend down the road. Whipping her stocking over the hasty bandage, she tugged on her boots, tied the laces, plastered a pleasant expression onto her hot face, and waited for the coach to reach her. It only took one glance to identify the driver, but Charley wasn't sure whether he would stop or roll right past her without a second glance.

"Whoa there, boys. Whoa." The deep command answered Charley's silent question.

Instead of relief, however, nervous trepidation filled her stomach and set her nerves to jangling.

The six-horse team tossed their heads impatiently and snorted but slowed to a standstill beside Charley's resting place.

Shifting the leather lines to one hand, Cooper Knight shoved his hat brim up and frowned at her from his high perch. "Are you lost?"

Charley countered his curt question with a bright smile. "No. But I could use a ride, if you please." The few times she'd crossed paths with Cooper since her first Sunday at church, he'd ignored her, but she needed a lift and a little sweetness might go a long way toward getting her home. Even if the thought of riding beside him rattled her nerves and threatened to crack her practiced composure.

"You have a ticket?"

Her breath hitched. He couldn't be serious. "No."

"That's what I figured." He jerked his head toward the coach. "Come on."

Charley studied his face. Was he teasing her? The beard made him appear forbidding, and it was difficult to decipher any other expression. She darted a glance toward the passengers who watched her curiously through the open coach windows, then she glanced back at the driver who watched her without a flicker of emotion. "I can ride with you?"

His short nod expressed nothing except maybe a hint of impatience. "But hurry up. I've got a—"

"I know. You've got a schedule to keep. Here."

He took her medical bag from her upraised hand and dropped it under the seat. This time his expression was readable. It held clear distaste, and she almost expected to see him wipe his gloved fingers on his pant leg.

She scrambled up the side of the coach to the waiting seat before he could change his mind. The moment her backside touched the coach seat, he divided the reins between both hands, released the brake, and clucked to the horses. All without saying a word. But she didn't care. After her long walk, the hard bench felt absolutely wonderful.

~

"What were you doing out here?" Cooper hadn't intended to give in to his curiosity, but Miss Adams' weary sigh and the grateful smile she sent his way had drawn the question out before he could stop it.

"I went to see a patient, but it turns out he didn't need my help after all." She sounded half irritated, half amused.

It was probably frustrating to be a sawbones with no patients.

Cooper shifted on the hard seat. Why was he feeling sympathy for the woman? She was a *doctor*.

But maybe it was a good thing the town had accidentally acquired a petticoat physician. People automatically distrusted her and that kept them from getting taken in by another quack.

"Why didn't you ride a horse? It's quicker than shank's mare." Cooper indicated her dusty brown boots with a jerk of his chin.

She grimaced. "I started out with a horse."

Heaven save him and the entire west from greenhorns. "Forget to tie him?"

"No. I never got the chance to tie him."

Cooper looked at her sharply. "Did you get thrown? Is that why you limped over to the stage?"

She shook her head. "No. Blisters." A quick grin bunched her cheeks. Big enough he could see its glow from the corner of his eye. "Today could have turned out a whole lot worse. In fact, now that I think about it, it would be funny if it hadn't happened to me."

The humor lighting her face appeared a lot more genuine than the phony smile she'd given him when asking for a ride. *That* particular expression had prompted his ticket question simply because he'd wanted to spark some kind of genuine emotion on her face.

The last of her statement registered. "*What* happened?"

She eyed him then seemed to come to a decision. "Well, there was this young man who said his friend was hurt."

Cooper listened to her tale of a red-headed scallywag, a non-existent emergency, and an owl-inhabited cabin in silence and growing anger.

"I must have looked a sight trying to get out of the way of that poor, panicked owl." Her light chuckle was dangerously entrancing. "After I got over being mad, I actually enjoyed most of my enforced walk—until the blisters joined me, that is. I was quite thankful to see you come around that bend in the road."

This time her smile lit up her green eyes. In the short time he'd known her he'd already discovered that a fake smile left her eyes cool and watchful, like a cat stalking a mouse. But a genuine smile turned them warmer and shinier than sunlight on rain-drenched spring grass. And he was in danger of drowning.

Cooper yanked his attention back to the team. The only reason he'd noticed was because a man accustomed to keeping his eyes peeled for danger naturally paid attention to details like that.

Miss Adams shifted against the seat and was quiet for several minutes before speaking again. "I was so excited about my first real case since arriving, too." All humor had disappeared from her voice "Only it wasn't real."

Cooper set his jaw. He knew exactly who her red-haired tormenter was. The young man worked at the ranch Cooper had bought a bull from a couple years earlier, and Cooper would make sure the fella knew that if he ever pulled another prank on Miss Adams, he might not live to regret it. Bears and wildcats roamed these hills, and a small woman alone made a tempting target for a hungry four-legged critter. Not to mention two-legged ones.

"Don't go on any more rides with strangers." Cooper guided the horses around a washed-out edge of the road. He wasn't changing his mind about doctors, but no woman deserved to be put in harm's way for the sake of a prank. And like it or not, since this particular woman seemed to lack a healthy sense of self-preservation—climbing around on rooftops and riding out of town with a strange man. He'd have to keep an eye out for her until someone else volunteered for the job of protector.

V

Charley woke with a smile on her face. Yesterday's prank had bruised her natural optimism, but then the short ride with a certain taciturn stagecoach driver had left her strangely invigorated. Even his gruff order not to ride out with strangers hadn't bothered her. She was a doctor and would go where she was needed, but Cooper's warning had made her feel like someone else in Puma Ridge besides Ma Jankins cared what happened to her. And that feeling gave her a burst of fresh energy for the challenges that still lay ahead.

Being a doctor had been her dream since she'd started tagging along on Uncle Eddy's house calls as a young girl. God had given her the strength to make it through medical school and an inheritance from her grandparents to live on until her skills could earn her a living, and surely, God hadn't brought her this far to fail—annoying pranks and unwelcoming townsfolk notwithstanding. Until He showed her different, Puma Ridge was where she felt she needed to be.

Tomorrow, she would accompany Ma Jankins on her rounds again, but today, she would busy herself with a different kind of patient. If the outside of her house had ever worn a coat of paint, it had long since disintegrated, leaving behind weather-beaten, almost-colorless gray clapboard siding. The interior of her home and office was now clean and in order, and soon the exterior would be, too. Ma had recommended a carpenter who'd bird-proofed her chimney and repaired a couple of soft spots on her roof, and now it was time to apply the finishing touches.

Charley assembled her supplies and set to work, a hymn humming through her head. It felt good to have a task, and the pale blue paint she'd found at the mercantile, along with white for the trim work, would make her little house feel alive and loved again. Cobwebs and spiders were no match for her vigorous broom, and when the squatters had been evicted, Charley wiped down the window frames with a cloth before painstakingly applying a thick coat of white to each one. She'd never painted an entire house before, but with her arms already tired from all the sweeping down of dirt and insect debris, the trim seemed the less intimidating part of the whole project.

Soreness burned along her shoulder muscles when she stretched to reach the top corner of the last frame. Her new home wasn't a large building, but it seemed to grow larger with each stroke of her brush. A muscle cramped in her neck, zinging pain through her shoulders. Right now, she'd cheerfully give away half of it to the first person who asked. And they could finish painting it. Lowering her arm, she gently rolled her neck and shoulders several times, wincing at their stiffness before dipping her brush in the bucket of white paint balanced on the top of her stepladder.

"Ma'am?"

Charley nearly knocked off her paint bucket at the sound of the small, unexpected voice. After steadying the container, she stepped down and faced her young visitor. "Yes?"

A boy of maybe eight or nine years with tousled brown hair and a dirt-smudged face eyed her paintbrush doubtfully. "Are you the petticoat doc?" He shifted a bundle of fur in his arms.

Charley propped the brush across the top of the bucket and wiped her hands on her apron. "I am. Is there something I can help you with?" He was a cute little thing with his solemn expression and wide brown eyes.

He stepped closer and held out his burden. "Digger's been hurt. Can you fix him?" His rapid blinks couldn't hide the sudden wetness shimmering in his eyes. "Please?"

Charley gave the bundle of dark fur her full attention. It was a dog. "Well, I normally work on people…"

The boy's thin shoulders drooped at her hesitation.

She sighed silently. It wasn't quite the kind of patient she'd hoped for, but who was she to be finicky? Yesterday's patient had been a sleepy owl, this morning, it had been an unpainted house. Now, it would appear to be a wounded dog. "But I'll see what I can do to help."

Relief kindled in the big brown eyes that met hers.

"Let's take him inside where I can get a good look." Leading the pup's owner into the examination room, she directed him to place the animal on the sheet-draped table. "What happened?"

Charley changed her grimy, paint-spattered apron for a clean work smock then scrubbed her hands and arms thoroughly but quickly. The dog had started whimpering painfully upon being placed on the table.

"We were coming home from fishing when Mr. Farnsworth's dog broke his rope and started chasing us. Digger thought he was going to hurt me and tried to stop him. But the other dog is bigger, and before I could run him off, he hurt Digger real bad." He fondled the dog's ear and pointed to an oozing gash on the pup's shoulder. "He's bleedin' in some other places, too. That old dog just picked him up in his mouth and shook him." A sniff indicated tears weren't far away. "I thought he was gonna kill Digger." The boy's voice trembled.

Charley gently examined the black terrier, carefully parting its shaggy, blood-matted fur to assess each wound. Several small punctures and scrapes oozed blood. They would need a thorough cleaning and ointment but should otherwise heal on their own if no infection set in. The gash on the dog's shoulder needed stitches, though. It was deep with ragged edges. More of a tear, actually.

Charley straightened and eyed the young boy who visibly struggled to keep tears from falling at his dog's distressed whines. "Well, young man. I know my patient's name, but what's yours?"

He sniffed, not taking his eyes off the little dog. "Benjamin Olson, ma'am."

"Well, Benjamin. I need you to wash your hands better than you've ever washed them before, and then do you think you can help me hold Digger while I clean his wounds and stitch up his shoulder?"

"Will it hurt him?" His voice trembled, but he walked over to the sink and indoor pump to scrub his hands.

Worried button-eyes tracked Benjamin, but the terrier was clearly in pain and barely moved his head.

Charley assembled the supplies she would need and tried to reassure both master and dog with her calm voice. "I'll do my best not to hurt Digger. I'm actually going to give him something to let him sleep, so he shouldn't feel any pain while I'm working on him." She also didn't want herself or Benjamin to be bitten by a frightened dog who didn't understand why she was causing him more pain.

Benjamin dried his hands haphazardly on the clean towel and hurried back to stand beside his furry companion.

"I'm going to hold this cloth over his nose until he goes to sleep, and I need you to watch him closely. If you see him starting to wake up while I'm working, let me know instantly, because I'll need to give him more anesthetic. I also want you to keep your hands on him in case he wiggles while he sleeps."

Nodding, Benjamin gently placed his hands on his dog's hip and back, rubbing his fingers softly in the animal's fur while he watched Charley with wide, worried eyes.

Lord, I can tell that this dog is precious to this little boy, so help me to do the right things. She'd never used anesthetic on a canine before, much less one small enough to fit in her shopping basket.

The dog drifted easily to sleep on the tiny amount of anesthetic Charley administered, and a whisper of relief slid through her when the dog's breathing and heartrate remained strong and regular. With quick, steady hands, she trimmed the hair away from the gash before cleaning it thoroughly. Then, dipping her threaded needle in a disinfecting solution, she set tiny, precise stitches, drawing the edges of the wound together.

Benjamin stroked the dog's back, flinching every time the needle pierced his dog's flesh.

Hoping to distract him, Charley asked the first question that came to her mind. "How did Digger get his name? Did he tear up somebody's prize roses?"

"No." A faint, lopsided smile peeked through the boy's palpable concern. "We were digging potatoes when he was a puppy—Mom and I raise vegetables to sell to the store and the miners around here. At first, Digger watched us with his head cocked, like he was trying to figure out what we were doing. Then all of a sudden, he started digging for his own potatoes. He'd bark and growl whenever he found one, and I taught him to carry his own potatoes to a bucket. He's been Digger ever since."

Charley grinned at the obvious pride in the boy's voice. "What a clever dog. What else can he do?"

Her achy spine protested her hunched position over the dog, and she worked quickly while Benjamin recounted another tale. After tying off the tenth stitch, she set the needle aside and stretched her back for a second before applying ointment and bandaging the gash. Then she cleaned and salved each of the dog's other wounds. If the little animal came out from under the effects of the anesthetic, he should heal well.

Charley gathered her instruments into a pan to clean later and washed her hands before opening a drawer to retrieve her stash of peppermint candy. She had overused them on the trip west and wasn't quite ready to taste their strong flavor again, but Benjamin might appreciate their sweetness after his distressing afternoon.

She offered him a piece, but he paused right before accepting it, and his hand lowered reluctantly to his side. "No, thank you."

"Go ahead. I have plenty more where this came from." She extended the paper-wrapped sweet again.

He shook his head and rubbed the toe of his dusty boot against the floor. "No, ma'am. I don't deserve it. I, uh…" He shifted uneasily.

"What's wrong, Benjamin? I think Digger will be fine after he has time to heal. You shouldn't worry. That's my job." She smiled to encourage him, but he didn't raise his head.

"No ma'am That's not… I mean…" He bit his bottom lip. "I should've told you when I first got here, but I was afraid you might not help Digger."

Charley's eyes widened at his outburst. "Tell me what?"

The small boy gulped and forced his shoulders back, appearing to brace himself for a blow. "I… I was one of the boys who stole your ladder when you climbed on the roof." His explanation spilled out in a rush. "I'm really sorry. I shouldn't have done it. The other fellas said it would be funny. But it wasn't." His hand rubbed the seat of his trousers, and he winced. "I'm sorry, ma'am."

Charley bit the inside of her cheek to keep the amusement off her face. It would seem someone had come to her defense. "No. It wasn't funny. But thank you for your apology. I forgive you. And I would have helped Digger even if you had confessed that earlier."

"You would have?" Relief brightened his dark eyes.

"Yes. Now how 'bout a peppermint to show there are no hard feelings?"

"Yes, ma'am! Thank you!" He reached for the candy, grinning shyly as he unwrapped it and popped it in his mouth.

Charley handed him a second one that he tucked in his pocket.

"Will he really be all right?" The boy's grin faded quickly, and he fondled a floppy ear of the unconscious terrier.

"He'll be in some pain until his injuries heal, but otherwise he should be fine." Charley breathed another quiet sigh of relief when a black-button eye blinked slowly open, and a long pink tongue clumsily swiped at the hand resting near his nose. "Why don't we leave him here overnight so I can keep an eye on him? If he's doing well in the morning, we'll talk about how soon you can take him home."

The boy nodded. "Can I go get his bed and bring it here so he won't be scared?"

"I think that is an excellent suggestion. Digger will be more comfortable with his own things. But since it's nearing supper time, why don't you eat before you return to check on him?"

Benjamin laid his brown head next to the drowsy pup's black one and wrapped his arms loosely around its body in a boyish, half-hug. "I'll be back quick as I can, Digger." He straightened and slowly shuffled toward the door, watching his pet the entire way.

He paused with his hand on the doorknob and looked at Charley. "Doctor, ma'am?"

She smiled at the note of respect in his sweet, young voice. "Why don't you call me Dr. Charley?"

"Yes, ma'am. If mama says it's all right, may I stay here tonight with Digger? I don't need a bed or nothin'. I'd sit beside him real quiet and make sure he doesn't get scared."

Charley's heart expanded two sizes, and her eyes prickled. Someone might be able to resist the pleading in those big, serious eyes, but it wasn't her. "If your mother gives permission, you are more than welcome to spend the night here with Digger."

A big smile replaced the anxiety that had pinched Benjamin's face since his arrival. "I'll be right back." He darted out the door.

"Don't forget to eat…" Charley spoke to thin air and shook her head, chuckling softly. Oh well. If he got hungry, she would feed him. She stroked the silky, black head resting on the examination table. "And let this be a lesson to you, Digger. Don't go picking fights with those who are bigger than you."

The dog whined, his eyes fastened to the door his master had disappeared through.

"I know. You were protecting that little scamp. Don't worry. I have a feeling he'll return before I have time to turn around." She laid a towel over the dog to keep him warm and quiet and began cleaning her instruments.

Her prediction wasn't accurate, however. Digger had dozed off, his nose pointed compass-needle-true toward the door, and Charley had cleaned and set the examination room to rights, put her painting supplies in the outbuilding, and was finishing her slightly scorched supper when a faint knock alerted her to the boy's return.

She hurried to the front. "Come in."

Digger lifted his head a fraction and whined, his tail limply beating the table at the sight of his boy and a tall, dark-haired woman entering the room. The terrier struggled to rise but fell back with a little yelp. Benjamin rushed over to soothe him, a folded blanket hanging over his shoulder.

"I'm Hannah Olson, Benjamin's mother. I'm sorry to bother you again this evening, but Benji wouldn't rest until he checked on Digger." The woman's eyes were a match to her son's in shape and color.

"It's nice to meet you. I'm Dr. Charley Adams, and you're not a bother. I expected Benjamin to return. Is he going to stay here tonight with Digger?"

"See, Mama? I told you she didn't mind. I can't leave Digger all alone. He'll be scared." Soulful pleading filled the two pairs of eyes that focused on Hannah Olson—one pair brown-sugar warm, the other pair inky black.

The woman was made of sterner stuff than Charley if she could resist that double-barreled load of pitiful.

She turned to Charley. "Are you sure Digger can't go home with us? We'll keep a close eye on him."

Charley shook her head. "Since I used anesthetic on him, I'd like to keep him here at least overnight in case he has a reaction. He might be able to go home tomorrow." She drew the woman aside and lowered her voice. "I know we haven't met before, but if you don't mind your son staying here, he would be a help. And Digger will probably rest quieter." She pointed to a long leather couch against the wall in the examination room. "He can sleep there. I have a pillow and blanket all ready for him. And you're welcome to stay as well. I have another bed in the small room off of this one that you can use."

"No. Ma Jankins has nothing but good to say about you, and I don't mind Benji staying the night as long as you're sure *you* don't mind him being underfoot."

Charley gave the woman a reassuring smile. "I wouldn't have offered otherwise."

Hannah Olson sighed and nodded. "Then thank you. That will make Benji feel better." She turned to her son who had wrapped his skinny arms around the dog on the tall table. "You can stay, Benji."

"Did you hear that Digger? I get to stay." The little dog responded with a quick lick across the bright smile so close to his snout.

Hannah smiled but shook her head slightly. "I don't know why he came to you. The blacksmith is usually the one Benji bothers with Digger's injuries."

"I was glad to help." Charley smiled wryly. "You might have noticed that I'm not exactly overrun with patients at the moment."

"From the way Ma Jankins sings your praises, I doubt that will remain the case for long. So, thank you for taking time to help my son and Digger." Mrs. Olson ran her fingers through her son's hair before kissing his head. "I guess I'd better run along home. Benji, behave, and don't cause Dr. Adams any more trouble. I'll be back in the morning."

"I'll be good, Mama."

Digger thumped his tail as if agreeing to the same terms, and Mrs. Olson stroked his head, too.

When she looked up at Charley, her posture was stiff and her expression tight. "I almost forgot to ask. What do we owe you?"

The woman's clean but carefully mended dress and Benji's patched trousers had not escaped Charley's notice. "Actually, if you don't mind, since Digger belongs to Benjamin, I'd like to strike a deal with him."

Mrs. Olson blinked in surprise, and Benjamin looked up curiously.

"If it's acceptable with your mother," Charley darted a glance her way, including her in the conversation, "I'd like to trade my medical services for an afternoon or two of your help painting my house. Does that sound fair?"

Benjamin eyed his mother, and when she nodded, he faced Charley, his shoulders squared proudly. "I helped mama paint our house last time. She said I was a good painter."

Charley clapped her hands together. "Excellent. My back and shoulders thank you. We can start tomorrow, if you're available, and that way, we can *both* keep an eye on Digger. He'll need to be kept quiet for several days and can rest on his blanket and watch us work."

"All right." The boy grinned eagerly, the idea of work not seeming to daunt him in the slightest.

His mother's shoulders lost some of their tension. "Thank you, Dr. Adams."

Charley followed her out the front door. "Don't worry. I'll keep a close eye on both of them."

"You've already proven that. And I don't know how I'll ever be able to thank you." She held up a hand to stop Charley's reply. "My brother gave Digger to Benji after my husband died, and…" A shaky smile followed her pause. "Benji said he told you how Digger got his name? Well, that pup's silly trick of digging up potatoes was the first thing to bring a smile to Benji's face after his father's death. To say Digger is pretty special is an understatement. I don't know what Benji would do if Digger…"

Charley laid her hand on the widow's arm, her heart squeezing over the loss the woman and her son had suffered. "Digger will be fine. Tonight's only a cautionary measure to ensure that. Now you go home and get some sleep. And don't worry. Doctor's orders." She softened her stern order with a wink.

Hannah squeezed Charley's hand and took her leave without another word, but her eyes glistened with a faint hint of tears.

Charley locked the front door behind her and returned to check on her furry patient. He appeared to be doing as well as possible, so she gently moved him to the bed Benjamin had made for him beside the leather settee.

Digger curled up stiffly on the faded, folded blanket, and Benjamin sprawled, stomach down, on the settee, one hand stroking his furry pal.

Charley turned down the bright, overhead lamp. "If you get worried about anything in the night, call me. My room is right down the hall, and I'll leave the door open so I can hear you. I'll also check on Digger several times throughout the night, but I'll try not to startle you."

"All right, Dr. Charley. Thank you."

She returned his grin, but a thought stopped her exit from the room. "By the way, why did you bring Digger to me instead of taking him to the blacksmith?"

The boy propped his chin on his arm and met her gaze with guileless brown eyes. "Because you're a woman doctor, and women are always more gentle."

Charley hurried to her bedroom to hide the sudden stinging in her eyes. The warm glow around her heart didn't care one whit that her first real patient wasn't of the human variety. Earning the trust of one small boy and his dog was as unexpected a victory as it was sweet.

VI

Cooper pounded on the door and rattled the knob.

Locked.

Nightmarish memories surged higher, swirling into the mixture of fear and panic that had locked his jaw shut since finding the note on Hannah's kitchen table. His lungs strained for a full breath. He beat on the door again and considered kicking it in. How could Hannah have brought Benji here? Her husband was dead because of bringing him to the last sawbones who'd inhabited this building. Why hadn't she gone to Ma Jankins?

"I'm coming, I'm coming." The muffled response preceded the click of the lock.

He shoved the door open and rushed inside.

The startled physician jerked out of his way. "Oh. It's you." Green eyes glinted drolly up at him. "I apologize for keeping you waiting, but a few more blows and you could have walked in over the debris."

Cooper's gaze darted around the tiny, empty waiting room, and he stomped deeper into the doctor's lair, fists clenched to hide their tremors. The larger room held a cloth-covered, narrow table in the center, a sink, cabinets, low couch, and chair along the walls, but no evidence of his family. The space looked no more dangerous than an everyday kitchen. But looks could be deceiving.

"Where. Are. They?"

Miss Adams' brows drew together in confusion. "Where's who?"

"Hannah and Benji. Her note said there was an accident, and they were here." Why weren't they here? Had something worse happened? The vise around Cooper's lungs tightened at the unthinkable possibility.

A door on the far side of the floor-to-ceiling cabinets swished open, and a small figure shot through it. "Hey, Uncle Coop. Did you come to see Digger?"

Cooper caught his nephew by the shoulders and squatted down on shaky knees. "Benji. You're not hurt?"

"Nah." Benji shook his head with the blissful indifference of youth. "But you should see Digger. Mr. Farnsworth's mean ol' dog tore him up somethin' awful, but Dr. Charley sewed him up real good. Come see." Without waiting for an answer, he pulled free of Cooper's grasp and darted through the open door and down a short hallway.

Swallowing down his racing heart, Cooper forced his weak legs to follow his nephew into the living quarters of the house.

Hannah looked up from the cook stove when he entered the kitchen. "Coop. What are you doing here?"

The feigned surprise on her face made Cooper's head itch, and he jerked off his forgotten hat to rub a hand through his hair. He smelled an ambush. "You left a note."

His husky growl didn't faze her.

She forked fried strips of bacon onto a plate and set it on the table. "Oh, that's right. I didn't want you wondering where we were, but I was in such a hurry this morning it's a wonder I didn't leave my head at home." She laughed lightly.

"You *said* there'd been an accident." And nearly given him heart failure.

"There was. Poor Digger." She shook her head. "He might have died if it hadn't been for Dr. Adams. Charley, I apologize. The grizzly who so rudely charged into your home is my brother, Cooper Knight. I hope you won't hold his boorish behavior against me." Hannah speared him with a reproachful glower before turning her attention to the woman who slipped between him and the doorway.

Cooper glanced between the two women. Since when was his sister on first name terms with Miss Adams?

"We've met. And so far, I've found his growl to be worse than his bite." Miss Adams grinned and motioned toward the table. "If you'd care to join us for breakfast, I think Hannah fixed enough for an army."

"He'll stay. He's not only grumpy as a bear, but he's always hungry as a bear, too." Hannah grinned but avoided Cooper's eyes.

Benji tugged on Cooper's arm. "Come see Digger."

Cooper hung his hat on the back of a chair and followed his nephew to the corner of the kitchen. The small black mongrel he'd given to Benji two years earlier lay curled on his favorite blanket, the tip of his tail thumping the floor a lot slower than usual.

"Mr. Farnsworth's big ol' dog got loose and chased me, but Digger stopped him. We just finished putting some medicine on his stitches when you got here. See?" Without waiting for an answer, Benji moved the folded cloth that covered the wound.

Cooper swallowed hard.

Blackened, tied-off threads held together an ugly, swollen gash on the dog's shoulder.

"He's got more scratches and bites other places, but that's the worst one. Didn't Dr. Charley do a good job? She says he'll heal up fine."

Digger, his nose resting between his paws, sighed as if he doubted his master's confident statement.

Cooper's attempt to return Benji's relieved grin was shaky at best. Injuries to man and beast were unavoidable parts of life, but in recent years, he'd grown shamefully weak kneed when it came to blood.

"All right, you two. Wash up, and let's eat."

Grateful for the excuse to turn away from Digger's injuries without offending Benji, Cooper obeyed Hannah's order and supervised his nephew's wash job before scrubbing and drying his own hands. His earlier panic was fading, but Digger's stitches had soured his stomach, and he kept his head down and took the remaining seat at the square table.

"May I ask the blessing, Dr. Charley?"

"That would be wonderful, Benji. Please do."

Cooper closed his eyes, relieved to have a few more seconds

before he'd be expected to speak. He had a lot to bless God for—his nephew and sister were safe and unharmed—but he was still trying to remember how to breathe normally and wasn't sure he could string a coherent sentence together.

The clatter of dishes told Cooper he'd missed the end of Benji's prayer, and he looked up. Straight into Miss Adams' concerned gaze.

"Are you feeling well, Mr. Knight?" She studied his face. "You've gone pale."

He opened his mouth to reply, but Hannah laughed—the hard-hearted female. "My brother shouldn't have looked at Digger's wounds so close to breakfast. He has a weak stomach."

"Oh. I have a tea that will help that." Miss Adams jumped from her chair.

He shoved his own chair back and stood. "Stop."

She paused, hand on a cabinet door, and looked over her shoulder. "It won't take but a few minutes to brew, and it'll settle your stomach."

"My innards are fine." Cooper willed his words to be true. "They're just empty."

She faced him, her eyes narrowing. Cooper wouldn't have been surprised if she'd walked around the table to press her hand to his forehead, but she finally nodded and slid into her seat without pressing him further.

Resisting the desire to take his "weak" stomach and hightail it home, Cooper returned to his chair, and Hannah slid a plate full of food in front of him.

Miss Adams probably thought him a chicken-hearted weakling—after all, it was only a dog—but he'd seen enough wounds and blood to last a lifetime. And when those wounds happened to someone under his care... The familiar sense of failure jabbed his insides.

He glanced at Hannah and Benji to reassure himself that they were indeed all right, and caught sight of a pair of grass-green eyes assessing him. Cooper's spine stiffened. If Miss Adams thought she could treat him like a patient, she had another think coming. He picked up his fork and speared a forkful of fried potatoes, shoving them into his mouth. His belly could protest later.

Miss Adams' scrutiny faded, and she began to regale his sister and nephew with a colorful version of her trip to the abandoned line shack. Despite the fact he'd heard the story already, he found himself listening to every word. And a reluctant grin tugged at his mouth when Hannah and Benji burst out laughing at Miss Adams' description of the mutual surprise between herself and the owl.

How long had it been since he'd heard his sister laugh so freely? It was a nice sound.

"My blistered feet were quite happy to see Mr. Knight and his stagecoach that day."

Cooper jerked his gaze away from the bright smile aimed full-bore at him and looked down at his plate. Surprise jolted him almost as hard as Miss Adams' smile. When had he emptied it?

Hannah pushed her chair back and stood. "Well, I'm glad Coop rescued you, but now we need to stop wasting this pretty day. Between the four of us, we should be able to get the first coat of paint done today."

Paint? Four? Cooper glanced from Hannah to Miss Adams.

She touched a napkin to the corners of her mouth. "That's not necessary. You already made breakfast. I'm sure you have plenty of other things you need to be doing."

"Come on, it'll be fun." Hannah coaxed, tossing a flour-sack towel over the remaining bacon, biscuits, and fried potatoes. "Cooper can do all the high work. You and I and Benji can do the low work and have a nice long visit."

Cooper stared at his sister. Since when had he volunteered to paint the doctor's place? This was his day to help Hannah with chores around *her* place.

Miss Adams protested again, gathering the dishes and taking them to the washtub.

His stubborn sister railroaded right past the objections. "Cooper works around my place once a week, but I don't have anything that needs attention right now. Instead of having him underfoot until supper—which is what he *actually* comes for—I decided we'd help you today."

"But I don't have enough paint brushes."

Hannah grinned. "You do now, I brought some with me."

Yep. Cooper's nose for trouble still worked. This *was* an ambush.

His interfering, high-handed sister ignored his attempt to get her attention and instructed Benji to carry Digger to the yard where the dog could watch them. "Do you have a ladder Cooper can use, or do I need to send him for one?"

"I have a new ladder in the barn." Miss Adams flicked a glance Cooper's direction. "Someone made kindling out of the old one."

The laughter twinkling in her smile robbed him of protest, and before he quite knew how it happened, he found himself perched on the sturdy new ladder, smearing pale blue paint over weathered gray boards. Nothing about Miss Adams was content to blend into the background, including her choice of paint color for her house. What was wrong with white? Or gray? But no. She had to have blue.

"What made you want to be a doctor?" Hannah quizzed from beneath him.

Cooper didn't have to glance down to know exactly where Miss Adams stood. His peripheral vision seemed determined to keep her in view.

"When I was young, my uncle Eddy lived near us. He was a doctor and would sometimes let me join him on his rounds. I loved watching him help people. One day, I told him I wanted to be a physician like him. Most men would have laughed and told me girls weren't allowed to do that sort of thing, but Uncle Eddy looked me in the eye and said it would be the hardest thing I'd ever do, but that when I succeeded, it would be the most rewarding."

"Do they actually allow women into medical school?"

Cooper wanted to know the answer to that question, too.

"Oh, yes." Miss Adams laughed lightly. "It's not illegal for women to be doctors. It's simply uncommon, and in many places, still frowned upon. There are a few all-female medical schools, but I attended a medical school in St. Louis that opened its doors to female students a couple of years prior to my arrival. When I attended, however, I was the only woman in my classes."

"How did the other students handle that?"

"Not very well." Miss Adams chuckled wryly. "Some of the professors weren't happy about it either. They couldn't kick me out or deny me access to the classes, but they did everything they could think of, short of murder, to get me to quit."

Cooper climbed down, repositioned the ladder, and ascended again, using the busy movements to hide the fact he listened as closely as Hannah and Benji.

"What do you mean?" Hannah asked.

"The second week in class—*after* they'd gotten over the initial shock of seeing a female in their hallowed halls," Miss Adams warmed to her storytelling, "They propped a bucket of dirty mop water from the surgery room floor over the classroom door. When I walked in, it fell and poured all over me."

"Eeww!" Benji giggled in morbid delight.

Hannah gasped in horror. "That's terrible!"

"Oh, mop water was nothing compared to the other pranks they pulled over the next few months." Miss Adams shook her head, her tone hard to interpret.

"What else did they do?" Benji's paintbrush dripped blue spots on the grass, and he watched Miss Adams in wide-eyed fascination.

"Well…" Miss Adams faced Benji, her voice lowering. "One time, after dissecting a pig, I opened my desk the next day and found the leftovers inside."

Hannah gasped again. "Oh, no!"

"Oh, yes. It was bad." Miss Adams shuddered dramatically. "They had already started to reek."

Benji looked more intrigued than disgusted. "What's diesecking?"

"Dissecting is when we cut up a dead animal to learn how things like hearts and lungs and other organs work. Or we practice surgery techniques and our stitches."

Hannah shuddered in real horror, but Cooper didn't feel sorry for her. His sister had brought this on her own head, and he had enough to do keeping his own queasy innards under control.

"What else did they do?" Apparently, his bloodthirsty nephew hadn't had his fill, though.

"The male students were constantly trying to embarrass me and prove that women couldn't and shouldn't handle certain parts of practicing medicine. So, at another time, we all went to the morgue to watch an autopsy—that's where we examine a dead person's body to try and discover why they died. Anyway, they asked me to remove the sheet covering the deceased." She dipped her brush in the container of paint and touched it to the boards again. "Except the deceased wasn't deceased. When I lifted the sheet, the student underneath jumped up and grabbed me." She darted a hand toward Benji, and he jumped away with a startled yell.

Hannah jumped, too. "Oh, my. I think I would have fainted on the spot." She stared at Miss Adams in shock, but that woman only chuckled.

Cooper slapped his wet brush against the wall and felt paint splat against his nose. He swiped it off with his shirtsleeve. How could she laugh about such crude shenanigans when she'd been the victim of them?

"It startled me, yes, but it was the last time they actually got me to scream. After that, I always stayed on guard, always expecting something. It irked them when they realized they couldn't get a reaction out of me anymore, and it took away some of their incentive to try. Then someone got the bright idea to try the silent treatment. For months, the majority of the school wouldn't talk to me or acknowledge my existence."

Cooper had a clear view of her face from his perch and saw her nose wrinkle.

"Some of the professors joined in on that one. If I raised my hand to ask or answer a question, they ignored me."

"How incredibly bad-mannered of them!"

The steam in Hannah's voice put a smile on Miss Adams' face. "I much preferred that to the messier things they tried, like pig parts and mop water." She bent to rewet her paintbrush, but Cooper's sharp ears caught the words she muttered under her breath. "And mice." Another shudder shook her frame. This one so slight he almost missed it.

His brows scrunched together. What was the story behind that? The woman laughingly recounted things that would make a lot of men cringe, including him, but had whispered about mice like they were worse than an outbreak of smallpox.

She straightened and continued like nothing had happened. "I eventually got my revenge, though."

"How?" Benji had abandoned his painting and sat beside Digger, petting his dog's head while he hung on Miss Adams every word.

"When we started assisting with real patients, I and the student who'd been my worst tormentor were called to help with an emergency surgery. When the surgeon made the first incision, blood spurted into the air. The other student fainted and hit the floor, leaving me to help the surgeon by myself. When he came to, the surgeon demanded to know why he was in medical school if he couldn't stomach a little blood. Then he ordered him out of the operating room."

"How come it didn't make *you* sick?" Benji questioned again.

"Because I am fascinated with the intricacies of the human body. Man is truly God's greatest work. It amazes me how every bone, muscle, tendon, vein, artery, and nerve work. They bear the mark of a divine Creator, and I never tire of studying them." Awe filled her voice. "God's fingerprints are all over us." She stroked her brush over a weathered board, leaving a glistening coat of pale blue behind.

It was a long minute before anyone broke the silence.

"Did any of those men ever apologize for the way they treated you?"

Hannah's question seemed to surprise Miss Adams, and her laugh sounded surprised. "No. They didn't bother me much after that, but I think we all breathed a sigh of relief at graduation because we wouldn't have to put up with each other anymore."

Cooper scowled at the rough siding that snagged the bristles of his paintbrush. The woman sounded as callous and indifferent as the sawbones who'd informed him his brother-in-law had died on the operating table. What well-bred woman willingly subjected herself to the type of rough treatment she'd endured and the immodest sights and situations she must have encountered?

"Did you come straight here after finishing medical school?" Hannah squatted beneath a windowsill and carefully painted the boards beneath it.

"No. After I graduated, Dr. Tidd, the doctor I assisted during that emergency surgery, asked me to work at his small, private hospital which serves the poorer population of St. Louis, and that's where I've been the last two years."

"What made you come all the way out here?"

"When I was fourteen, my aunt died and Uncle Eddy headed west. We got a few letters from him over the years before he died, and several times, he mentioned the great need for doctors in the rapidly expanding west. I decided then that I wanted to follow in his footsteps and serve where it was most needed. When Dr. Tidd pointed out the advertisement in the paper that Puma Ridge was looking for a physician, I replied and started packing my bags."

"Me and Digger sure are glad you decided to come." Benji piped up.

"I am, too." Hannah agreed. "And don't you worry. The men will put aside their silly notions about female doctors when they're actually sick. Pride doesn't last long when you're in pain."

That made *three* people glad the female doc was in town: Ma, Hannah, and Benji. Cooper wasn't ready to join the welcome wagon, however. Miss Adams had managed to stitch up a wounded critter, but that was no proof she was competent with human patients. The last two physicians Coop had had the misfortune to know hadn't been. The former Puma Ridge doctor had been little better than a butcher, and the Army doctor had been worse. His addiction to his own medicinal tonics had made him a murderer.

Miss Adams was a beautiful woman, and if she wasn't a physician, Cooper might have been interested in getting to know her better. But she *was* a doctor, and all he could do was keep an eye on his family and pray they would never need to test her competency for anything more serious than an impetuous terrier's injuries.

~

Sooner than Charley would've believed possible, they were finishing the last side of her house. It would have taken her a week to accomplish what four pairs of hands had done in one day. She'd tried to send them away after lunch, but Hannah had gaily refused, saying she never left a job half finished, and that she was enjoying Charley's company too much to quit.

Cooper moved the ladder to reach the last unpainted section under the eave, drawing her eyes when he ascended the sturdy rungs. He'd worked all day with the same unstoppable efficiency as the wheels of the locomotive that had carried her west. Hannah had had to threaten him with bodily harm before he'd descended the ladder for food at noon. Charley ached from two days of painting, and she shrank from thinking what her legs would have felt like if she'd gone up and down the ladder as many times as he had today. Yet, he showed no signs of the fatigue that slowed her movements and dampened the conversation that had flowed so easily earlier in the day.

Not that he had any conversation to dampen. He responded to direct questions and occasionally spoke to his nephew in that low, deep voice that made the hairs on the nape of her neck stand to attention, but he'd taken no part in the friendly chatter bouncing between the three painters on the ground.

The seeds of friendship had been planted today, though, or she was sorely mistaken. Hannah's genuine interest and easy acceptance was a nice change from the prune-faced disapproval or outright rejection she was accustomed to, and Benji was a pure delight.

Each time Charley had caught Cooper watching her, however, there'd been more than a hint of disapproval on his face, and she'd reacted by jabbering like a crazy mockingbird. What a surprise to find out medical school hadn't surgically removed her nervous bone. She wasn't bothered by the other men in town who were clearly uneasy with her gender and profession. It had become second nature to hide behind a shield of unflappable aloofness while taking occasional, secret delight in being able to fluster someone like the mayor with a pretty smile and flattering tongue. But somehow, those defenses weren't effective against Mr. Cooper Knight. His silence made her sound like an emptyheaded chatterbox, and her smiles felt insipid and contrived when they bounced harmlessly off his solid frame.

Hannah and Benji took their brushes to the pump to clean them with soapy water, and Charley gave herself permission to watch Cooper for a few more seconds before joining them. The man's rolled shirtsleeves displayed the tanned, muscle-corded forearms that had lifted her down from the stagecoach more than once now, and her heart did a quick double tap and pounded faster. His thick beard might possibly hide a weak chin or sagging jawline, but anyone who found fault with his build or the way he moved with effortless grace needed to have their eyes examined. He might growl like a grizzly, but he moved like the big cat the town was named for.

And apparently the strong sun had fried her brain like it had seared her tender nose. She wrenched her eyes from the mesmerizing subject above her. Why did her stomach wobble whenever she caught sight of the man? Why did her breath forget its reliable rhythm whenever he turned those steely eyes on her? Maybe *she* needed her eyes examined. A person would have to be blind to miss his disapproval of her. Besides, she wasn't on the lookout for a potential suitor. She'd already learned that painful lesson. A man wanted a wife to tend his home and children not a physician who could be called out any hour of the day or night. And this stern, bearded man was no different. He might even be more adamant about not wanting a physician for a wife. So why did she allow him to rattle her? She didn't even like beards. They masked the face God created and made expressions hard to read.

She turned her back on the enigmatic man and carried her brush over to the pump where Hannah and Benji were laughing and splashing. She would enjoy the camaraderie Ma Jankins and Hannah and Benji offered and chalk up her reaction to Mr. Knight as the strain from a cross-country move and trying to get her practice up and running.

Because that's all it was.

All it could be.

VII

"Hi, Dr. Charley!" Benji opened wide the front door of his home. "Come in. Digger's in the kitchen."

"Thank you." Charley stepped inside the little white cottage on the north side of town. The furnishings in the front room showed faint signs of wear, but like the flowerbeds around the front of the house and the large vegetable garden in the back that she'd caught a glimpse of, everything was clean and neat as a pin.

She followed Benji to the kitchen where his mother was stirring a large pot on the stove. "Oh. I'm sorry to intrude at mealtime, Hannah. I intended to drop by earlier, but a patient came in to see me." The older woman had really only wanted someone new to listen to her imagined ills, but she had let Charley examine her, and hypochondriac or not, she was the first human patient who'd come to see the new female doctor of their own accord.

"I didn't want Benji to think I'd forgotten all about Digger, so I headed this way when I was free, but I forgot about what time of day it was."

Hannah laid aside the spoon and wiped her hands on her apron. "Nonsense. I told Benji you'd come when you could, and I had already planned to ask you to stay to supper. We're waiting on Coop to get in from his stage run. He was planning on eating with us before riding out to his place."

Charley shook her head, nervousness replacing the hunger pangs that had flared to life the instant she'd caught a whiff of Hannah's simmering stew. "You don't have to feed me. You don't owe me anything for checking on Digger. I'm in debt to *you* for all the work on my house."

Hannah closed the oven door and pinned Charley with a stern look. "This is not about who owes what. It's about a friend asking a friend to share a meal." The woman's eyes might be warm-brown, but she did an impressive imitation of her brother's steely glare.

Charley grinned at the pushy woman. "In that case, I'd love to stay. And thank you." Despite the uneasy tickle in her belly at sharing another meal with Cooper Knight, she was a trained physician and could put aside this odd interest she had in a man who seemed to only tolerate her. After all, she'd barely thought of him in the three days since he'd helped paint her house.

"You're welcome." A smile bloomed across Hannah's face. "Coop will be here any minute and supper's almost ready, so you and Benji better get a move on if you're going to check Digger's stitches and get washed up in time."

"Yes, ma'am." Charley knelt to examine the terrier whose tail had thumped with each mention of his name. "Hello, Digger. How are you feeling?" The dog licked Charley's hand when she gently grasped his snout, and she rubbed his ears with her other hand while checking his eyes for any dullness. They were bright, and his tail beat a steady rhythm against his blanket even while she checked each of his injuries.

She settled Digger back on the blanket when she was finished and looked over at his worried young owner. "You've done an excellent job of keeping him quiet and clean, Benjamin. His wounds are healing nicely, and they don't show any evidence of festering. In a few more days, I should be able to remove the stitches."

The gangly frame that held hints of one day rivaling his uncle's swelled with pride. "I can tell he's feeling better because he wants to play each time I take him outside. He's bored in here."

"That's a good sign. I'd be worried if he wasn't." Charley scratched the base of a black silky ear, much to the dog's satisfaction.

"Digger's not the only one who's been bored. I'll be glad when they're *both* out from under my feet." Hannah eyed her son and his dog with a fondly exasperated expression before stirring the stew again.

"Then you'll all be glad to hear that if Digger stays away from other dogs and doesn't play too rough or hard for a few more days, Benji can start taking him on longer walks and spend more time outdoors. The fresh air and sunshine will do them both good."

Benji's grin displayed a space where a side tooth had gone missing since she'd checked on Digger two days earlier. "Did you hear that, boy?" He cradled the furry nose in his hands. "We can go exploring again."

Digger yipped, his lips parting in a doggy smile.

Benji's eyes held a seriousness far older than the ten years his mother had declared him to be when he looked back at her. "Thanks, Dr. Charley."

"You're more than welcome, Benjamin. I'm honored you asked for my help. You two just stay out of trouble from now on." Charley tousled the soft fur on the dog's head and winked at the boy.

A happy sparkle appeared in his eyes. "Yes, ma'am."

The back door burst open and boots thudded against the kitchen floor as Cooper entered the room.

Pulse skittering, Charley watched him from her spot beside Digger's bed. Was that an actual smile on the man's face?

Cooper removed his hat and hung it on a peg by the door. "Sure smells good in here." He wrapped an arm around Hannah's shoulders and leaned over to sniff the contents of the stewpot. "I'm hungry enough to eat an entire buffalo. When do we eat?"

"As soon as you help Charley to her feet, and all three of you wash your hands." Hannah grabbed a couple of towels to shield her hands from the hot pan she transferred from oven to table."

Cooper stiffened and turned. No trace of a smile remained, but something flickered through his smoky eyes when he spotted her kneeling beside Digger's bed.

If only she could read that emotion. Figure out what it meant. Figure out why her knees didn't want to push her to her feet.

Stop it.

Only this morning, while peering through her curtains to watch him climb aboard the stage and drive out of Puma Ridge, she'd determined to treat him like any other person who disapproved of her. She would remain polite and pleasant and keep her professional distance firmly in place. Her plans to gain the confidence of the town's citizens and establish her practice had no room for figuring out what secrets lay behind those intriguing, enigmatic gray eyes.

"Hurry up before the food gets cold." Hannah urged.

"Miss Adams." Cooper held out a hand to assist her to her feet.

"Mr. Knight. I hope you had a pleasant trip today." She ignored his hand and attempted to rise without his help, but the toe of her shoe pinned the hem of her skirt, and she tripped forward.

Strong hands caught her around the waist, holding her steady until she untangled her feet. Which took longer than it should have because of an abrupt inability to draw a full breath.

"You all right?" Cooper's voice rumbled quietly above her bent head.

Charley pulled away and brushed off her skirt, giving her unsteady hands a task. "I'm fine. Thank you." Thanks to years of practice, she was able to blank her expression before she looked up.

She must have imagined the hint of softness in his voice, because there was no give in his granite-hard eyes. They searched her face like he knew she was lying. Like he wanted to pry off her veneer of composure and prove that she was nowhere close to calm and collected. Which was ridiculous. No one had ever figured out that she protected herself behind the barriers of an unruffled smile, good humor, and feigned obliviousness to scorn and insults.

Charley sidestepped his probing gaze and scooted to the sink where Benji washed his hands. If a whole school full of narrow-minded men couldn't trick her into losing her composure, giving up, or quitting, neither would one disturbing stagecoach driver. Either he'd get over his aversion to female physicians, or she'd learn to ignore him. *And* the disturbing feelings he stirred up.

The hearty stew and cornbread were delicious, and Charley concentrated on enjoying Hannah's hospitality and Benji's happy chatter rather than her own scattered emotions. Even Cooper relaxed enough to recount, at Benji's request, several funny occurrences from his stagecoach travels. Charley briefly wondered whether she had been the subject of his more recent stories to Benji then shoved the thought aside. It was probably better that she didn't know the answer.

She dried her hands on a towel when she finished helping with the dishes. "Thank you for a wonderful meal, Hannah. It was a nice change to have someone besides myself to talk to."

Hannah gave her a quick hug. "Come over anytime." She released Charley and tapped Cooper on the shoulder. "Have you picked up your horse from the livery stable yet?"

He looked up from his task of adding the finishing touches to a whistle Benji had carved. "No. Why?" His nephew hung over him, watching the sharp knife shave away the rough spots on the slender piece of wood.

"Then you can escort Charley home on your way there."

"Oh, no. I don't need an escort. It's not even dark yet." If any of the room's occupants heard Charley's protest, they ignored it.

Cooper slid the knife into its sheath at his waist and stood, handing Benji the whistle. "Remind me to sharpen your knife next time I'm here. You had that one almost perfect."

"Thanks, Uncle Coop." Benji beamed.

Charley inched toward the door, intending to slip away while he was distracted, but the sight of the big, brawny man ruffling his nephew's hair and tenderly hugging his sister stopped her in her tracks. The softness of those actions made her want to linger, to learn more about the man.

And that was a bad idea.

Cooper crossed the room, retrieved his hat from the wall peg, and glanced down at her, appearing neither pleased nor displeased at being asked to accompany her home. "Ready?"

She nodded and managed to wave goodbye to Hannah and Benji before stepping outside. Cooper followed her, pulling the door closed behind him, before jamming his hat over his thick, chestnut-colored hair.

The action snapped her out of her befuddled thinking. "I appreciate Hannah's offer of an escort, Mr. Knight, but I'll be fine. You must be tired after driving all day. You should go on home. Good evening." Thankful that her voice didn't betray her nervousness, Charley started toward her house.

She hadn't gone two feet when he fell in beside her and blandly answered the unspoken question in her glance. "This is the shortest distance to the livery stable."

Charley didn't protest again. It would be outright rude to tell him to find another route. Unfortunately, she failed to think of a single, coherent topic of conversation and stiff silence stretched between them until her house came into view.

She nearly signed in relief when she saw its crisp, blue paint. "Thank you for the escort, Mr. Knight. I can make it from here. Have a good evening."

Cooper stopped, pulled off his hat, and scrubbed his fingers over his scalp. "Thank *you*, Miss Adams."

Charley blinked in surprise and paused to face him fully. "For what?"

Cooper replaced his hat and jammed his hands in his pockets. "For taking care of Digger."

It had cost him something to say the words, but Charley couldn't have explained how she knew that. She decided to accept them at face value. "You're welcome."

When she didn't say anything else, his shoulders lowered and lost some of their tension.

He opened his mouth to reply, but a shout interrupted him.

"Hey! Dr. Adams!"

Charley jerked toward the two figures that staggered from the twilight shadows gathering around the buildings across the street, and a pained groan carried easily on the clear evening air.

"Get inside. I'll handle this." Cooper planted himself squarely in the path of the oncoming men.

Charley stepped around him, determined to investigate the cause for the sound of pain she'd heard, but stopped when she recognized the freckled-face redhead who'd taken her on the wild owl chase. She plopped her fists on her hips and frowned at him. "Do you have another sick bird for me to visit?"

The redhead yanked his hat off and nearly dropped his friend in the dirt. "No, ma'am, uh, Doctor, ma'am. And I'm right sorry about that. It'll never happen again."

"Then why'd you do it in the first place?" The young man didn't appear to have the kind of mean streak that had driven some of the pranks she'd experienced in medical school.

Cooper loomed at her side, irritation at her disobedience of his order evident by the fierce glare he shot her way before turning it on the redhead.

The young man swallowed and jostled his companion who leaned heavily against his shoulder. "Jonesy, here, bet me I couldn't make the pretty new doc go with me anywhere. I won the bet when you rode out of town beside me." His quick grin disappeared when a low rumble came from Cooper's direction.

Charley looked at the arms-crossed, formidable-looking bear beside her, but surprisingly, his ire wasn't aimed at her. Was he *protecting* her? She'd thought he barely tolerated her, much less liked her.

She returned her attention to the redhead. His unsteady companion did seem unwell, but... "How do I know you aren't trying to trick me again?"

"Because Cooper said he'd wallop me if I did. Warned the other fellas to leave you alone, too."

"What?" She gaped at Cooper.

"Is there a reason you're bothering Miss Adams, Oscar?" His snarl made the young man flinch.

"Aw, come on, Coop. Jonesy needs the doc's help. Don't ya', Jonesy?" He shook the fellow beside him again and took the resulting groan for adequate affirmation. "He's got a tooth that's painin' him somethin' awful. He wants you to pull it."

Charley shook her head. "I'm a medical doctor. Not a dentist." She couldn't stop herself from assessing Jonesy's condition, though.

Beneath the shadow of his hat brim, the side of his face appeared swollen. She had some rudimentary dentist tools and knowledge of dentistry, but it was not an aspect of medicine she cared to practice. In fact, she'd been relieved to learn a dentist regularly visited Puma Ridge. Pulling teeth was hard work, and if you didn't have the strength to yank the tooth out quickly, it prolonged the agony of the patient.

"Please? The dentist won't be through for at least two more weeks, and it's already been painin' him for a month. I told him you were a woman doc, but he said he didn't care who took it out. He's been taking Wizard Oil, but it's not helping anymore."

Charley barely refrained from rolling her eyes. Hamlin's Wizard Oil and its slogan were all too familiar. *There is no sore it will not heal, no pain it will not subdue.* The patent medicine promised to treat and cure a whole list of things, including toothaches. But at best, the only thing it was capable of was numbing pain for a few hours. And one whiff of the contents explained why.

The poor fellow moaned again, and Charley didn't have the

heart to turn him away. "Mr. Knight? Will you please help Oscar bring his friend inside? "I'll go light the lamps."

Cooper grunted his disapproval, but he went to Jonesy's other side and none-too-gently assisted him and Oscar into the examination room.

"Put him there." Charley gestured to the leather couch, and the men lowered the groaning man onto it while Charley washed up and gathered the instruments she would need. "Cooper, I'm going to need you to help hold him down. Even with the Wizard Oil, Jonesy's gonna feel this, and I don't think *he's* going to be much help." She motioned to Oscar who stared open-mouthed at the full-length chart of a human skeleton she'd tacked to one wall of the examination room.

Cooper stiffened, and the skin over his tanned cheekbones paled.

"Or go find me someone else to help." She had momentarily forgotten how green he'd turned after looking at Digger's wounds the other day.

He straightened to his full height, his face hard. "What do you need me to do?"

Charley suppressed a grin. If Cooper Knight gritted his jaw any harder, he'd have his own dental problems to worry about. "Oscar. *Oscar!*"

The wide-eyed young man wrenched his eyes off the skeleton. "Huh?"

"Can you hold Jonesy's legs down?"

Oscar hesitated before moving to do her bidding, noticeably less brash than he'd been minutes earlier.

"Cooper, I need you to hold Jonesy's shoulders down."

Grim-faced, Cooper stepped to the raised end of the couch where Jonesy's head rested and planted his large hands firmly on the sufferer's shoulders.

Charley placed her tools within easy reach, repositioned a lamp, and leaned over her patient to open his mouth. His fetid, whisky-soaked breath nearly knocked her over, but she easily spotted the offending tooth.

After placing a tool in his mouth to hold it open and prevent him from biting her, she grasped the rotting tooth with a pair of forceps, and prayed it wouldn't crumble before she got it extracted. "Hold him tight, please. This will hurt."

She pulled, closing her ears to Jonesy's bellow of pain. If he'd come to see her before pickling himself with that snake oil, she could have used an anesthetic and saved him a lot of misery.

Jonesy bucked in the chair, dislodging her grip on the tooth.

Cooper firmed his grip on the man's shoulders, the move bringing his head inches away from hers. The scent of leather and horses was a pleasant reprieve from Jonesy's breath, but Charley shoved the thought aside and forced her attention back to the rotted tooth.

She grabbed it again, and feeling it give slightly, she tugged harder.

The poor man bucked violently, and Oscar lost control of his legs. Cooper fought to hold Jonesy on the couch as he twisted and kicked to escape the pain in his mouth.

Charley jumped back with a yelp. Somehow, Jonesy had managed to swing one booted foot back far enough to hit her in the side of the calf with his spur.

"What's wrong?" Cooper's complexion lightened by several shades.

"Nothing. Except next time, I'm going to require that spurs be removed before I work on a patient." Charley resisted the urge to rub her stinging leg.

"Oscar, if you don't hold his legs down, I'll thrash you." The words snarled past Cooper's gritted teeth.

"Sorry, Doc." Oscar pushed Jonesy's legs back on the couch and sat on them to hold them down, his freckles standing out in sharp contrast to his pale face.

Charley wrapped her forceps around the tooth again. *Lord, I need some help here.* With a deep breath, she yanked. Hard.

The tooth broke free with a grinding, sucking noise.

Jonesy gargled a pained yell then sagged limply into the couch.

Charley blew out a breath, hating that she'd had to cause the poor man so much additional agony. But at least it had only taken three tries to get the tooth extracted.

~

Miss Adams calmly dropped the offending tooth into the bowl on the table beside her then swabbed out Jonesy's mouth several times while peering closely into that gaping cavern, seemingly unaffected by the sight or the smell.

Cooper swallowed hard and looked everywhere *but* Jonesy's mouth.

Finally, she packed a piece of cotton wadding inside Jonesy's cheek and removed the torture device that had held his mouth open. "You can both let go of him now. It's done."

Cooper retreated to the far wall, his knees nearly giving out before he leaned against it. He'd come perilously close to losing his supper until he'd glanced up and realized how close Miss Adams' head was to his nose. Focusing on her shiny hair and breathing deeply of her subtle, floral fragrance had kept him from embarrassing himself by vomiting or passing out.

"What does he owe you, Doc?" The interminable minutes that had just passed had sobered Oscar from whatever liquid courage he'd imbibed with Jonesy. Then again, a grown man's wounded shrieks would do that.

"One dollar." Miss Adams moved her instruments of torture away from her now-passive victim and to the sink.

Oscar dug into his friend's pocket, extracted a coin, and laid it on the table. "Can he go now?"

She shook her head. "Your friend is going to be unsteady for a while. He should stay here until he feels better."

Jonesy roused enough to mumble an objection and used an elbow to lever himself into a slouched sitting position. His hand cradled his swollen jaw.

"Nah. He was hurt worse than this when Outlaw bucked him off and tried to stomp him into the ground a couple years back. We'll take it slow to the bunkhouse, and then he can sleep it off." Oscar pulled Jonesy to his feet. "Come on, partner. You're all right now. The doc fixed you right up."

Jonesy mumbled something unintelligible, and Oscar half dragged his wobbly friend toward the door. "Thanks for your help, Doc."

"You're welcome." Charley tucked a bottle of something in Oscar's vest pocket. "Have him swish his mouth out with that three times a day until his gum heals, but come get me without delay if you see any signs of infection. I'll have Ma Jankins drive me out tomorrow to check on him."

The door closed behind the two men, and Miss Adams shook her head slightly before moving to the basin to wash up.

The burning question shot off Cooper's tongue. "How do you do it?"

"Do what?" She glanced over her shoulder, her green eyes questioning.

"How do you stand causing so much pain it makes a grown man scream?" Cooper welcomed the anger washing through him. It stiffened his knees.

She dried her hands slowly then turned and spoke softly. "He was *already* in pain. If I'd left that tooth alone simply because it would hurt him to pull it out, infection would've set in and most likely killed him. Sometimes additional pain is necessary for the body to have a chance to heal itself."

"Couldn't you have given him something to make it less painful?" How had she endured those awful groans and cries of pain? He'd nearly bolted from the room like a yellow-bellied coward.

The lady's chin lifted and firmed. "Yes. I would have preferred to give him an anesthetic to put him to sleep and block the pain. It would have made that procedure easier on both of us. But that *medicine* Jonesy has been treating himself with is about 80% alcohol, and with that already in his system, I didn't want to risk him going to sleep permanently under the anesthetic I have."

Her cool explanation made sense. Sort of. But Cooper had had more than enough of this torture chamber for one evening. He strode toward the door, but his hand froze on the doorknob when a terrifying thought penetrated his nausea and irritation.

A woman alone. At night. Inviting two unknown men inside her house. The danger in that scenario churned his already uneasy stomach into painful knots.

He whirled to face her again.

She took a startled step backwards, but her veil of aloofness remained firmly in place. "Did you have another question, Mr. Knight?"

"Do you have a gun?"

VIII

"What?" A crack appeared in Miss Adams' composure, and she blinked at him like he'd started speaking gibberish.

Maybe he had. She *was* an easterner.

Cooper slowly repeated each word. "Do you have a gun?"

"Why?"

Cooper knew no way of putting it delicately, so he put it bluntly. "To protect yourself from anybody who decides they want more from you than your doctoring skills."

She blinked again, swallowed, and her skin lost some of its rosy color.

Cooper felt a grim sense of accomplishment at finally shaking the woman's annoying self-control. Turnabout was fair play. The blood had drained from his own face when she'd made him hold Jonesy down.

He held back a shudder at the memory of Jonesy's yells and the gruesome sound of his tooth coming out. "Do you own a gun?"

"Yes. I do." Miss Adams' tone echoed the stiffness of her frame.

The woman might have a speck of common sense after all. "Let's see it."

With an annoyed huff that reminded Cooper of Hannah humoring a request she thought was ridiculous—it must be a sound all women were born with—Miss Adams retrieved her medical bag, dug through its contents, and pulled out a derringer.

Cooper sidestepped quicker than a beetle on a hot rock. "Lady, don't ever point a gun at someone unless you're planning to pull the trigger."

She pointed the small weapon toward the floor. "It's not loaded."

The flash of annoyance in her eyes hinted she might wish otherwise, and Cooper snagged the firearm from her hand, unwilling to give her time to prove his suspicion. "Always treat a gun like it's loaded. *Always!*"

The empty chamber that winked up at him when he flipped the derringer open failed to bring any relief, and his stomach lurched as he examined the decrepit gun. The fragile old piece needed to be retired to the gunsmith's display of antiques. If she'd actually fired the thing, there was a distinct possibility it could have blown apart in her hands.

Cooper shoved the derringer into his pocket. Sawbones or not, he couldn't leave a woman defenseless. Especially one who insisted on putting herself in dangerous situations.

He pulled his revolver from its holster, checked the cylinder, and then laid it on the table. "Keep my gun for tonight. It's loaded. All you need to do is point at what you fully intend to shoot and pull the trigger. But keep your doors locked and hopefully you won't need it. I'll be back in the morning." He stomped to the door and yanked it open. "Be ready, and don't shoot me." One of these days, he'd learn to mind his own business and stick to driving coaches and raising cattle.

"Why?" Her puzzled question followed him.

He kept walking. "To teach you how to use it."

Even if I live to regret it.

Twelve hours later, he walked back up the path to her door. The house looked inviting with its fresh coat of blue paint, white trim, and tidy yard, but less than a month ago, if anyone had suggested Cooper Knight would voluntarily visit it and the sawbones inside, he would've laughed in their face. It hinted at cowardice for a grown man to break out in a cold sweat at the thought of needing a doctor, but too many people in his life had ended up dead under their so-called care.

He hadn't heard of Miss Adams causing any lasting damage to

the few patients she'd had, but so far, she'd done nothing the blacksmith couldn't have done. The man had a knack for treating injured animals and he'd even been known to pull a bad tooth before the circuit-riding dentist had arrived in the area.

Cooper squared his shoulders and knocked. Although she'd teased him about the purpose of it, Hannah's breakfast had made the trip into town worthwhile. But now he itched to forget last night's half-baked scheme and run for the hills. Ranch work provided more than enough work to keep him busy without adding keep-an-eye-on-the-petticoat-doc to his list. Unfortunately, the woman had his favorite pistol, and he wanted it back. The one he currently carried would work in an emergency, but he didn't like the weight or the feel of it.

He banged on the door again. The sun had been up for over two hours. Surely, she was up.

A muffled shriek came through the wood panel, seizing his lungs, and before he'd consciously thought about it, his weapon was in his hand. Had Oscar and Jonesy returned? He'd never known either of them to be anything more than harmless, high-spirited cowboys. Had that changed? Or had someone else decided to take advantage of the lone, pretty woman?

Thank the Lord he'd left his other revolver with her last night. But had she had it within reach when she'd needed it? Would she have the courage to use it?

Caution reined in the instinctive urge to bust down her door and rush inside. Announcing his presence that way could get the doc hurt. If he snuck in and caught the ruffian off guard, he would have the upper hand and hopefully protect Charley from further harm. If she didn't shoot him in the process.

Pistol at the ready, he tried the door and found it unlatched. *Thank you, God.*

But he was going to have a long talk with the woman about disobeying his order to keep it locked.

He eased it open—silent hinges giving further evidence of its owner's industriousness—and peeked into the tiny waiting room.

Empty.

He crept across to the examination room and found it empty as well. Silently, he deposited the satchel he carried on the couch and tiptoed toward the hallway.

"Please! Just go away." The desperation in Charley's voice drilled straight through his chest.

Jaw hardening and eyes narrowing, he slid down the hall on cat feet, gun trained on the doorway where Charley's whimpers came from.

"Please! I know you were here first, but this is my home now. You have to leave."

Cooper's fist tightened around the butt of his pistol. This building had supposedly been uninhabited for over two years. Had Charley surprised a drifter breaking back in?

He inched closer, his eyes studying the slice of sitting room visible from his position.

"Oh, stop! No! Stay over there." Charley's voice rose in alarm. "No! No! No!"

Cooper whipped around the door casing, his gun sweeping the room. "Drop it!"

Crack! Bang! Thud!

A stack of books crashed to the hardwood floor, sounding like a young war.

The lone occupant of the room teetered on the seat of a straight-back chair, her now-empty arms windmilling.

Cooper holstered his gun and darted forward as Charley lost her fight for balance. His arms closed around her, and she crashed into his chest instead of the floor. Relief hit him with the same force the thick volumes had struck the floor, and then chaos disintegrated into frozen silence.

He stared down into startled, unblinking emerald eyes. Wispy tendrils of blonde hair had escaped a loose chignon to frame her face, and one long lock had snagged the corner of her mouth. He reached up to free it, and the feel of her smooth cheek against the calloused pads of his fingers jolted him to his senses.

He dropped his hand and forced his other arm to uncurl. But before he could step away, she darted a wild glance over her shoulder and pressed closer.

"What's going on?" The question shot out harsher than he'd intended, but the feel of her curves wreaked havoc on his senses.

Charley whipped her head to the other side, eyes wide. Searching.

Cooper wrapped his arms back around her to steady her. And

him.

"Where is it? Where did it go?"

Cooper hauled his eyes off his distracting armful and glanced around the room, seeking the intruder. With books spread across the floor and a bookcase pulled away from the wall, the room appeared to have been ransacked. But there was no sign of man or beast. "Where's what?"

It shouldn't have been possible for Charley to cling any tighter because his arms were already anchored tight around her waist, but she did, darting another fearful peek behind her. "It was right there! Oh, where did it go?"

Her feet did a little tapping-hop, giving Cooper the distinct impression that if it had been possible, she would have climbed him like a frightened kitten up a tree. He had no idea what she was trying to escape, but holding her wasn't what he'd call a hardship.

Bending and twisting, he scooped an arm behind her knees and straightened, cradling her against his chest. Her right arm lassoed his neck, and her left hand tethered the front of his shirt while her head continued to swivel back and forth, searching the floor.

Cooper swallowed hard, willing his breathing to settle. He shouldn't have picked her up. Holding her was doing peculiar things to his insides. Or maybe he should have picked her up sooner. He was seeing an entirely different side of the woman who'd so coolly introduced herself to the flabbergasted welcoming committee. "Charley—I mean Miss Adams—"

She shrieked and nearly choked him with her arms.

For a woman whose soft tone was normally the embodiment of calm control, she sure could deafen a man when she wanted. "What is it, Charley? *Where* is it?"

Charley jabbed her finger at something. "There. Make it go away. Please!"

His gaze followed her frantic gesture, and he finally spotted the vicious brute terrorizing the doc. A mouse, no bigger around than his thumb, scurried along the base of the opposite wall then darted under the bookcase. Frankly, he couldn't blame the critter for trying to find some place quieter.

"*That's* what you're screaming about?" He must be missing something. Charley's proximity was hindering his ability to think straight.

Her arms squeezed tighter, halting his attempt to set her down. "No. Don't. Please! It might crawl on me." Worried eyes met his for a split second before refastening on the bookcase.

"It's only a little mouse."

"I hate...mice." A shiver rattled her entire frame.

Understanding dawned on Cooper. She'd shuddered like that after she'd recounted her experiences at medical school and said the other students' silent treatment was better than *the mice*. He tightened his lips around the laughter that threatened to explode. The sawbones who'd calmly walked back to town after Oscar's practical joke and who'd unflinchingly extracted a rotten tooth from a yelling, bucking, intoxicated cowboy last night was terrified of a tiny rodent.

Holding her snug against his chest, he walked out of the room, pulled the door firmly shut behind him, and entered the kitchen. With each inch of distance he put between her and the frightening beast, her arms loosened from around his neck, and her head drooped until he couldn't see her face. When he lowered her feet to the floor, she darted away to the pump at the sink.

The immediate feeling of loss startled Cooper.

Avoiding his gaze, Charley poured herself a glass of water, her hand trembling when she lifted the drink to her mouth.

Cooper's heart squeezed at her lingering distress and all trace of humor evaporated. A single mouse was a tiny, fairly harmless creature, but it inspired profound terror in Miss Charley Adams. In fact, the exhibition of fear he'd just witnessed might be worse than his fear of doctors. And that was saying something.

He pulled a chair away from the table, straddled the seat, and folded his forearms across the back. "Why are you so afraid of mice?"

Charley lowered the glass and lifted her chin. Her attempt at a pleasant half-smile failed miserably, however, and her eyes clouded with chagrin. "I suppose I do owe you some explanation after that disagreeable display of hysterics."

The display had exercised his heart pretty good, but there had been nothing disagreeable about holding the woman in his arms. To be honest, if she didn't stop looking like she expected the mouse to jump out of hiding at any second, he was going to scoop her back into his arms.

He stood and left the kitchen before the impulse could get him into more trouble. When he returned a minute later with the satchel he'd left in the front room, Charley had unearthed his revolver from some hiding spot and handed it to him without comment.

He stuffed it behind his belt and opened the back door. "Come on."

"Where are we going?" She exited the house with a faint sigh of relief, lifting her face to the morning sunshine like she was trying to shake off a nightmare.

"I'm going to teach you how to shoot while Benji removes the mouse and any of his friends." And maybe satisfy his bewildering need to find out more about Charley Adams while her habitual mask was down.

Charley shuddered again but nodded her head. "Good!"

~

Why couldn't it have been a big old spider that had run out from under the bookshelf and over her feet? Even a snake wouldn't have been as terrifying. *Why* had it been a mouse? And why did it have to be Cooper who'd witnessed her loss of control?

Mortification heated Charley's cheeks, but she continued to trail her rescuer, eager to put the rodent far behind. They'd stopped at his sister's place, and after ordering Benji and Digger to rid Charley's house of vermin, Cooper had led her into the woods beyond Hannah's large garden. The twenty-minute walk in silence didn't eradicate Charley's embarrassment, but by the time a grassy clearing opened out in front of them, she'd regained some of her equilibrium.

Cooper sat the satchel he'd been carrying on a weathered stump. "Have you ever shot a gun before?" He pulled a small revolver out of its depths. Smaller than the one he'd loaned her or the one he currently carried at his hip.

Charley wet her lips. "A long time ago, when I was a little girl. I preferred going with my uncle to visit his patients over going hunting with my brother, though." She was relieved to find that her voice had lost its betraying quiver. And even more relieved that Cooper seemed willing to ignore the scene he'd interrupted in her sitting room.

He dumped shiny brass shells out of the cylinder of the revolver and snapped it closed. "Where'd you find that old derringer?"

She cleared her throat of the roughness that lingered from her fright. "Dr. Tidd gave it to me after a male patient thought my work as a doctor meant I was…well, not a nice woman and acted ungentlemanly. After that, I carried it in my pocket in case I needed to reinforce a refusal to an unseemly proposal."

He grimaced. "That corroded old thing couldn't have reinforced a piece of string."

Charley hated the feeling of foolishness that welled through her. Again. "Dr. Tidd spread the word that I carried it, so I never had to actually use it. Eventually, I tucked it into the bottom of my bag and sort of forgot about it."

Walking to the base of a small hill about fifteen yards away, Cooper gathered up twelve fist-sized rocks and set them along the trunk of an old, fallen pine tree. Then, returning to the stump, he motioned her over and handed her a wad of cotton lint he'd taken out of his bag.

She eyed the cotton in her palm. "What's this for?"

"Stuff some into each ear. It will dull the sound of the shots and help you not flinch when you fire."

She followed his instructions, but he continued speaking—his words only slightly muffled by the cotton in her ears—and she had no time to wonder at his odd determination to teach her to shoot after she'd thoroughly humiliated herself in front of him.

"I want you to face the targets I put on that log, and hold the gun like this." He held the pistol in a two-handed grip then demonstrated how to aim it before easing the weapon into her hands, all the while keeping it pointed away from them and at the ground.

Charley worked to ignore the internal havoc and confusion his close proximity created and focused on gripping and pointing the gun he'd handed her. It was heavier than the derringer she'd carried in her bag, but lighter than the revolver he'd loaned her the previous evening.

"Now, gently squeeze the trigger." Cooper stood close enough that his breath tickled her ear.

She barely managed to hide her shiver. "But it's not loaded." She'd seen him empty it.

"You need to get used to holding the gun on the target while pulling the trigger." Cooper's impassive instruction did nothing to settle her nerves.

Instead of trying to decipher his enigmatic gray eyes, she lined her gun up with the targets, and pulled the trigger at his command, realigning the barrel after each sharp click of the falling hammer. Before her arms could tire of holding the gun up and steady, he took it away from her and walked her through loading the firearm. Then had her face the condemned rocks once more and stepped behind her.

Charley had to be imagining the instant warmth on her back. Her skin burned with the sensation that he'd touched her, but he hadn't. He hadn't even looked her in the face since they'd left her house. Shoving the odd sensation away, she aimed and squeezed the trigger. The loud bang and buck of the gun made her flinch. It had been too many years since her father and brother had tried to interest her in shooting, and she'd forgotten how hard a gun could kick.

She lowered the revolver and blinked against the powder smoke. "Did I hit it?"

"Nope. You only scared it. Try again." He sounded like he'd expected her to miss, and it stung Charley's raw pride.

Firming her shoulders, she tried again. And again. Until the hammer fell with a dull click. She lowered her arms, disgusted with her ineptitude. Failure didn't sit well. Had she been this poor of a shot when she'd been a girl on her parents' farm? If so, she'd blocked it from her memory.

Cooper passed her six more cartridges. "Reload. And this time, when you get ready to fire, take a deep breath, release it until it feels comfortable, then hold it while you gently squeeze the trigger."

She nodded and reloaded the revolver. In other words, control her breathing. Easier said than done. Her breathing hadn't been normal since that mouse had darted out of hiding. And Cooper's presence wasn't helping.

Her next two shots missed everything but dirt.

He must have seen her growing frustration because he touched her arm to get her attention. "Pretend the big rock in the middle is a mouse."

A tingle started up Charley's arm but promptly ran into a wall of surprise when his words registered. She looked over at him and saw that a twinkle had turned his gray eyes to liquid silver.

Oh, my!

The tingle shook itself off and continued up her arm, across her shoulder, and down her spine, making her breathing stutter. Beard or no beard, if the man ever combined a smile with that twinkle, she would be in serious trouble.

She jerked her attention back to the line of targets and made herself concentrate on his advice. What had he said? Pretend it was a mouse? Right. The disgusting creature that had turned her into a flinching, babbling idiot earlier.

Holding her breath, she aimed and slowly tightened her trigger finger. With a sharp crack, the middle rock cracked and flew off the log.

Charley stared at it for half a second. "I hit it!"

The corners of Cooper's mouth twitched. "Lucky shot."

She scowled and turned back to the targets, determined to prove him wrong. But he was right. Her next two shots plowed dirt.

Charley squared her shoulders, acrid smoke stinging her nostrils. One round remained in the revolver, and she intended to make it count. Aiming carefully, she slowly squeezed the trigger.

Another rock flew off the log.

"Ha! Take that!" She lowered the gun to her side and eyed the log. The remaining rocks mocked her burst of triumph, but she squinted at them in defiance. The day wasn't over.

Without a word, Cooper held out six more cartridges.

"Thanks." She swiped the ammunition from his hand and reloaded without looking up at him. She didn't want to know if he was silently laughing at her ineptitude. She had mice to kill.

Twenty-four rounds later, she had finally cleared the log of all twelve of them.

A smile stretched her cheeks, and she lowered her tired arms. "I did it."

Cooper held out his hand for the gun. "Not bad for a beginner." His soft expression wasn't quite a smile, and it wasn't quite approval, but it *was* a nice change from the suspicious disapproval he'd worn around her ever since she'd announced herself to the town's welcoming committee.

Returning to the stump, he dumped the empty cases from the revolver's cylinder into the satchel and wiped the gun down with an oily rag.

Charley pulled the wadding from her ears and folded her arms across her middle while she watched him work. The man was an enigma and altogether too interesting for her comfort, but a question had bugged her since last night and she wanted to know the answer.

"Did you actually threaten to wallop Oscar?"

"Not in so many words." He shoved a small square of cloth through the barrel with a short metal rod, not sparing her a glance.

"But 'in so many words' you told him not to trick me again?"

He finished cleaning the gun then reloaded it and returned it to a leather holster before replying. "I suppose."

"Why?" And how had he known who to talk to? *She* hadn't known the cowboy's name until last night.

He handed her the holstered gun, his face expressionless. "Carry this with you from now on and run an oily rag over it once in a while to keep it from rusting. It's loaded, and I'll give you a box of extra cartridges after I walk you home."

She took it but sank to the grass in a sitting position, determined to satisfy her curiosity before leaving. "You didn't answer my question."

The man was a complete mystery. He frowned and growled yet he always seemed to appear right when she needed help. He also hadn't laughed her to scorn upon seeing her reaction to a tiny rodent. Although it hadn't looked that tiny when it darted over her feet.

Cooper squatted on his heels beside her, broke off a long stem of grass, tucked it between his teeth, and looked out across the clearing. Seconds ticked by without a response, almost as if he'd forgotten she sat beside him.

Charley let the silence lengthen, and little by little, the cheerful birdsong returned. A few flowers dotted the grass, dark evergreens ringed the pretty glade, and a gentle breeze tempered the sun's strength. She drank in the serene landscape. When time hung heavy on her hands, she missed having her family nearby, but her new home was beautiful, and she didn't regret the move. Despite the obstacles she faced.

"I'll answer your question after you answer mine." Cooper's voice was low and quiet, barely disturbing the now-peaceful setting. Until he spoke again. "Why are you so frightened of mice?"

IX

The fragile bubble of peace that had enveloped Charley instantly evaporated. She grimaced and looked away. "You have my permission to forget about all that."

"You can sew up a mangled dog and pull a rotten tooth without flinching." He sat down against the stump and relaxed, looking comfortable enough to wait all day for an explanation. "Why are you frightened of mice?"

Charley inhaled slowly and fingered the leather holster. With the exception of mice, she didn't run from hard things, but this discussion would be about that very subject. She couldn't jump up and escape to her home, though, because that's where the mouse was. Her skin crawled at the memory. If Benji and Digger were unsuccessful in catching it, she would have to move back to the hotel.

"A lot of people don't like…rodents in their house. It startled me, and I suppose I overreacted a little. I'm sorry you had to see it. I would have calmed down eventually." Which might have involved burning the house down.

She *had* to learn to control her reaction to the dreadful creatures. If other people saw that kind of hysterics from her, they'd never trust her to be their physician. But when she'd moved the bookshelf to get the paper that had fallen behind it, that *thing* had scurried over her feet, and the only thought in her head had been to arm herself with books and get off the floor before it could dart up her skirt.

Another shiver shook her, but then a flush worked its way up her throat when she remembered where she'd ultimately ended up—in Cooper's arms, hugging his neck like her life had depended on it. Which at that moment, it had.

She slid the gun from its holster, pretending to examine it, and changed the subject. "Thank you for the shooting lesson." If she kept practicing, she might become good enough to shoot the next tiny invader of her home.

Cooper didn't reply, and she peeked over to see if the distraction had worked.

His eyes caught and held hers, and he shoved his hat brim up to let her feel the full weight of their probing intensity. "You still haven't answered my question." The arms that had held her so effortlessly crossed over his chest, his whole attitude one of patient watching.

Charley rammed the pistol back into its covering and groaned silently. She'd managed to keep her fear hidden from an entire school of medical students whose whole goal in life had been to find new ways to make her life miserable. But this man had found her shrieking in panic, standing on a chair, ready to hurl her armload of books the second she spotted the tiny creature again, and although he'd barged in with his gun drawn like he'd expected to find an entire gang of armed bandits, he'd rescued her without one word of ridicule or teasing.

Pretending a calmness she didn't feel, Charley folded her hands in her lap and fastened her gaze there. "You probably heard me tell Hannah and Benji how I didn't react in medical school when the other students tried to scare me in the autopsy room and so they tried to ignore my existence instead?"

"I did." The hardness in Cooper's voice reminded her that the man thoroughly disapproved of her profession.

He would probably think she'd gotten what she deserved for being presumptuous enough to attend medical school, but he'd asked for an explanation and he was going to get it. "Before they stopped talking to me, they tried one more thing to run me off." She gripped her hands so hard they ached.

"Mice?"

Charley's head jerked up at his soft question. The concern on his face surprised her. Maybe the disapproval that remained there wasn't completely directed at her.

The notion made her words come easier. "A professor sent me to get a couple of items from a supply closet. I had already learned to be careful opening doors, but nothing fell when I opened this one, so I walked inside to get what I needed. The door was yanked shut behind me and locked, and in the dark, I tripped over a cord that was rigged to a container of mice taken from the laboratory. It fell off the shelf onto my head." Nightmares had plagued her for weeks afterwards. If she closed her eyes, she'd feel their tiny, clawed feet darting frantically across her body.

Charley kept her eyes open and her voice rigidly emotionless. "I was in there for over three hours before the janitor found me."

The angles of Cooper's face appeared to have been cut from stone. "A practical joke is one thing, but how could men who were training to be *healers* ignore cries for help that long?"

Grim satisfaction spilled into her voice. "I didn't scream. Or cry. I wouldn't give them one second's satisfaction of knowing they'd succeeded in terrifying me—not that they would've heard me over their own laughter. Besides, before it happened, mice didn't bother me. It was the hours spent with them squeaking and crawling around me in the dark that created that quirk."

"What kind of men attended that *medical* school?" His voice dripped with contempt. "No *gentleman* would ever do that to a lady."

"Some people believe I'm not a lady because I chose this work." Was he one of them?

It was impossible to tell exactly what he thought of her, but somehow in all their interactions, although he'd made her feel a lot of things, he'd never made her feel *less* than a lady. And today, he'd made her feel safe. Uncomfortable, but safe. Maybe that's why telling him the tale had been easier than she'd expected.

Cooper's scowl faded while he eyed her. "What'd you do after that?"

"Classes were over for the day by the time I got out, so I dragged myself to my boarding room, bathed twice, consigned my clothes to the woodstove, and crawled into bed and cried. It was the closest I ever came to quitting. But I dug out Uncle Eddy's old letters, reread how he encouraged my dream, and remembered why I chose this profession in the first place. I wanted to be able to competently help sick and injured people. The next morning, I marched into class like nothing had happened."

For the first time, Charley was able to chuckle when thinking about the incident. "However, I stayed away from closets and *never* walked through a doorway first if I could possibly help it. Although it seems I forgot that hard-learned lesson when Oscar took me to see the owl."

Cooper's eyes brightened with something that looked like grudging admiration. He pushed himself to his feet, brushed off his hands, and then offered her one. "You might be tough enough to make it out here after all, Miss Adams."

She grasped his hand and let him tug her to her feet. The warmth of his palm ran up her arm and thawed a corner of the icy walls she'd built around her heart to protect her while she'd pushed through obstacle after disapproving obstacle on the way to her goal. Cooper Knight might not like petticoat physicians, but the kindness that lay beneath his rough-and-ready exterior made him more of a gentleman than all the suit-clad doctors she'd graduated alongside.

He dropped her hand abruptly, and his face hardened. "Unfortunately, we have bigger, more dangerous things out here than mice." He turned and stalked toward the path leading to his sister's house.

She shook her head. It was a good thing it was firmly attached or she might have attributed the tingles from his touch to attraction rather than to the mental strain of revisiting a terrifying memory.

Gripping the firearm in her right hand and lifting the hem of her skirt with her left, she hurried to catch up with her confusing companion. "I realize you don't approve of women doctors, either, so why have you gone to all the trouble of warning Oscar to leave me alone and making sure I know how to handle a gun?"

He didn't break stride or look at her. "A lady should be able to defend herself, but it doesn't hurt to spread the word that someone's keeping an eye on her."

"But why bother if you don't approve of me?" She liked that he considered her a lady, despite her profession, but his disapproval irritated her. And it shouldn't. If she wanted approval, she'd have put away her medical bag, married, had half a dozen babies by now, and never left Missouri.

He bypassed the turnoff for Hannah's place and continued into town without speaking.

"I answered your questions, and now I'd like an answer to mine." Charley prodded him.

Cooper exhaled roughly. "It's not you I disapprove of. It's doctors in general."

Charley tilted her head. "You're only cantankerous because I'm a doctor? Not because I'm a *woman* doctor?"

He stopped and stared at her. "I am not cantankerous."

"Yes, you are. But that's okay. I forgive you." She walked past him, grinning and suddenly feeling almost brave enough to face a whole horde of mice, or at least the one in her sitting room. It wasn't *her* he disliked, just her profession. She wouldn't examine why that distinction was important. Nor would she think about how safe and capable his arms felt when he'd carried her out of range of the mouse.

Benji and Digger bounced off her front stoop when her house came into view and met her at the edge of her yard. "We caught the mice for you, Dr. Charley." Benji beamed proudly up at her, and Digger flopped at his feet, panting with the satisfaction of a job well done.

Charley stopped in her tracks. "Mice?" There had been more than one in her house?

Benji nodded. "Yep. Digger caught two of them, didn't ya' boy?" The dog sat up and barked sharply in agreement. "But we didn't find any others, so I think we got 'em all, but we'll come back tomorrow and check again."

Charley patted Digger on the head to disguise the tremor in her hand and ruthlessly shoved away any notion of additional rodents lurking in her home. "I thank you both for your services. What do I owe you?"

"Nothin'." Benji shook his head. "You're Digger's doctor, and we had fun. Come on, Dig. Let's go see if we can catch some fish for Mom for supper. I might even let you eat one of those, too."

The boy and his dog took off down the street before Charley could protest, and she turned to his uncle with a small shudder. "I'm assuming by that last statement that Digger *ate* what he found in my house?"

Cooper's brows rose in amusement. "Digger's a natural-born mouser and eating what he catches is the best way to prevent them from coming back."

Charley eyed her house with distaste and reluctantly approached it. "I suppose." If she did spot another rodent, at least she now had a weapon to protect herself with.

"Would you like me to go through the door first and make sure there's no sign of life before you go in?" Cooper's eyes glinted with humor, but at least he wasn't outright laughing at her.

Charley halted at the base of her front step and felt her cheeks flush. "I know I should be brave enough to do it myself, but would you mind terribly?"

His expression softened. "I wouldn't have asked if I did. Wait here." He disappeared through her front door.

Five minutes later, he reappeared. "All clear. And I put your bookcase back against the wall."

Charley breathed an internal sigh of relief. Somehow, she believed his "all clear" verdict even more than Benji's assurance that the mice were gone. "Thank you for all your help today." Her cheeks warmed again, remembering how he'd seen her at her worst. "If you'll wait a moment, I'll get my purse and pay you for the gun."

"Gifts aren't for sale." He shook his head, sounding almost offended.

Her eyes widened. "You're giving this to me?"

He regarded her like the answer should be obvious.

"But why?"

"Because you need it." He spoke matter-of-factly. As if the statement explained everything.

It didn't. "But—"

"Don't argue, Miss Adams." His voice softened to a gentle rumble." Simply accept the gift. Even though you live in town, you need a way to protect yourself out here."

At their first meeting, Charley would never have picked this big, bearded man to be a potential friend, but appearances were incredibly deceiving. In hindsight, he'd been as kind to her, in his own brusque way, as Ma Jankins or Hannah. And in a way, his kindness meant more—maybe because he was kind to her in spite of his aversion to doctors. "I'll accept it on one condition. My friends call me Charley."

Cooper scratched behind his ear then nudged his hat back into its proper position. The one that shaded his eyes from her. "Fair enough. And my friends call me Coop."

A full-blown smile parted Charley's lips. "Thank you, Coop. For everything."

He nodded again, and a faint smile peeked out of hiding before he walked away. "See ya around, Miss…uh, Charley."

~

The razor-sharp axe bit into the side of the tree with a ringing thwack. Cooper levered it out and swung again, his muscles warming to the practiced rhythm. Pine-scented wood chips flew while he chopped an angled notch in first one side and then the other of the thick trunk. When about two inches separated the notches, the tree creaked and started to lean.

He stepped back and shouted to the two men working nearby. "Timber!"

The tall pine barely moved at first then it picked up speed and hit the ground with a splintering crash that left its branches waving wildly.

Cooper took a long swig of water from the covered bucket sitting in the shade of the supply wagon, then poured a dipper-full of cool water onto his handkerchief and wiped the sticky sweat from his face. He was a good stagecoach driver and enjoyed doing it, but there was nothing more satisfying than working his own land.

He returned to the downed tree and began trimming branches from the trunk, while his two hired hands worked on taking down their own trees. Clearing this section of land would give his cattle more grazing land, and he'd sell the trees to the lumber mill for cash profit. The trees he'd harvested early on had also been sold to the lumber mill, but he'd taken his payment in finished lumber, and now he had a house, barn, and a couple of other outbuildings to show for it. His stage job had provided a steady income, allowing him to get his ranch up and running without incurring debt, but God willing, the place would be able to support itself within a couple more years, and he could go to ranching full time. Hopefully, before the advancing railroad put him out of a stagecoach job. The fulfilment of his long-held and long-worked-for goal was so close he could taste it. If he had a wife, she would complete the picture and make his house a home.

Cooper swung his axe faster to rid his head of the image that thought inspired. He hadn't seen the golden-haired doctor for four days, yet if he'd seen her four minutes ago, she couldn't be any fresher in his memory. He'd always planned to marry some day in the future, but that hazy idea had sharpened into a particular person. One with green eyes and blonde hair that looked like it would be long, soft, and wavy if allowed to escape its confining pins. Why did those beautiful features have to belong to a sawbones, of all things? Why couldn't Charley Adams have been a teacher, or a dressmaker, or some such thing? And why couldn't he manage to stay out of range of her fearless personality?

Fearless until it came to a certain small creature, that is.

The pressure in his chest expanded. If only he could forget the feel of her against him, the sensation of her arms around his neck, the genuine, excited smile she'd blinded him with when she'd shot that rock off the log. If only he could forget her face when she'd said, "My friends call me Charley." Forget the unreasonable hunger that had welled up inside him for a deeper relationship than that of friends.

Dr. Charlotte Adams had elevated his opinion of doctors slightly above what it had been, but his skepticism remained. His bad experiences were too many and his wounds too deep to change his opinion overnight. Moreover, he couldn't see that determined female physician giving up all she'd worked for to become the wife of a simple rancher. Not to mention she was afraid of mice. How would she be able to handle all the other kinds of wildlife that were an inevitable part of ranching?

Cooper yanked his axe free of the wood and swung it again. It was better to chop down that budding idea before it sunk roots that would be painful to dig out. If he was serious about a wife, then he should quit looking at pretty, impractical distractions and search out a sturdy woman unafraid to tackle the hardships of building a life in the wilds of Dakota Territory. One who could cook and would be content to stay home and work beside him where she belonged.

"Hey, Boss?"

Cooper flinched at the unexpected interruption, and his axe bit soil rather than the tree limb he'd aimed at. "What?"

"Whoa! No need to bite my head off. What's got you grumpier

than a winter-starved bear lately'?"

Cooper jerked the blade out of the dirt and inspected it. Another stunt like that, and he'd have to stop and sharpen it. A dull axe made the work harder, and instead of biting into the wood, it could bounce off and into the softer flesh of his leg. Thinking about Miss Adams was dangerous. But lately, no matter what task he was working at, he was constantly distracted by thoughts of her. When he should be on the alert for the bandits that had robbed multiple stagecoaches over the last several months, he found himself remembering her sitting beside him on the driver's bench. Or he would remember something she'd said along a particular stretch of road. And today, instead of keeping his mind on the business end of his axe, he was daydreaming about how she'd felt when he'd caught her to his chest. Lifted her in his arms and held her close.

He *had* to banish the woman from his thoughts or risk getting hurt. In more ways than one. "I am not grumpy."

"If you say so." The graying cowpuncher sunk the dipper into the water bucket and lifted it to his mouth. After draining it three times, he hung the ladle back on the handle and covered the bucket. "Your attitude doesn't have anything to do with that pretty little doctor you threatened Oscar about, does it?"

"If I'd known your penchant for gossiping like an old woman, I'd have thought twice about hiring you, Martin." A single blow severed another limb from the fallen pine, and he kicked it out of the way. If only he could cut Charley out of his brain so easily.

Martin's eyes sparkled gleefully. "Where else could you find a man who'll play carpenter one day, lumberjack the next, and cowpuncher in between? You found a rare specimen in old Martin here. I am good at all those things." He puffed out his chest and hooked his thumbs in his suspenders.

Cooper's mouth twisted into a reluctant grin. "I beg your pardon, Martin. You are absolutely correct. I wouldn't have lasted a week here without your expertise."

Martin nodded, accepting the sarcastic praise as his rightful due.

"Did you come over here for something more important than bragging on yourself?" Cooper rested the axe head on the ground and propped his hands on the end of the handle, giving his banty-rooster friend a mock glare.

The man grinned but sobered quickly. "Lyle's got a

widowmaker hanging uncomfortably close to a big pine he wants to harvest, and he doesn't want to risk his tree twisting into it when it falls. If we get a couple of ropes around the big pine, we can keep it from snagging any of the broken limbs when it comes down."

"I'm on my way." Cooper sank the blade of his axe into the stump of the tree he'd cut down and retrieved the coiled ropes he brought along for situations like this.

Big limbs and occasionally even entire treetops broke off due to storms or decay and became entangled in branches of nearby trees. They then hung suspended until wind, gravity, decay, or some other disturbance—like harvesting the surrounding lumber—brought them down. They were dangerous and had more than earned their ominous nickname of widowmaker. Working under one was foolhardy, and Cooper had given his men orders to leave them alone. If a widowmaker hung near where they were working, they took precautions like roping the good tree to ensure it fell where they wanted it to. That way they prevented the freshly cut tree from snagging and slingshotting the nearby widowmaker at them as it fell.

Cooper breathed easier when Lyle's tree was safely on the ground. The widowmaker remained undisturbed and well away from where Lyle would be trimming limbs off in preparation for dragging the pine log out of the woods and down to the sawmill. There were plenty of accidents waiting to happen when clearing land, building a ranch, and growing a cattle herd, and it was impossible to totally avoid risk, but Cooper's caution and commitment to the welfare of his men and animals had paid off. So far, none of them had had anything worse than splinters, blisters, and occasional scrapes and bruises in the five years since he'd purchased the land. Puma Ridge might have a new physician, but the thought of having to make use of her services for him or his men made the hair on the nape of his neck prickle like a bad case of poison ivy.

He might be intrigued with Charley Adams, but as a sawbones, she scared him to pieces.

X

Charley eyed her kitchen floor while she warmed a piece of ham and a couple slices of Mrs. Whipple's fresh bread for her supper. Although she hadn't seen evidence of any more mice, she still flinched each time she caught movement out of the corner of her eye. It had helped to join Ma on her rounds around the countryside, not only to escape the possibility of encountering another rodent in her house but also to escape the memory of her behavior in front of Cooper.

    He'd been kind throughout the whole incident, but embarrassment continued to plague her. When he'd strode out of the stage office this morning and caught her watching instead of sweeping her front steps, her skin had flushed instantly and fiercely hot. Although she'd had years of practice smiling and pretending calmness when she was anything but calm, Cooper Knight had seen her at her absolute worst, and she'd had to force herself to smile and nod and not duck inside and hide from his probing gaze. Hopefully, the distance between them had prevented a good view of her rosy cheeks, but when he'd paused and tipped his hat with a slight smile before driving away, the glow of her cheeks had spread to her heart. Try as she might to deny it, Cooper's quiet, across-the-street greeting thrilled her more than Mr. Porter's grudging admission that her prescription had eased his rheumatism pains and Mrs. Whipple's ecstatic declaration that her baby's colic had all but disappeared.

Charley smiled and slid the hot ham between the slices of buttered, toasted bread. It had been a good day all around. Two women had even been brave enough to come to her office after she'd finished with Ma to seek medical advice—not just gossip or complain of imagined ills. She poured a glass of milk and carried her food to the table, but before she could sit down to eat, someone knocked on her office door. Tossing her napkin over her sandwich, she hurried to the front of the house.

The man who'd distracted her thoughts more than once during the day stood on her doorstep, using his hat to knock the dust off his pant legs.

"Hello." Charley willed her cheeks to remain cool.

The hand holding the hat fell to Cooper's side. "Have you seen any more mice?" Not a hint of mockery or teasing colored his abrupt question.

"No. Thanks to Benjamin and Digger, I think they're gone." It made no sense to be so excited to see a man who admitted he didn't like her profession, but her heart skipped like a little girl released from school early on a bright spring day.

"Good. This should discourage any others from coming in." He lifted a pocket flap on the long duster he wore, and a golden, furry head popped out.

Bright blue eyes blinked sleepily at Charley, and the kitten meowed softly, almost inquisitively.

She stared in surprise. "Oh, it's beautiful."

"No, it's a cat." Cooper scooped the feline out of his pocket with one hand. Despite his gruff description of the animal, his motions were gentle as he offered it to her.

Charley lifted the small, velvety kitten from his proffered hand and cuddled it to her chest. "Where did you get it?" The kitten yawned then licked Charley's chin with a tiny, rough tongue, making her giggle.

Cooper's mouth softened in an almost-smile. "One of Hank's barn cats had a litter a few weeks ago. He asked me today if I knew who might want one. I said you had mice trouble, and he told me to deliver this furball to you with his compliments and to say that her momma's one of the best mousers on his place." Cooper indicated the kitten with a jerk of his chin. "She's little, but it won't be long before she's big enough to earn her keep."

"Thank you. This is a wonderful, thoughtful surprise." Charley suppressed another giggle when the kitten's soft head burrowed into her neck.

"I'll pass along your thanks to Hank next time I see him." He shrugged as if carrying a cat in his pocket for several hours while handling a team of horses was an everyday occurrence for stagecoach drivers. "Have a good evening." He plopped his hat on his head and turned to go.

Charley stopped him with a hand on his arm but quickly withdrew it when he glanced down at it. "Thank *you* for thinking about me and bringing her to me. It couldn't have been easy."

He scratched the hair behind his ear and avoided her gaze. "It wasn't any trouble. She slept most of the way."

Charley's grin broadened. Was it her imagination or was the color across the bridge of his nose and cheekbones more than the remnants of a day spent in the sun? She cuddled the kitten, enjoying the throaty purrs that vibrated through its small body. "Thank you anyway, Coop."

His nod was brusque. "You're welcome, Charley."

She watched him stride away then reentered her house, still smiling while she ate her supper sitting on the kitchen floor while the tiny tabby licked milk from a saucer. She'd lost her heart the instant it had poked its head out of Cooper's pocket. To the kitten. Not to the taciturn man who'd single-handedly made her comfortable again in her new home.

"What am I going to name you? I can't keep calling you kitten." She ran her hand over the thick, silky fur, and the feline arched her spine into the caress. "Any suggestions?"

After a few more licks, the tabby sat up and skimmed a tiny pink tongue around her mouth to capture any stray drops of milk. She was a sweet-looking cat. Orange stripes crisscrossed a plush, light yellow coat, and white fur surrounded her pink nose and mouth before running down her throat to give her a white bib. She crawled into Charley's lap, her innocent blue eyes blinking sleepily. After tucking her tiny white paws underneath her body, she closed her eyes with a contended purr.

"Oh, well. I guess there's no hurry to come up with a name."

Charley caressed the small, warm furball and smiled. Cooper Knight was as full of surprises as medical school had been, but she actually liked his idea of a surprise.

The smile hovered around her mouth for the rest of the evening and returned the instant she awoke to a miniature tiger standing on her chest roaring for breakfast. Playing with the furball nearly made her late for church, and when she hurried up the front steps, she found Benji waiting for her.

"Good morning, Dr. Charley. Do you want to sit with us today? I don't think Ma's coming."

Charley glanced the direction Benji gestured and found Cooper watching her. She lowered her gaze back to the boy, willing her heart to quit stuttering and attend to what he'd said. "Is anything wrong with Ma?"

Benji shook his head and explained while he led her to the pew where his mother and uncle chatted with Pastor Schwartz. "Uncle Coop said he passed her and Mr. Jacob on his way in to town. Mrs. Jacob's having her baby, and Ma went to help."

The words punctured Charley's good mood. Ma Jankins had delivered plenty of babies and could handle almost any difficulty that might arise, but it hurt that the father-to-be hadn't asked for Puma Ridge's new doctor and that Ma hadn't invited her along. And here she'd thought she was starting to make headway on being accepted.

Pastor Schwartz greeted Charley before walking to the front platform, and Cooper gave her a small smile. "Morning." He tugged Benji out of the way so she could step into the space between the pews.

"Thank you, and good morning to you both." Cooper's smile momentarily lightened Charley's growing sense of disappointment, but then Hannah stood and hugged her, and Charley blinked back a sudden sting of tears.

"Hi, Charley." Hannah spoke under the cover of the pump organ's wheezing opening notes. "Will you join us for lunch today? Coop's taking us on a picnic."

Charley laid her Bible on the seat when Hannah released her and remained standing for the singing. "I don't want to intrude." All she wanted to do was make it through the service then hurry home to salve the sting of being rejected by burying herself in a good book or a medical tome.

"You won't intrude. I told Coop I was going to ask you. It'll be fun, and you'll disappoint Benji if you don't come with us." Hannah sounded determined to convince her.

Charley hesitated but then acquiesced. If they kept whispering, they were going to get another stern stare from the deacon in the pew in front of them, and Cooper would definitely be more distracting than a book—as soon as the latest blow to her professional pride quit stinging.

"Good." Hannah faced the front and joined the singing, adding a pretty alto to Cooper's rumbling bass and Benji's tremulous but energetic tenor.

Charley took the hymnal Benji offered her and pretended to read words she knew by heart. When would people start accepting her? Dr. Tidd had recommended her to Puma Ridge's town council as one of the best young physicians he'd ever worked with. Unfortunately, it took patients to prove what he'd said about her.

Pastor Schwartz announced his text and interrupted Charley's descent into feeling sorry for herself. "Open your Bibles to Galatians chapter six and verse nine, please." He waited for people to locate the passage then began to read. *"And let us not be weary in well doing: for in due season we shall reap, if we faint not."*

He lowered his Bible to the lectern and glanced over his audience. "Most of you are familiar with the difficult task of preparing soil for a garden. You have to break up the hard ground and remove rocks and roots and stubborn weeds. You might even have to work in some smelly fertilizer." Muffled laughs greeted the pastor's grimace. "But finally, you're ready to plant seeds. Now, I don't know about you folks, but when I'm all done planting my garden, I can already taste that first bite of sweet corn, the first bowl of crisp green beans." He closed his eyes and smiled. "And that first juicy tomato."

"Amen, Brother!" The deacon's hearty agreement sparked a ripple of laughter through the congregation.

Pastor Schwartz grinned. "I see you know what I'm talking about. But let me ask you this. How many of you go out to your gardens the morning after you planted ready to harvest all your vegetables?"

Heads shook from side to side at the ridiculous question, and

Benji snorted. "That's silly."

Hannah leaned around Charley to shush him.

Pastor Schwartz tilted his head. "So, you're not surprised you don't have overnight results? You're not disappointed in the lack of immediate reward for all your hard work? You don't start digging up the seeds in disgust because they didn't yield a bumper crop while you slept?"

Chuckles rippled through the congregation again and more heads shook no.

Benji grinned but eyed his mother and remained silent.

The preacher waited until the laughter faded then spoke quietly. "In the same way we're not surprised seeds don't mature and produce fruit instantly, or we're not surprised that we have a summer of pulling weeds and maybe even watering those plants before fruit develops, we shouldn't be surprised when the work we do for the Lord doesn't always show results right away. If you don't see anything happening, don't be discouraged. God is working under the surface, behind the scenes. Our job is to keep on. Don't faint. Don't grow weary. When we're where God wants us to be, doing what He wants us to do, one day we *will* reap the reward and see results."

The truth of the Pastor's sermon sank into Charley's soul, and her customary determination returned as strong as ever. She had never been one to faint or give up, and she wasn't starting now. She'd been blessed in several ways over the last weeks, and despite the morning's setback, she *was* making progress in breaking up the hard ground of distrust and suspicion. And on top of all that, she was going on a picnic with her new friends—one of whom had rescued her from a mouse, taken time to teach her to shoot, and given her the sweetest kitten.

Her smile returned. It had been a long time since she'd gone on a picnic. That explained the excitement tickling her insides.

~

Cooper stretched out in the shade and watched Benji throw a stick for Digger. From a distance, he couldn't tell the dog had recently been injured. It would be a few more weeks before the fur grew long enough to hide the remaining scar, but the terrier didn't act like it pained him. He had to admit, Charley had done a good repair job on the little mutt.

Closing his eyes, he listened to Hannah and Charley chatting. He could almost imagine he was on a picnic with a wife and child of his own. Maybe a little girl with gold hair and emerald eyes like her mother. His eyes flew open, and he sat up to shake off the fanciful notion. Children daydreamed. He was not a child. He was a grown man.

He sensed someone beside him and looked over to see Charley standing a few feet away.

"I'm sorry. I didn't mean to wake you."

Cooper shoved his fingers through his hair to push it off his forehead and bent his legs to stand. "You didn't. I wasn't asleep."

"Don't get up." Charley plopped onto the grass, seemingly unconcerned that her fancy church dress might get damp or grass stained. "Can I ask you something?"

Cooper glanced around the deserted picnic area. "Where are Hannah and Benji?" Maybe he had actually dozed off because he didn't remember hearing them leave.

"Benji wanted to show her something down at the creek." Charley tucked her feet to one side and clasped her hands in her lap. "So, can I? Ask you a question?"

His muscles tensed involuntarily at her grave tone. "What do you want to know?"

She exhaled slowly before speaking. "What happened to Hannah's husband?"

The old anger flared up, and Cooper barely managed to hide it from view. "He died. Two years ago."

Emerald eyes narrowed at his simplistic answer. "I gathered that. But how?" She didn't retreat at his silent warning stare. She simply watched him and waited.

Fine. If she wanted an answer that badly, he'd give it to her. "The sawbones killed him."

Her eyes widened at his snarl, but again, she only watched and waited in silence.

Cooper's hands fisted as they'd done around the doctor's throat before three men had managed to haul him off. "My brother-in-law, Ben, was a hard-rock miner. Two years ago, there was a partial cave-in where he worked, and he was trapped beneath the debris. When they dug him out, his right leg was badly busted up. They carried him to Dr. Engstad who hardly looked at him before declaring that the only way to save his life was to cut off the leg. Ben begged him not to take it, but Engstad made the men hold him down so he could hack it off."

Cooper swallowed hard. "If I'd gotten there sooner, I would have stopped him." In his nightmares, he continued to hear the spine-crawling screams coming from the blood-spattered surgery room he'd approached at a dead run. And then Ben's dreadful, permanent silence.

"I was too late." The words scraped through his tight throat. "Ben died on that table."

Cooper sucked in a harsh breath. "After pronouncing my brother-in-law dead of a heart attack, the sawbones wiped his hands on a towel and calmly stated that Ben probably would have died from gangrene anyway and at least the shock-induced heart attack had been quicker and more *merciful*." He sucked in another rasping breath and blinked away furious tears. "Ben was a good man. But Engstad killed him as surely as if he'd put a gun to his head and pulled the trigger. Robbing my sister of her husband and my nephew of his daddy."

A long silence followed his statement, and then a hand rested on his forearm. "I'm so sorry." The softness of Charley's touch contrasted sharply with the constricted muscles that pulled his fist into a hard knot.

Cooper yanked his head up and glared at her. "Do you think you could have done any better?"

She shook her head gently, her eyes shimmering like mossy green pools. "I don't know. Without being there—"

Cooper wrenched his arm from her touch. "I should have known a *doctor* would protect one of their own."

"I'm not trying to protect him. Amputations are risky and complicated." Charley held her hand up, forestalling his protest. "*However*, what he *said* to you was unconscionable!"

The quiet fury in her voice mollified his anger a fraction. "Have *you* ever cut off someone's limb?"

She held his gaze. "Yes. Once."

He gritted his teeth. She looked too soft and delicate to saw off someone's arm or leg. "Did they die?"

"No. But when I was finishing my medical training, I assisted on an amputation where the patient died a few hours later. It's a dreadful procedure, but sometimes it's the only chance we have to save a life."

"And yet they *died!*" Agitation propelled him to his feet. Her gentle answer made sense to some small part of him. And it felt like a betrayal to Ben.

He began walking with no particular destination in mind.

Charley caught up with him and walked alongside him in silence for several minutes. "When you came to find Hannah and Benji the morning after Digger was injured, was that the first time you'd been back inside that house since…since Ben?"

Cooper exhaled sharply. How had she guessed that? "Yeah."

"No wonder you were in a panic." Her quiet comment held no criticism and felt like forgiveness for his ill-mannered entrance to her home that morning.

A forgiveness he hadn't asked for and wasn't exactly sure he wanted. Pretty or not, he shouldn't care what a sawbones thought about him or his attitude.

He directed his steps to the section of creek where Hannah and Benji waded in the shallow water.

"Come on in, Uncle Coop! The water feels good." Benji urged him. "You, too, Dr. Charley."

Cooper sat down on the bank to tug off his boots. He wasn't in the mood to play, but he desperately needed a distraction from the bad memories, the anger, and the unwanted allure of Dr. Adams.

"Thanks for telling me what happened." Charley spoke under her breath. "I'll be more sensitive around them." She nodded in Hannah and Benji's direction.

Oddly enough, the weight of the old memories lightened with her concern. "Don't worry about them. They don't hold that against you."

"Unlike you?" A crooked smile softened her question.

He shook his head, surprised by the dawning realization. "No. I guess I don't hold it against you, either." Uncomfortably pleased with her relieved smile and ready to put the subject behind them, he pushed to his feet and pointed to the water. "You coming?"

"Yes. Let me take my shoes off first." She walked over to a large rock and sat with her back to him to discretely remove her shoes and stockings.

Cooper splashed into the chilly creek to give her more privacy and inspected Benji's attempt at constructing a dam, shoving the painful memories back where they belonged. In the past.

Charley joined Hannah in the edge of the creek, and Cooper avoided a second glance at her bare calves by turning his back and helping Benji with his building project. But when he bent to place a large rock on the lengthening dam, a splash erupted beside him, spraying him full in the face.

Feminine giggles told him who the culprits were, and he straightened, wiping his face on his shirt sleeve. "Ladies, you are going to regret that decision."

Charley held out her hands in defense, her green eyes bright with laughter. "I didn't throw the rock. Your sister did."

He picked up the last rock he'd placed on the dam. "But you obviously didn't do anything to stop her. Therefore, you get to share the consequences." He gently lobbed the large, flat rock to land at their retreating feet, sending water spraying up on them in sparkling droplets.

Both women screeched in protest but stopped retreating and advanced instead, kicking water at him and Benji as they held their skirts up nearly to their knees in a futile attempt to keep them dry. Benji wholeheartedly joined the water fight, and shrieks and laughter echoed off the creek banks.

When Hannah finally negotiated a truce with the promise of cake, Cooper's heart felt lighter than it had for many years.

His sister led the soppy foursome onto the bank. "Oh, Charley. Your dress! You should have gone home first and changed. Now it's ruined."

Charley wiped at the water dripping off her face. "I'm sure I look like a drowned cat, but I wouldn't trade the fun we've had for all the pretty dresses in the world, Hannah." She stopped at the edge of the picnic blanket to wring out the hem of her skirt.

With her flushed cheeks, bright eyes, and liquid diamonds sparkling in her hair, she was the prettiest thing Cooper had ever seen, but he was relieved when she sat down. The way the damp fabric clung to her wasn't indecent, but it sure showed off her figure better than the dry full skirt had. Why hadn't someone snatched the pretty woman up already and changed her last name?

Or had they tried and found that playing doctor meant more to her than being a wife and mother?

Digger dropped a stick in Cooper's lap, derailing the depressing train of thought. Accepting the invitation, he threw the piece of wood for the enthusiastic dog, and accepted the piece of cake Hannah gave him.

"Speaking of cats, I'd better get home and check on mine—soon as I finish my cake, of course." Charley laughed lightly. "This is delicious, Hannah. Thank you."

"You have a cat now?" Benji mumbled around a mouthful of sweet treat.

"I do. A beautiful little kitten, thanks to your uncle."

"Don't speak with your mouth full, Benji. What do you mean thanks to his uncle?" Hannah shot Cooper an inquisitive glance then looked at Charley. "Coop hates cats."

"He does?"

Cooper's head itched when two pairs of feminine eyes turned on him, and he curled his fingers into his palms to keep from scrubbing at his scalp. "I don't *hate* cats."

Hannah's brown ones began to sparkle suspiciously. "Interesting. I thought he did."

"But he brought me the prettiest little blue-eyed, gold-and-white tabby I've ever seen. He carried it in his pocket all the way from Hank at the swing station, yesterday."

"All the way from Hank's. Wasn't that sweet of him?" The syrup in Hannah's voice could have drowned four stacks of flapjacks.

"She needed something to keep the mice away, and Hank needed to get rid of his latest litter of kittens." Cooper tugged the slobbery stick from Digger's mouth and tossed it. But not too far. He needed something to keep his hands busy and out of his hair. His sister's eyes were all too keen, and she'd not miss that betraying nervous gesture.

"You never brought *me* a kitten." Hannah's teasing smile spoiled her attempt at pouting.

"You don't have trouble with mice." Cooper ignored Digger's obvious disappointment in his stick-throwing abilities and tossed the crooked piece of wood again.

"That's because Digger is as good a mouser as a cat." Benji proclaimed proudly. "Can we come see your kitten sometime, Dr. Charley? Digger won't hurt it. I promise." The dog dropped the wet stick at his master's feet, and when Benji sent it sailing through the air, the terrier bounded after it, barking happily.

Cooper frowned at the furry little traitor who'd abandoned him.

Charley smiled at Benji. "You and Digger are welcome at my house anytime. You're my heroes, you know."

"We are? Why?"

"Because you took care of that nasty pest." She matched Benjamin's happy grin then looked straight at Cooper. "Anyone who rescues me from mice is my hero and has my undying gratitude." Her pretty eyes held his for three full seconds before she turned back to Benji. "I need some ideas for a name. I can't keep calling her 'Cat' for the rest of her life."

Hannah sent Cooper another teasing grin then gave Charley a couple of feline name suggestions.

Cake finished, they picked up their things and returned to town, but Cooper didn't join in the carefree conversation that swirled around him. It was only a silly cat. The sentiment sounded nice, but he wasn't a hero. He'd failed to protect the ones under his care too many times to qualify for that title.

The stern reminder did nothing to shake the image of a pair of shining green eyes peering straight into his and promising her undying gratitude, however, and Cooper was almost to his ranch before his heart rate returned to its normal pace.

XI

Charley stepped out of the cramped cabin into the bright noon sunshine and stretched her sore spine. The seeds of approval and recommendation Ma had sown on her behalf had begun to sprout, and requests for Charley's help had increased so much she'd been able to use her skills on an almost daily basis for the last two weeks. It was exhilarating.

And exhausting. A yawn threatened to crack Charley's jaw. Nearly twenty hours earlier, a frantic husband had pounded on her door, seeking help for the wife he'd left at home in labor. Ma was out of town, nursing a family with seven children through chickenpox, so he'd turned to the new doctor for help. Although she hadn't been his first choice, Charley had jumped at the chance to assist a new life into the world. The infant had had her own time schedule for arriving, however, and it had been a long afternoon and a longer night.

But as the first rays of sunrise had burst across the sky, the little one had finally made her squalling, red-faced appearance, bringing tears of joy to her mother's eyes and a beam of pride to her father's. Mother and daughter were worn out from the grueling birthing process, but now that they were fed, cleaned up, and resting, Charley didn't expect them to have any serious problems recovering from the ordeal.

The tired father led Charley's mount from the barn and leaned against the porch post with a gusty sigh. His two sturdy little boys had kept him thoroughly distracted and hurrying between them and their mother well into the night. "Thank you for coming, Dr. Adams. I would have been terrified without you here. Our boys didn't take near the time this one did, and I thought something was bad wrong."

Charley fought back another yawn and smiled. "I was happy to help. Each baby is different. Your daughter had her own schedule, and unlike her brothers, she had no intention of rushing."

The strapping farmer chuckled in agreement then sobered and cleared his throat nervously. "I don't have any cash money to pay you with, but when we butcher the hogs this fall, I'll bring you a side of meat. If that's acceptable?"

"That sounds more than fair, Mr. Svensson. I'll return tomorrow to check on your wife and daughter, but come get me if you need me before then."

Mr. Svensson's shoulders relaxed, and he gave her a wide smile. "Thank you, Dr. Adams. Have a safe ride home."

"I'll do my best." Charley hoisted her weary body into the saddle and waved to the two boys who raced around the side of the cabin with rowdy goodbyes and sticky faces from the peppermint candies she'd given them in celebration of their new sister. Mrs. Svensson would have her hands full with three children under the age of six, but Charley had no doubt Ma Jankins would ensure that the woman also had time to snatch a few naps over the next few weeks.

Leaving the happy family behind, she followed the wagon ruts back to the stagecoach road, another yawn stretching her jaw. She pointed the mild-mannered gelding toward town and gently urged him to quicken his pace. A pillow and soft mattress sounded better and better with each tick of her watch pin.

Charley patted the gentle animal's neck. "If I fall asleep, you're responsible for getting us both home." Despite the horse's bouncy trot, her eyes were blinking slower and slower. She should have drunk *two* cups of coffee while she'd prepared breakfast for everyone.

Her head jerked hard, waking her from a light doze, and she opened her eyes to find that her mount had slowed to a walk. It took another second to realize that the drumming hoofbeats she heard weren't coming from him. She straightened in the saddle and looked over her shoulder. Someone was in a big hurry. Charley guided the gelding off the side of the road to get out of the rider's way, and reached inside the saddle bag where she'd tucked the revolver Cooper had given her.

The rider thundered past her, then slid his horse to a stop and wheeled it toward her. He pointed to the black leather case strapped to her saddle horn, while he easily controlled his snorting, prancing mount. "Are you the doctor? Hank at the swing station said there was a woman doctor in Puma Ridge."

"Yes. I'm Dr. Adams. What's wrong?" Charley left her revolver where it was and returned both hands to the reins.

"There's a sick baby at Hank's. Can you come?"

She turned her horse the direction the messenger had come. "How far away are we?"

"About an hour's hard ride." The man scrutinized her closely but not unkindly. "You look tired. Can you make it?"

She nodded. Fresh energy had jolted through her the second he'd mentioned a sick child, and she was wide awake. "I can. Let's go."

Their horses shot down the trail with a speed that suggested they knew their errand was vital, and although the young man slowed them twice to give them a breather, they rode into the hard-packed yard of the waystation less than an hour later.

Hank took the reins of her sweaty horse and pointed her into the front room of his house with a concerned expression. Inside, a weary-looking woman rocked a lethargic little girl, and worry creased the gaunt face of the man pacing beside them.

He looked up at the sound of her feet on the plank floor. "Are you the doctor?"

"I am." Charley knelt beside the woman's chair. "What seems to be the trouble?"

Tears rolled down the mother's hollow cheeks, and her eyes never left her baby. "I don't know. She's been poorly and fussy since she was born, but she's gotten worse the last few weeks. We heard about a new doctor in Puma Ridge and were coming to see you. We'd made it this far when she had some sort of fit. Hank let us bring her out of the sun and said he'd send someone for you."

Charley knelt on the floor and took her stethoscope out of her bag. "How old is she?"

"Almost a year old now." The woman gently shifted the baby from her arms to her lap for Charley's closer inspection while the father hovered over her shoulder.

Hiding her dismay, Charley examined the little girl. She was too small for her age and painfully thin, her eyelids were swollen, and her breath came in short, labored pants. Charley lowered her stethoscope after listening to the tiny heart's faint, erratic rhythm. "Has she been able to nurse?"

The mother shook her head, looking both ashamed and bone weary. "I haven't been able to since right after she was born. I've had to use canned milk."

A check of the baby's gums confirmed Charley's suspicion. Scurvy. She'd seen a similar case one other time with Dr. Tidd while visiting a poverty-stricken tenement house in St. Louis. Scurvy could be treated in its early stages with fresh milk or fresh fruits and vegetables. Left untreated for too long, however, and the body eventually passed a point of no return.

Throat aching, Charley locked away her emotions and softly stroked a pale, sunken cheek that should have been plump and glowing with health. The parents bore the scars of a hard-scrabble life and inadequate living conditions, and their careworn eyes pleaded silently for her to heal their dying child.

She shook her head slowly, forcing the hope-killing words out her tight throat. "I'm so sorry. I'm afraid I'm too late."

"No!" The mother sucked in a sobbing gasp and cradled the tiny girl to her chest. "You're a doctor. You *have* to do something!"

"What's wrong with her?" The father demanded hoarsely.

Charley explained as gently she could, but all the gentleness in the world couldn't soften the diagnosis, and agony filled the small room with its palpable presence. This was the side of medicine she hated. She had identified the problem, but now she could do nothing but keep vigil and helplessly await the inevitable while the little girl's shallow breathing grew ever fainter. *Why* hadn't they sought help sooner? When she could have treated the condition and made a difference?

Silent tears slid down the mother's face, and she rocked and tenderly stroked the pale face of her child who struggled for each breath.

Minutes or maybe hours later, Charley dimly heard the stage

arrive, but she paid little heed to it until the door of the dusty front room opened. She glanced up, ready to shoo away whoever had wandered into Hank's house by mistake.

Cooper stood in the doorway, hat off, taking in the scene, but before either of them could speak, a sobbing intake of breath jerked her attention back to the dying child. Instantly, she saw what the mother had recognized, but she pressed her stethoscope to the child's frail chest, hoping she was wrong. Praying for a miracle.

Slowly, she straightened and shook her head, unable to meet the desperate eyes that watched her. Life, ever fragile, had tiptoed irrevocably away, and there wasn't a thing she could do to recall it.

The world seemed to pause, and no one moved for several minutes. Then with tears still cascading down her cheeks, the mother gathered her baby to her bosom and rose with heartrending dignity and sorrow. "I want to take her home."

Her husband's arm wrapped around her thin shoulders, and he gently ushered her outside into sunshine that shone too brightly and too cheerfully.

Charley accompanied them to their wagon, searching for any words of comfort that might ease their anguish, but her own heart was too sore to supply anything but questions. Thick silence seemed to insulate them from the noise and hustle of the busy stage station yard.

After helping his wife onto the seat where she continued to quietly weep and cradle their lifeless child, the man turned to Charley. "If we have more children…" His voice broke, and he swallowed hard. "How…how do we keep this from happening again?"

His hoarse whisper nearly shattered Charley's fragile grip on her emotions. She dug her nails into her palms. "If your wife is able to nurse, she will need plenty of fresh vegetables on a regular basis. If she's not able to nurse, then feed the baby fresh milk not canned. Babies don't get scurvy on a diet of fresh milk. And if you can get goat's milk, babies tolerate that better than cow's milk." She swallowed a rush of sorrow. "I'm so sorry I wasn't in time to save your little girl."

The man's face twisted. "I don't blame you, Doctor. Thank you for coming. I know it gave her comfort." He glanced in his wife's direction then eyed the ground. He scuffed the dirt with his cracked-leather boot. "I can't pay you for your time until I have enough cattle to sell a few."

She touched his stooped shoulder and waited until his tormented eyes met hers. "In times like these, money is unimportant. The only thing you owe me is a promise that you'll bring your wife to see me when she's in the family way again, and that you'll follow my advice about the milk and fresh vegetables."

"I will." He nodded solemnly before climbing up beside his wife.

Charley watched the heartbroken couple drive away and sucked in a hot, painful breath. She *despised* being powerless to alleviate suffering. Especially that of a child.

Heavenly Father, hold those parents in your arms and remind them, and me, that their little one is safe and healthy in your arms.

"Doc?" Hank stood beside her, thumbs wrapped around his red suspenders. "Coop's ready to pull out. Would you like to ride home with him? We can tie your horse to the back of the coach."

Fatigue settled onto Charley's shoulders, heavier than a wet wool blanket. The thought of the long ride home physically hurt. "Do I have time to use the wash facilities?"

The grizzled stationmaster nodded. "I'll fetch your medical bag and tell Coop you're coming. Better hurry, though." Concern creased the corners of his eyes, but he turned and hustled away without speaking it.

Charley slumped with relief and forced her weary legs toward the privy. If Hank had given voice to his sympathy or concern, she would have broken down. And that was something she couldn't do. Those who disapproved of women doctors liked to pounce on any little show of weakness to prove their belief that females didn't belong in medicine. Her tears would have to wait until she reached the privacy of her bedroom.

~

"She's comin'. I'll tie her horse to the back."

Cooper caught the bag Hank tossed him, and when Charley disappeared behind the small station building, he eyed the harmless-looking leather satchel. Its secrets would be easier to discover than those hidden behind the unshaken composure of its owner.

After a quick glance around, he gave in to the growing impulse and opened Charley's physician case. A row of leather loops held small medicine bottles neatly in place around the sides, a paper-wrapped package took up one end, and an assortment of metal instruments lay in the bottom. The wicked teeth of a small saw glinted at him, sending a shiver up Cooper's spine.

He slammed the bag shut and rebuckled its two straps before depositing it in the boot more gingerly than if it were a live rattlesnake. Maybe those strange tools held the secret to doctoring because the mere sight of them were more than enough to scare *him* healthy. Except they hadn't worked for the doctor's most recent patient.

Cooper's fists tightened around the reins, and the team shuffled impatiently. Why did the first woman he'd been attracted to in a long time have to be a cold-hearted doctor?

"Here you go, Dr. Adams. Plenty of room inside today." Hank held the stagecoach door open for Charley, but like she had on their first meeting, she balked and darted a desperate peek toward the driver's bench.

Cooper didn't understand her aversion to riding inside the stagecoach, but he intended to use it to his advantage. "Hand her up here, Hank. She's riding with me." He had something to say to the unruffled woman who showed no distress at witnessing a couple lose their only child.

Hank latched the coach door and assisted Charley aboard. With a quiet word of thanks, she settled onto the seat and arranged her riding skirt. As if the only thing that concerned her was wrinkles.

"I 'preciate you comin', Dr. Adams." Hank touched his hat brim.

"You're welcome, Hank. Oh. I almost forgot. Thank you for the kitten. I'm very happy with her."

The grizzled old hostler grinned. "Glad to do it, ma'am. Coop said you needed one, and I was glad to find a home for the little critter."

Cooper set the horses in motion before the man could give away any more information about where the idea for Charley's kitten had originated. He didn't want her thinking the gesture had been anything more than self-preservation from having to rescue her from another mouse.

The team wanted to run, but he held them in until they settled into an efficient, ground-eating pace. The jingle of harness chains and thud of hooves magnified the silence stretching between himself and Charley. Aggravated equally by his awareness of the petticoat doc and her complete lack of emotion, he eyed the unblinking female who stared straight ahead. Her emotionless response to the baby's death proved just how big a fool he'd been to start to hope she might be different from the other sawbones who'd brought so much heartache to his life. Dr. Adams exhibited the same lack of compassion they'd shown.

He couldn't take her silence any longer. "Why didn't you even try to save that baby?" She been sitting there doing nothing when he'd walked in.

She flinched like she'd forgotten he sat beside her then exhaled before replying in a quiet monotone. "Because I couldn't. We don't know exactly what causes scurvy, but when caught early, it's easy to cure. Fresh vegetables, fruit, and milk—any one of them can heal the problem."

Scurvy? The disease sailors used to face on long sea voyages? His brow puckered. "If it's easy to cure, why didn't you?"

Charley shook her head. "She'd had it too long, and it caused her little body to shut down. She was dying before they ever came to find me." Her voice trailed off.

Cooper concentrated on guiding the team around a tight, rutted bend. Her explanation didn't entirely make sense, and he didn't understand how she could be so calm and unaffected.

The road straightened out and Cooper thought he heard a muffled sniff. But Charley's head was down and turned slightly away, preventing him from seeing her expression.

"I hate it!" Her furious whisper caught him by surprise.

"Hate what?" Cooper's anger faded in the face of hers.

She brushed her knuckles across her cheek before looking at him. "Death."

Cooper stared at her. The mask she habitually wore had disappeared, leaving him an unobstructed view of the aguish that darkened her eyes. "I helped bring a new life into the world this morning, and within a matter of hours, I was forced to tell another mother and father that I couldn't help *their* baby. I had to sit by helplessly while they watched it die." She swiped at the tears wetting her cheeks. "*Why* didn't they come for help *sooner*?"

Charley demanded the answer of him, but he could only stare at her, thunderstruck by the depth of emotion she'd concealed so completely. Until now.

"I could have *helped* her if they hadn't waited so long." She spat the words at him like their decision was his fault.

The sudden, intense desire to give her the outcome she wished for surprised and rattled him. And yet, if it had been his child who'd been sick, he would probably have been guilty of the same delay and reluctance to seek a doctor's help.

The thought knifed ruthlessly through his conscience. "I'm sorry." He didn't know what else to say, and her tears were tearing him to pieces.

Charley sagged against the backrest. "I love being a physician and helping people. But times like this, when the limits of medicine have been reached and passed, and there is nothing I can do…" She sniffed again and shook her head before growing quiet.

To Cooper's utter relief the tears quit falling.

She wiped her eyes with a soggy handkerchief. "I'm sorry to be such a watering pot. It took all I had to keep from crying in front of that poor couple."

A couple of minutes ticked by before Cooper gave voice to his growing curiosity. "Why couldn't you let them see you cry?"

"If I'm upset and crying, it will scare my patients and their families and make it harder for them to calm down and trust me and my skills." Charley's flushed cheeks and damp eyelashes were worse than her previous tears.

Because they made her much too appealing.

Cooper cleared his throat and shoved the notion away. "Or maybe they'd think you cared."

Charley's brows drew together, and for the first time, he noticed the faint, bluish circles under her eyes. "But I do care." She faced forward again. "I do! I almost wish I didn't. That way it wouldn't hurt so bad when I lose a patient."

Cooper searched his mind for an answer that didn't sound trite but came up empty. He'd misjudged her based on previous experiences, and that had been unfair. She wasn't like the other doctors he'd dealt with. His losses caused him to lump them all together in one harshly judged pile. But during their conversation after their picnic lunch, Charley had made him see that *maybe* Dr. Engstad wasn't totally responsible for Ben's death.

His jaw hardened. There were still plenty of bad physicians out there, though. That good-for-nothing Army doc was *directly* responsible for Captain Vandever's death. It was bad enough that the doctor's soused incompetence had killed Cooper's best friend, but the man hadn't even been held accountable for it.

The coach hit a rough stretch of road, and Charley fell against his arm.

Cooper glanced down when she didn't immediately straighten and retreat to her side of the bench. A smile softened his face. Dr. Charley Adams was asleep, her head bouncing limply with each jolt of the coach.

Thankful that he had a well-seasoned team at the end of the lines, Cooper gathered the reins in his right hand and slipped his left arm around her waist, gently tugging her closer until her head rested in the hollow of his shoulder. She twisted into him with a sigh, but her breathing slowly deepened, and she didn't wake.

Cooper momentarily froze at the sensations stabbing through him, and he tightened his arm around her. He wasn't used to holding someone while he drove—much less a pretty woman—but the awkwardness of it quickly faded. The swing and sway of the coach box on its leather suspension straps was rocking-chair comfortable and familiar to him, but he didn't want an unexpected bump to knock Charley off the high seat. Doctor or not, he was getting kind of used to having her around.

XII

Charley repositioned her head to a more comfortable position then frowned. Her pillow felt more like smooth leather than soft feathers, and her sheets smelled of the salty tang of sweat and earthy scent of horses rather than clean, sun-dried cotton. The combination of odors wasn't unpleasant—they reminded her of Cooper—but if her bed didn't stop swaying like a drunk stagecoach, she was going to wake from her dream with a sick stomach. The sensation intensified even as the fog of sleep lifted, and her eyes flew open. She wasn't in her bed.

Catching her breath, she tilted her head and came nose to bearded chin with Cooper.

He glanced down at her, his surprisingly soft beard tickling the tip of her nose. "You were tired."

The voice vibrating against her cheek jolted her fully awake. She was pressed up against Cooper more shamelessly than her new kitten at naptime. She jerked upright but went no farther than the arm circling her ribcage.

"Easy now. Hold on." His low, husky voice was oddly soothing, and he raised his elbow while maintaining easy control over the six-hitch team.

Charley ducked underneath it and scooted to the left side of the bench, putting as much distance as possible and sitting straight and stiff as a fireplace poker while her hands fisted together in her lap. "I'm sorry."

Cooper rested his elbows against his knees and looked over at her. "For what?"

"For…well, for…" Her fatigue-muddled brain couldn't come up with anything that didn't sound indecorous. "It must have been difficult to drive and hold…" She'd thought medical school had forever cured her of blushing, but then she'd met Cooper Knight and continually found new ways to embarrass herself in front of him. How long had she slept against him?

"I didn't mind." A gentle smile reinforced his quiet statement.

She turned her head away from the gray eyes that somehow saw too much. "Where are we?"

"In a few minutes, you'll be able to see Puma Ridge."

Charley suddenly recognized her surroundings, and mortification burned deeper. She'd slept for nearly two hours. What had happened to the female physician who never let anyone see her get upset? The man must think her a weak-kneed female—witnessing her panic over a mouse and then having to keep her from tumbling off his coach when she'd fallen asleep after crying all over him.

"Did you ever decide on a name?"

"What?" Charley squinted at the confusing question.

"Your cat?"

Her cat? "Oh." She gathered her scattered wits. "Pockets."

It was his turn to give her a bewildered frown. "Pockets?"

"In memory of the way she arrived."

Understanding lit his face. "In my pocket."

She nodded and felt a smile work its way through her embarrassment at the thought of the tiny feline in the care of this brawny coachman. For all his bluster, he had a habit of quietly taking care of those around him.

"It'll do, I suppose." He pressed his boot into the brake lever and spoke to the horses as they crested the edge of a downward slope. "Whoa, team. Easy does it."

"What name would you have given her?"

Cooper shrugged and guided the horses around a deep rut. "I don't know. Pussycat?"

The residue of her discomfiture disintegrated at his blank look. "Pussycat? Where's your imagination?"

He met her laugh with a stern glance before a cynical grin broke through. "When it comes to cats, I have no imagination. Give me a dog any day."

"Then why did you give me a cat?"

"Hank needed a home for it, and you needed a mouser." His fingers curled into his palms, tightening the tension on the reins and slowing their entrance into town.

Her smile grew at the awkward note that crept into his reply. "It was exceedingly thoughtful of you. Pockets and I both thank you. That is, if she's still around. She might think I've abandoned her by now."

The team trotted toward their regular stopping place with little visible guidance from Cooper. "That dumb cat probably slept all afternoon and didn't realize you were gone."

The horses came to a halt, dropping their heads and relaxing with noisy, blowing snorts. Cooper set the brake and wrapped the reins around its handle.

"She isn't dumb." Charley twisted her feet over the side of the coach and climbed down without waiting for help. She was getting the hang of mounting and dismounting the tall conveyance. "And if it was only one afternoon, I wouldn't be worried. But I've been gone since yesterday morning."

His boots puffed miniature clouds of dust when they hit the ground beside her, the medical bag she'd almost forgotten gripped in his fist. "I thought you said you delivered the baby this morning."

"I did. But I went out there yesterday." Her stomach burned at the reminder of how long it had been since she'd last eaten.

Cooper handed over her bag, and without warning, their easy companionship dissipated. What exactly did one say to the man you'd used for a pillow?

She gestured toward the stage office, her nerves grabbing her tongue. "Would you tell the ticket agent I'll settle the price of my fare with him tomorrow? I'm going to have to set up an account if I make a habit of catching rides."

Cooper dipped his head in a nod.

"Thank you for the ride and for not letting me tumble off onto my head." Even with the nap, she was nearly silly with fatigue. Otherwise, she wouldn't be so nervous around a man who merely tolerated her.

She spun and reached for the reins of her rented horse, surprising the baggage handler who was leading the animal to the hitching rail.

He pulled them out of her reach. "If you don't mind, ma'am, I have to deliver something to the livery stable in a few minutes, and I can ride the horse over and return it for you. Save you and me both a few steps."

"You would be doing me a favor." Charley dug in her pocket for a coin.

The man waved it away. "Keep your money, Doc. That little one you brought into the world this morning is my niece." He finished looping the reins of the rented horse around the rail and started unloading the luggage boot. "I figure you're due a rest."

"Thank you." Charley smiled and turned toward home. News had traveled fast.

She heard Cooper speak to the groom who was unhitching the team, then he dashed across the street to catch up with her. "Were you up all night?" His disapproving frown had returned.

"Yes, but that's the way it is with babies sometimes. They have their own time schedule."

"No wonder you fell asleep."

The unexpected compassion in his voice made her turn and face him. "Would you like coffee or something cooler to drink?"

Why was she reluctant to lose his company? Especially since her self-consciousness about falling asleep against the grumpy man had returned in full force.

Cooper shook his head. "I've got to make tracks toward home." Gloved fingers touched the brim of his hat. "Go get some rest." He started to leave then paused and spoke over his shoulder. "And you can ride with me anytime. I enjoyed the company."

She watched his tall figure stride away, and a warm sensation enveloped her. The man was a bewildering mass of contradictions, but right now, she was too tired to decipher how she felt about it.

Pockets greeted her with a yawn and sleepy meow from her spot on a padded chair in Charley's private parlor. Scooping up the yellow fluff ball, she snuggled the animal to her neck, the noisy purr bringing a smile to her face. "Cooper was right. You did sleep the afternoon away, didn't you?"

~

Wispy dreams that created a vague sense of longing vanished with the dawn, and Charley met the sunrise determined to put confusing emotions behind her and focus on doctoring. Thankfully, a frantic pounding on her door around midmorning made it easy to do, and she hurried after another anxious father whose two boys had tumbled out of a tree. After setting one arm, patching numerous scrapes and bruises, and admonishing the undaunted young men to stay out of trees, Charley followed her growling stomach to Ellie's Kitchen.

"Miss Adams. Good afternoon." The editor stepped onto the boardwalk from the door of his newspaper office.

"Good afternoon, Mr. Farnsworth." She paused to return his greeting.

"How are you enjoying our fair town? Are you settling in all right?"

Charley studied the man's inscrutable expression. "I'm finding it quite welcoming, thank you." She'd done little more than exchange polite greetings with him, and she'd assumed that, despite his civil reaction when she'd first arrived in Puma Ridge, he avoided her because he disapproved of her.

"That's good to hear. However, as a newspaper man, I must admit I'm curious why a woman of your obviously genteel breeding would choose such an unusual vocation."

Charley stiffened at his question, but she didn't hear any criticism in his words. Maybe, like he'd said, he was genuinely curious.

She smiled slightly. "You can blame that on my Uncle Eddy. He was a physician in Missouri before he headed west, and he often let me accompany him on his house visits. When I expressed interest in helping people like he did, he encouraged me to pursue becoming a doctor."

"Why not be a nurse instead? That's what most women would've chosen."

His question was mild, but Charley had had too many people—women included—try to persuade her that nursing was the only acceptable place for females in the practice of medicine. "I'm not most women."

Mr. Farnsworth chuckled lightly. "I get the feeling you've heard that question before."

Charley acknowledged his teasing statement with a slight tilt of her head. "I will admit that it's unusual for women to become doctors, but that is changing with each passing year."

"So it would seem." He leaned inside his office door and came out with his hat. "You looked like a woman on a mission when I stopped you. I have a meeting with the mayor in a few minutes, but may I escort you to your destination first?" He offered his elbow.

"No, thank you. I don't have far to go. I'm going to Ellie's for an early lunch. I was called out before I could eat breakfast."

"I won't take no for an answer. Ellie's is right on my way." He offered his arm again, and she reluctantly took it.

He led her down the plank walk along the front of the buildings that lined the south side of the main street. "Did you have to patch up another wounded dog?" Humor warmed his voice.

Charley bit back a sharp retort. "My patients were of the human variety this time, and not a dog bite among them."

He cleared his throat and had the grace to appear chagrined. "Ah, yes. I've been warned about the consequences of further misbehavior by my canine. I apologize for the trouble he caused you."

Charley hid a grin. She had a good idea who'd done the warning.

"You shouldn't have to worry about Benji bringing you his injured dog again. At least not due to my dog's actions. I found a new home for him farther away from town where hopefully, he won't cause any more trouble."

Charley wasn't sure whether to thank him for addressing the problem or sympathize over losing his dog, but he continued before she could come up with an appropriate response.

"I'm happy you're starting to have a steady supply of two-legged patients, but I don't mind admitting I'm a little surprised." He led her around a barrel of brooms and crates of fresh vegetables displayed in front of the mercantile.

"Why?" She couldn't decide if the chatty newspaper editor was interviewing her or merely passing the time of day.

He tilted his head. "I didn't think the townsfolk would accept you quite so quickly."

It hadn't seemed quick to her, nor had the entire town accepted her. However, as the editor of the only newspaper in town, Mr. Farnsworth had influence, and if he accepted her, it would possibly sway all but the most stubborn—like Cooper. "I *am* a physician, and when people are in pain, that's usually who they turn to."

"Quite true, Miss Adams, quite true." He patted her hand with a fatherly air. "I'm glad you have that attitude. I have overheard more than one disparaging remark about our new 'petticoat' physician. I'm happy you're not taking it personally because I've also heard from your first few patients that you seem to be competent." He lowered his voice. "A fair newspaper man should remain neutral on issues like this, but off the record, I hope you stay here. You're an attractive addition to our town."

Charley bit her tongue and merely smiled politely. A more roundabout, backhanded compliment she'd never received. Mayor Hennessey had better watch out for his job. With doublespeak like that, Editor Farnsworth could easily slip into the role of politician.

The mayor stepped out of the bank across the street, and Charley welcomed the timely distraction. "Thank you for the escort, Mr. Farnsworth. We're nearly to Ellie's, and there is Mayor Hennessey, so I will let you go on." She freed her hand from his arm.

He tipped his hat. "Thank you for a lovely stroll, Miss Adams. I enjoyed our chat. Good day."

"Good day." She continued down the boardwalk when the newspaperman crossed the street toward the mayor. She was happy he wasn't using his paper to run her out of town, but she wasn't sure he actually approved of her beyond the fact she was an "attractive addition" to Puma Ridge.

Charley snorted under her breath at the piece of flattery. She'd much prefer to be a useful, *needed* addition to town. She'd also earned the right to be addressed as *Doctor* Adams rather than simply *Miss* Adams. Women had nursed people for centuries, but the minute one had the audacity to add Medical Doctor to their name, people got their antiquated notions in a twist and acted like a scandalous crime had been committed.

She shook off the spurt of aggravation and stepped off the end of the walk to cross the alleyway between the gunsmith's shop and Ellie's café.

A body hurtled to the ground in front of her, brushing her skirt and just missing knocking her down. She jumped back, blinking at the ragged bundle of humanity at her feet.

Cruel laughter yanked her gaze around to three adolescents standing in the alley.

The tallest boy leaned lazily against the side of the gunsmith's building and sneered. "You should watch where you step, ol' man."

The snickers that accompanied the taunt riled Charley to hot fury. It was as clear as the sneers on their faces that the boys were more than mere observers to the older man's fall.

Two strides brought her face to face with the ringleader. "You have five seconds to disappear before I scream for the sheriff."

The bully's lip curled, and he held her gaze for four long seconds, but when Charley opened her mouth and sucked in an exaggerated breath, his companions turned tail and ran, and his resolve broke. He spat a curse word in her face then turned and followed his friends.

Charley knelt beside the scrawny, grimy man who struggled to push himself upright. "Are you hurt?" She helped him to a sitting position, and the odor of long-unwashed body assailed her senses.

He squinted up at her. "Who're you?"

"I'm Dr. Adams." She brushed a strand of greasy hair off his forehead to examine the bloody scrape beneath it.

The man swatted her hand aside. "Go 'way. I ain't dead yet."

She dropped her hand to her side. The abrasion didn't appear deep. "I can clean that for you so it doesn't get infected and scar."

A sneer lifted thin lips, showing yellowed, crooked teeth. "Why should you care?"

Charley breathed through her mouth to avoid the worst of his body's odor. "Because I'm a doctor, and you need help."

"I'm a long way past help." He lurched to his feet and staggered sideways.

She stood and grabbed his arm to steady him. The self-contempt in his tone wrung her heart. "Then how about a meal?"

Several slow blinks met her question. Probably trying to clear the dizziness the sudden rise had caused him. "I don't want your pity." He yanked his arm away only to weave on his feet again. If he was drunk, she couldn't smell it over the other stronger smells that lingered about him.

She smiled and reached for his arm again, wrapping her hand around the grimy shirt sleeve to keep him from toppling over. "I've never liked dining alone, and if you would care to join me, I'd love to have you join me at Ellie's."

The old man squinted at her. "Are you real?"

Charley started toward the restaurant door, and he followed unresistingly. "I should hope so, otherwise you'd be talking to nobody. And wouldn't that look silly?"

Her nonsensical reply disarmed him, and before he could gather himself enough to protest further, Charley had seated him at a corner table.

She placed her order with the clearly disapproving serving girl who approached. "I'd like two specials please and plenty of hot, black coffee."

The girl eyed the dirty man with distaste then glanced back at Charley. "Are you sure you—"

"Would you please bring me and my *guest* our food and some coffee?" Charley interrupted her protest.

Her expression shouted her disapproval but she nodded. "Yes, Dr. Adams."

The coffee arrived first, and with a little persuasion, Charley's skeptical dinner companion accepted a cup. After a tentative sip, he downed half the mug in one gulp and looked more alert by the time fried ham, beans, and cornbread were slid in front of them. The food disappeared almost as fast as the coffee, and Charley had the serving girl bring him another helping.

When the man finally set his fork aside and leaned back in his chair, his earlier, glazed appearance was gone. "I'm obliged, ma'am. I was hungrier than I realized."

Charley dabbed her mouth with her napkin. "What's your name?"

"Hiram Beckenback, ma'am." A dignity almost as tattered as his soiled clothing threaded through his soft reply.

"It's nice to meet you, Mr. Beckenback. I'm Dr. Charley Adams." She gave in to a sudden, half-formed impulse. "Would you care for some peach pie for dessert?"

The man had piqued her curiosity, and she wanted to find out more about him. But not in the busy café where the gathering lunch crowd had their ears perked for gossip.

Mr. Beckenback's dull eyes brightened. "I haven't had peach pie in a coon's age." The tiny gleam faded. "But they don't serve that here."

"No, but I do."

His wiry gray brows wrinkled. "What do you mean?"

Charley laid several coins beside her plate and stood. "Follow me."

XIII

A tuneless melody whistled through Cooper's lips while he and Martin checked on his growing cattle herd, and he kept finding himself smiling for no reason. Unless he counted the picture of a bright head tucked under his chin as a reason.

He noticed Martin watching him when they returned to the ranch house and washed up for lunch.

"You're awfully chipper today, boss."

Cooper stripped off his shirt and dunked his head and shoulders under the pump to rinse off the morning's sweaty grime, then he straightened and shook the water from his hair, grinning when Martin jumped back to avoid the spray. "Any law against being chipper?"

Martin took his turn at the pump. "Nope. But you *ain't* been lately."

Cooper grabbed the worn strip of material they used for a towel and dried his face. "Are you saying I'm a grump?" He'd been called that a lot lately. It was enough to annoy a fella.

Martin lifted an eyebrow and smirked, water dripping off his scruffy chin. "If the boot fits…"

Cooper threw the towel at his ranch hand's face. "Some friend you are."

The shorter man snatched it out of the air. "Just callin' it like I see it, boss."

Cooper ignored him and the teasing ceased while they filled their bellies from the pot of beans Cooper had left on the back of the stove and cold biscuits.

Martin dumped his empty tin plate into the kitchen washtub. "What are your plans for this afternoon?"

"I'm headin' to town to pick up my pay at the stage office and a bag of coffee from the mercantile. We've worked hard this morning, so when Lyle returns from checking on that south pasture, why don't you two take it easy for a couple of hours?"

"Sounds good to me." Martin grinned slyly and strode toward the door. "Say hello to Miss Adams for me." He ducked when a burnt biscuit sailed past his head. "It's a good thing you're courting a doctor. Your biscuits could kill a man." He dodged another flying biscuit and laughed all the way to the barn.

"I'm not courting her." Cooper shouted the protest to his retreating ranch hand and scowled at the remaining biscuits. They might be slightly scorched on the bottoms, but they weren't all burnt. He covered them with a cloth and put the beans on the back of the still-warm stove for Lyle. If they didn't like his cooking, one of them could take over for a while.

He changed into a clean shirt and headed to the barn where he found a fresh horse waiting.

Martin grinned from his seat in the shade of the barn door and rubbed oil into a leather harness. "While you're at the doc's, ask her if she can make good biscuits."

Cooper swung into the saddle without replying. Just because thoughts of a certain green-eyed, blonde-haired petticoat physician had put a small spring in his step lately, it didn't mean he was courting her. What exactly he *was* doing wasn't a question he wanted to answer or even ask yet.

His horse wanted to run, and less than an hour later, Cooper reached Puma Ridge. After he deposited his pay at the bank and purchased a bag of coffee beans, he rode to Charley's house and hitched his horse to her railing. Halfway to her door, he stopped. He'd come up with a flimsy excuse for riding into town, but what excuse could he give for visiting Dr. Adams? He was thirty-four years old, yet he felt more awkward and nervous than a boy who'd noticed girls for the first time. Why had he given in to this crazy, ill-thought-out impulse—

"Mr. Knight?"

Cooper yanked off his hat and spun around faster than Benji caught with a grubby hand in Hannah's cookie jar. "Miss Adams."

She walked up the street toward him, sunlight glinting off the shiny strands of hair that escaped her hat and framed her face. She carried her familiar leather bag, but even its ominous presence couldn't detract from her fresh prettiness or her welcoming smile.

He swallowed hard and glanced at the person behind her in an effort to keep from staring. He felt his forehead crease. Why was old Hiram following her? Had no one warned her about the town drunk? Plunking his hat back on his head, he stepped forward to deal with the nuisance.

Charley smiled brightly. "Isn't this a nice surprise? You're just in time to join us for some peach pie."

Cooper stopped short. *Us?*

She sailed past him to the front door, old Hiram right on her heels. Cooper could almost *see* the stench that hovered around the man. The smell was bad. But oddly enough, he hadn't caught a whiff of anything stronger than a serious lack of soap. Maybe it was too early in the day for the man to be drunk.

Charley glanced over her shoulder after she and Hiram crossed the threshold. "Are you coming?"

Cooper caught up to the unlikely pair in three long strides.

"Watch out for Pockets. She likes to get underfoot, and I don't want anyone to trip or step on her." She nudged the kitten aside with her foot and strode toward her kitchen. "Take a seat at the table. I'll have the pie cut and served in just a second."

Hiram's aroma nearly overwhelmed that of fresh baked goods, and Cooper's disapproval intensified. It went unnoticed, though. Charley was busy cutting slices of thick, golden pie, and the old man's longing eyes were firmly locked on the pastry.

"Mr. Knight? Have you met Mr. Beckenback? He was kind enough to join me for lunch so I wouldn't have to eat alone."

Since when did Hiram have a last name? "We've met." Cooper sent the man another warning glare. He should have headed into town sooner. Not only would Miss Adams have made a more pleasing dinner companion than Martin, Cooper's presence would have spared her from Hiram's begging.

She served them mouthwatering wedges of peach-filled pie, and Cooper slid into the chair opposite the old man when she'd taken her seat.

Hiram forked a bite into his mouth and closed his eyes as he chewed and swallowed. "This reminds me of my mother's."

Charley beamed at the threadbare tramp. "I'm glad you like it." She chewed and swallowed a tiny bite before looking at Cooper. "Did you need to see me about something, Mr. Knight?"

He hastily swallowed his delicious mouthful of dessert. "Uh, no. Uh, that is…I came to town to pick up a few things and thought I'd see if you'd recovered from yesterday."

A pretty shade of pink tinted her cheeks. "I did. I'm not in danger of falling asleep at inopportune times today."

More's the pity. He'd rather enjoyed seeing that side of her.

Hiram scraped his fork across the plate then licked it off while casting a covert glance toward the remaining pie.

"Would you like some more, Mr. Beckenback?" Charley reached for the pan.

He wiped the back of his hand across his mouth. "Oh, no, thank you, ma'am. It was mighty delicious, though."

"Please. I couldn't possibly eat this whole pie myself. You'd both be doing me a favor if you helped finish it." Charley cut another large slice and started to set it on Hiram's plate but paused. "Tell you what. I'll trade you. A second piece of pie for letting me clean that scrape."

For the first time, Cooper noticed the abrasion on the man's forehead.

Hiram's smile displayed a small gap between his front teeth. "Never let it be said that Hiram Beckenback wasn't willing to help a lady."

Cooper coughed to clear the chunk of peach that went down wrong and took a swig from the glass of water Charley had provided along with the pie. The person sitting catty-corner from him looked like Hiram and smelled like Hiram, but he sure didn't *sound* like the Hiram that Cooper knew.

Charley smiled like she'd won first prize at the annual baking contest, and she refilled both Hiram's and Cooper's plates before hurrying out of the room. She returned almost before Cooper could blink, and while Hiram polished of his second slice of pie, she efficiently cleaned the bruised-looking scrape on the man's forehead and gently applied salve to it.

The minute she finished, Hiram pushed away from the table. "I've trespassed on your hospitality long enough, ma'am. I'm sure this young fella would like some of your time without an old man getting in his way. Thank you for the meal and the most delectable peach pie I've eaten in more years than I care to remember. If I can ever do anything to repay your kindness, please, don't hesitate to let me know." Hiram's slight bow at the end of his speech contrasted sharply with his filthy appearance.

Charley's voice halted his exit from the kitchen. "Mr. Beckenback? You may decline if it makes you uncomfortable, but I would enjoy having you join me at church some Sunday morning."

Hiram paled beneath his beard. "I don't think the church folk would appreciate that offer, ma'am."

The older man didn't so much as glance in Cooper's direction, but Cooper's conscience cringed anyway. He wasn't one of the people Hiram referred to, but the man wouldn't know that since Cooper had never done more than nod whenever they'd crossed paths. Why had he assumed Hiram had no interest in church? Why had he never reached out and asked?

"Mr. Beckenback, if other people's opinions were something I considered important, I'd never have become a doctor." A smile accompanied Charley's words, but a core of solid iron ran through them.

A rusty chuckle escaped Hiram's throat. "I'll think about it, ma'am. Good day." He slipped out the kitchen's rear door, closing it softly behind him.

Charley relaxed against her chair, gazing at the closed door in silence.

Cooper broke it after several seconds. "Are you sure it was a good idea to invite him into your home?" Maybe someone should have reached out to the old man before now, but a woman living alone? That was foolish.

He must have succeeded at keeping any accusation out of his tone because her eyes met his calmly. "It was a spur of the moment decision. I hope you don't mind that I dragged you in with us."

He grinned at her. "For peach pie, you can drag me in anytime you want. Who made this anyway? Old Hiram was right. It's delicious."

"I did."

The petticoat doc cooked? He eyed his empty plate and could almost hear Martin wanting to know if she could make good biscuits. "It was *really* good."

"Why do you sound so surprised?"

"I didn't expect you to know…" Cooper had learned to read sign a long time ago, but it didn't take an Army scout to see that he'd blundered smack-dab into an ambush.

"You didn't expect a woman doctor to know how to cook? Then I imagine you'll be even more surprised to hear I canned those peaches, too. From the trees on my father's farm."

Cooper raised his hands in a placating gesture. "Now, don't shoot. That's not what I—Yeow!" Sharp needles digging into his thigh made him jump and bang his knee on the underside of the table, rattling the dishes on top.

"What's wrong?" Charley sprang from her chair.

He scooted his chair back and gingerly unfastened the furry critter hanging from his leg. He held it up by the scruff of the neck. "Your cat."

The concern disappeared off her face, and she snickered. "Pockets obviously didn't care for your condescending tone, either." She rescued the tiny animal dangling from his hand, cuddled it in her arms, and returned to her chair.

"I wasn't being condescending. I was trying to compliment you."

Her left eyebrow rose. "Could've fooled me."

Rubbing his stinging leg, Cooper returned to his initial concern. "Why'd you invite Old Hiram home with you anyway?"

Indignation replaced amusement, and Charley's eyes glinted green sparks. "Three adolescent troublemakers sent him sprawling on his face and then taunted him. Nobody deserves to be treated like that, I don't care how bad they appear or smell. He wouldn't let me tend the scrape on his head, but he did accept the offer of a meal at the café." Her voice lost its hard edge as she explained.

"But why bring him here?"

She shrugged. "Like I said, it was spur of the moment. He looked so lonely I didn't have the heart to abandon him right then. And that scrape needed attention that he wouldn't have given it."

The woman's willingness to invite a strange man into her home bothered him, but he couldn't help but marvel at her kindness. Once again, he had to admit—if only to himself—that he'd been altogether too hasty in tarring her with the same brush he'd used on Dr. Engstad. The man barely had compassion for the patients who could pay. He had absolutely none when it came to the outcasts of the community. However, Charley Adams, without hesitation, had brought the dirtiest, smelliest man in town into her kitchen to feed him a mouthwatering peach pie before gently patching up his injury.

Her compassion was going to get her in trouble, though. Cooper would have to keep a closer eye on her to make sure the man didn't take advantage of it. But for the life of him, he couldn't figure out whether the emotion in his chest was annoyance. Or something far more disturbing.

Cooper suddenly knew why he'd come to see her. "It's a nice day. How would you like another shooting lesson?"

Charley's eyes lit up, and she set the kitten on the floor. It scurried over to stalk Cooper's boot. "Are you sure you don't mind? It *was* fun to knock off those rocks last time."

He nudged the attacking feline aside before it could decide to use his leg for a climbing post again. "Go get your gun, and we'll see how well you remember your last lesson."

~

Charley whooped when the last rock flew off the log. "I did it. Twelve times without missing." She bounced on her toes in excitement. "Pretty good for a beginner, no?"

One of Cooper's rare grins peeked out. "Yep. And since you've almost cleaned me out of cartridges, that concludes our lesson for today."

Charley was almost prouder of luring his smile out of hiding than she was of her newfound shooting ability. "Oh, I'm sorry. You didn't get to shoot."

"I don't need the practice." He took the gun from her hands and dumped out the empty cases before wiping it down with an oiled rag.

She propped her hands on her hips, unwilling to examine the reason she was in such a lighthearted, teasing mood. "Do you realize how boastful that sounded?"

"Telling the truth isn't boasting." His dancing gray eyes belied his bland expression when he glanced over at her.

She pointed to the revolver strapped against his hip. "Prove it."

"And how do you want me to do that?" He set her gun aside and pulled his own from its holster, rolling the cylinder to check each round.

Charley silently set about placing six smaller rocks on the log then stepped off a distance twice that of where she'd stood to practice. Cooper observed her movements with a growing smirk, and she added several more paces for good measure. "You have to hit all the rocks from here."

He joined her, and studied the targets. "Are you sure this is far enough away to satisfy you?"

So, he wanted to be a smart-aleck about it, did he? She crossed her arms. "Where would *you* prefer to shoot from?"

Cooper added ten long strides to the distance before turning to face the log again. "This will do."

She raised a brow at his quiet confidence and joined him. "I have a feeling I'm going to regret challenging you to prove—"

The gun flew into Cooper's hand with a blur, and he cleared the log so fast, his shots rolled together in one long burst of sound. Then, in a well-oiled move, he ejected the spent cases and reloaded the gun before returning it to his holster and hooking a small leather loop over the hammer. "Satisfied?"

Charley knew her mouth hung open, but she couldn't help it. She swallowed and cleared her throat. "That was the fastest thing I've ever seen! How did you *do* that?"

A smile teased the corners of his mouth. "Years of practice. A few years defending my scalp against Indians didn't hurt, either."

Her eyebrows were probably in danger of disappearing into her hairline. "You fought Indians?"

His smile disappeared. "I served with the Army down in Arizona Territory before moving here to be close to my sister and her family." He picked up the revolver he'd given Charley and stuffed it in his belt, the subject clearly over. "We'd better head back before it gets dark."

She nodded. The tone of the afternoon had taken a somber turn, but she was sort of relieved. She was in danger of letting her imagination run away with her good sense and needed the reminder to take whatever this was slow. They'd done nothing remotely romantic. Her hands were smudged with burnt gunpowder, and she felt the grit of it on face and neck, but her insides fluttered like he'd done something sentimental like bring her flowers and candy and take her on a buggy ride. And if Mr. Cooper Knight heard *that* thought, he'd hightail it into the hills without a backward glance.

She dug a handkerchief out of her pocket and surreptitiously wiped her cheek. A black streak marred the white cloth when she lowered it. Hastily, she scrubbed at the other cheek.

Cooper slowed and glanced down at her. "Something wrong?"

"I must look like a chimney sweep." She grinned, pretending she didn't care what he thought. Because she didn't.

The serious expression he'd worn since mentioning the Army faded. He tugged the fabric out of her hand and stepped close. Very close.

"No." He gently dabbed the end of her nose. "Not a chimney sweep." Calloused fingers smoothed the cloth over her cheek twice then lowered it slowly.

Silver eyes fastened on hers, and Charley's breath snagged in her throat. If either one moved more than a fraction of an inch, they'd be touching.

His voice was barely above a whisper. "You're too pretty to be anything but you."

Her heart slammed into her ribs when he picked up her hand, tucked it underneath his elbow, and continued walking. And he didn't seem to mind the way her skirt bumped and brushed against his leg.

Only when they reached her door did he release her arm and speak again. "Don't forget your gun." He handed over her small revolver.

"Thank you. I had a nice time." Why couldn't she come up with something cleverer than that?

"I did, too." The corner of his mouth lifted with a hint of uncertainty that further charmed her. "I'm not as interesting a dinner companion as Old Hiram, but would you care to join me for supper when I return from my stage run tomorrow evening?"

The grin that bounced to Charley's lips resisted all efforts to tame it into a demure smile. "I'd like that."

Cooper's smile grew. "I'll see you tomorrow then. I'll come for you after I've washed up." He touched his hat and sauntered away through the evening light.

Charley stood on her door stoop and watched until she couldn't see him anymore before entering the house. Closing the door behind her, she leaned against it and closed her eyes. He'd asked her to dinner. Did that mean he felt the same flicker of attraction that grew inside her?

If she'd read the expression in his eyes correctly when he'd wiped her face, then yes.

Her eyes flew open. Her handkerchief. He hadn't given it back.

Her grin scrunched her cheeks again. Gunpowder might not be romantic, but keeping a lady's handkerchief sure was.

You're going to get hurt again.

The memory his fingers against her skin drowned out the pessimist in her head.

Tiny paws batted at the hem of her skirt, and she picked up her kitten and cuddled it. "Pockets, is it crazy to be attracted to a man who doesn't like doctors?"

Pockets purred loudly, too contented with the fingers caressing her ear to worry about trivial matters like human relationships.

XIV

Cooper's nerves thrummed under his skin, echoing the tattoo of his knuckles against Charley's front door. The surprised reactions and speculative grins he'd received on his way down the street were enough to make any fella nervous. It wasn't like he never visited the barber shop. He'd simply let the bothersome chore go longer than usual.

His fingers tightened around the stems of the fragile blossoms Hannah had carefully selected from the beds around her house. He must look ridiculous standing here holding the silly things, but Hannah had insisted he couldn't show up at Charley's door emptyhanded, and it had been quicker to accept them than to waste time arguing.

Tucking his hat under his arm, Cooper smoothed his newly shorn hair with his free hand.

Faint footsteps sounded from inside, and Charley was already talking when the door swung inward. "I'm sorry. I'm running late. I was called out this afternoon…" Her voice trailed away, and her eyes widened in astonishment.

Cooper rubbed the tender skin of his jaw. He'd avoided the mirror above the barber's chair after one glance. That's all it had taken to see that the freshly shaved skin of his chin and jaw looked like it belonged to a sickly city dude. He should have dug out his razor at the first hint of warm weather like Hannah had pestered him to do. "I, uh, got tired of Hannah and Ma Jankins nagging me to get a haircut." The weak explanation made him want to wince.

Her hand reached up. Paused. Was she going to touch his face?

"You shaved, too." She yanked it down to her side. "And here I thought you were hiding behind all that brush because you were homely." Her gentle taunt wavered slightly.

Cooper stood a little taller. All day, he'd alternated between anticipation of this evening and regret at giving in to yesterday's momentary emotions. But the second-guessing beat a hasty retreat at her indirect compliment.

Breathing a bit easier, he handed her the flowers and tried to read the expression in her eyes before she lowered her gaze. "These are for you."

Lifting the blooms to her nose, she inhaled deeply, her eyes drifting closed. "They smell wonderful, thank you. Come in. I'll put them in water before we go."

He stepped inside, and she whirled away toward the back of the house. It was absurd to be jealous of a handful of showy weeds, but when those petals had brushed her soft-looking lips, he'd wanted to take their place for just an instant.

Or longer.

Had he nearly overlooked the woman he'd been waiting for all his life because of his prejudice against physicians?

"Meow." The gold kitten sat primly at his feet, her bright blue eyes peering up at him.

Cooper squatted on his heels and shook his finger at the animal, thankful for the distraction from his unsettling thoughts. "You'd better be protecting her from mice, or I'll know the reason why."

Pockets rubbed her face on his outstretched finger, ignoring his warning. Cooper opened his hand, and the kitten arched her head, back, and tail underneath his palm. Purring loudly, she turned to repeat the process.

He stood and brought the tiny critter to eye level. It didn't even make a decent handful. "I'm serious, cat. If you don't earn your keep, you can be replaced."

Pockets butted him in the nose, tickling that sensitive member with her soft, furry head, wholly oblivious to her precarious position.

Charley laughed upon entering the room. "Are you threatening my cat?" She pointed a dangerously long pin at him before stabbing it through the pretty, flower-trimmed hat that adorned her upswept hair.

He set the furball on the nearest chair and rubbed his nose with his knuckles to relieve the tickle. "No, ma'am. Simply inquiring about her health."

Her eyebrow rose. "I'm sure you were."

Her teasing erased his earlier nervousness, and he ran his gaze over the green dress that set off her eyes—and her curves—to perfection. "Miss Adams, you make that dress look real fine."

"Thank you." The twin emeralds sparkling at him from beneath her lashes did curious things to his insides. They buzzed and fluttered like a wasp trapped inside a window.

She took his offered elbow, glancing up at him while they strolled out of the house toward the street. "I noticed a man riding on top of the stage with you this morning. Between the two of you, there was a bit more weaponry than usual. When he returned with you this evening, I realized he wasn't a regular passenger."

For a city woman, Charley had sharp eyes *and* the sense to keep her voice low.

Her fingers tightened around his arm. "Are you expecting some sort of trouble?"

"Nope. You plannin' on startin' some?" The possibility that she cared enough to worry about him was appealing and attractive.

She sent him an annoyed scowl. "I might if you keep avoiding answering my question." Her dainty bootheels clipped a little harder against the boardwalk.

He grinned at her threat but kept his voice low. "We're not expecting trouble, but we wouldn't want to disappoint any that comes along, either."

"That means you are." She studied him with a furrowed brow. "I suppose your avoidance of my question also means you aren't going to explain any further?"

"Nope."

She huffed a disgusted-sounding sigh. "That's what I was afraid of. You'll be careful, though. Right?" Her hand tightened on his arm.

Cooper touched his calloused fingers to the slender, gloved ones that were curled around his forearm, gratified by her concern. "Always am. You know I'm not eager to visit a doctor."

Her lips lost their worried slant. "And yet you're visiting *this* doctor." She tapped her dress collar with her free hand.

"But not for the usual reasons." Although the *unusual* rhythm of his heart caused by her saucy grin might cause some fussbudgets to seek out a sawbones' advice. "This is a purely social call."

Their eyes caught and held as he reached for the café door, and the spark of awareness he'd experienced when he'd wiped the gunpowder residue off her face arced between them again. Maybe he needed his head examined more than his heart.

"You folks comin' or goin'?"

The impatient question startled him out of his daze, and Cooper shoved open the door and ushered Charley out of the way of the man waiting behind them.

Once seated at a table, his slightly flushed companion's eyes avoided his own. But strangely enough, Charley's unexpected bashfulness increased his confidence and the desire to learn more about her.

Unfortunately, he hadn't taken into account the time of day, and the busy, noisy dining room limited their conversation while they ordered and waited for their food. They'd have had more privacy at Hannah's dining table. Why had he thought the café at supper time was a good idea? He'd told Martin that he wasn't courting Charley, but after this meal, the whole town would know he'd stepped out with Dr. Adams. He nodded at a few acquaintances, but pretended not to see their pointed grins. Mercifully, by the time their waitress served them coffee and dessert, the room had emptied of all but a few stragglers.

Charley's unexpected shyness faded with each pair of curious eyes that departed, and Cooper finally saw her relax.

She toyed with her fork, smashing a fat cake crumb against the saucer. "May I ask you something?"

He swallowed the last bite of his own spice cake, a prickle of caution brushing the back of his neck. "What is it?"

"After what you experienced with your brother-in-law, I can understand why you'd be worried about a new doctor, but I think your dislike of my profession goes deeper than that one event." She kept her voice low and leaned forward, her expression equal parts curiosity and sympathy. "What else happened to you?"

Cooper lifted the mug of steaming coffee to his lips and stared into the brown liquid. He'd certainly given her plenty of reasons to speculate about his behavior, but she'd caught him off guard, and he wasn't sure he wanted to discuss it. It had been hard enough when Hannah dragged the story out of him several months after it had happened, and he hadn't talked about it since. The emotions that accompanied the memory were black and ugly and not something he was proud of. He couldn't get rid of them, but he tried to disturb them as little as possible.

Lowering the cup, he looked at Charley, intending to brush aside her concern. But her soft, compassionate gaze and unwavering focus slipped past his guard and took him hostage.

He exhaled heavily and surrendered. "My parents contracted cholera when I was thirteen and Hannah nine, and the doctor couldn't do anything to help them. After they died, our nearest neighbors gave us a place to stay for a couple of years until I could provide for the two of us on my own. I did my best to look after and raise Hannah, but not too many years later, Ben came along and took her off my hands." Cooper managed a small grin.

Ben had been a good man and Cooper hadn't had any reservations about giving him permission to marry Hannah, but the change hadn't been easy. In fact, it had been downright difficult. Hannah had been the only family he'd had left, and he'd handed her over to someone else's care.

"Once she had a husband to take care of her, I started scouting for the Army. It was a lonely job, but I liked it, for the most part. Several months after I signed on, we got a new captain. I didn't think much about it at the time, because it didn't really affect me. I didn't quite fit in with either the enlisted men or the officers since I wasn't regular Army, and to me, he was merely another set of stripes who'd try to tell me how to do my job. On our first assignment, however, we discovered we worked well together, and by the end of our second long patrol we were friends. Within a few months, I felt like I'd gained a brother—something I'd never had. We even planned to go into ranching together." He turned his cup in slow circles and old memories swirled to life like the coffee it contained.

Over the course of the next few months, their friendship had deepened, and Van's zest for life and genuine love for God had challenged Cooper to dig around the roots of his own beliefs. Consequently, the faith of his childhood that had grown dormant for lack of attention sprang to life with new vigor. Until he'd failed Van. And that failure had dealt Cooper's faith a severe blow it had never quite recovered from.

The clatter of tin plates jerked him to the present. How long had he been staring at his coffee in silence?

He looked up and found Charley sitting motionless, watching him with her head tilted in concerned patience.

More words grated to the surface, and he didn't try to restrain them. "During that time, the fort physician died of a heart attack, and our commander contracted with a civilian doctor to replace him until another Army physician could be assigned to us. I don't know who the man knew or what strings he pulled to get the position..." He sucked in a breath to control his rising emotions. "It didn't take long before we realized he was addicted to his opiates and laudanum, and within a few weeks, a sick soldier would only go see him after they were given a direct order by a superior officer. The charlatan lost more patients than he saved." Cooper's jaw clenched hard. "Actually, those that survived did so in spite of him."

A slug of lukewarm coffee moistened his throat. "Van and I normally went on the same patrols searching for renegade Apaches, but one night, I ate something that disagreed with me, and the next morning, Van ordered me to stay behind and rest while he took a different scout." Cooper's drum-tight chest made breathing painful. "He and his troop walked straight into an ambush that afternoon."

Regrets had haunted him ever since. If he hadn't gotten sick... If he'd disobeyed Van's order... He might have been able to change the outcome of that deadly patrol.

"A messenger managed to make it back to the fort, and we rode out as fast as we could. But by the time we arrived, Captain Vandever had lost over half his men and had caught an arrow in his upper thigh. We chased off their attackers while he and the other wounded men were evacuated to the fort." Cooper's eyes burned. "When I got back there, Van was dead."

Sympathy filled Charley's face. "The arrow?"

"The sawbones." Cooper spat the words. A small part of him was surprised the mug didn't crack under the pressure of his doubled-fisted grip. "That fraud was so full of his own medicines that when he tried to cut the arrowhead out of Van's thigh, his scalpel slipped. Van bled to death on that table, and I never got the chance to say goodbye."

A warm, slender hand slid over his left wrist. "I am so sorry."

"If I'd been there, I would've stopped that butcher from touching him and taken Van to the nearest town. There was a woman like Ma there who had experience taking out arrows." Cooper's voice rasped to a stop, and he cleared his throat. "But if I'd been with Van in the first place, maybe I could have kept them out of the ambush in the first place."

Charley squeezed his wrist. "You can't know that for sure."

Maybe he couldn't, but that didn't stop the vicious guilt from gnawing at him whenever he gave himself permission to think about that day. The nightmares didn't wait for permission, though.

"They had to drag my hands off the doctor's throat when I found out what had happened. He was transferred from our fort a few days later, and I was confined to my quarters for a month, but I promised myself if I ever saw him again, I'd kill him with my bare hands."

"No." Large, troubled eyes emphasized Charley's horrified whisper. "Did you...?" She left the rest unasked.

Another question that plagued him. Given a chance, would he have carried out his threat? "No. He died a few months later. Poisoned by his own medicines." His stomach writhed at the venom coming from his mouth. It had been a long time since he'd stirred the memories this much. They reeked.

He rubbed the bottom of his coffee mug against the scarred tabletop. What a way to impress a woman. Telling her he'd been so filled with hate he'd wanted to kill a man. At least *that* desire was gone. If only because the man was beyond his reach. The grief and anger lingered, though, and festered deep below the surface. But not deep enough, given the way it had oozed out over Charley.

Her other hand slid across the table, and she gripped both his wrists in hers. "I don't know what else to say except I'm sorry, and I hurt for your loss. I wish I knew what I could say or do to make it better."

He shrugged and tried to relieve the tension he'd created with a thin smile. "I suppose I let my experiences with a few medicine men dictate my opinion of all of them."

Charley looked at him for a long moment, her expression

unreadable.

Had his gruesome story destroyed their fragile relationship?

"Then it's a good thing I'm a medicine *woman*." Her raised chin was pure impudence, and it did what his sorry excuse of a smile hadn't. It lightened the heavy atmosphere by several degrees. "I can't say I blame you for your opinion, though, now that I've heard what happened."

Some of the pressure in his chest evaporated. "You don't?"

"No. I'll warn you, though. I intend to change your opinion of doctors, and I don't quit when I set my mind to something." Emerald determination glinted fearlessly at him.

This time his smile was genuine and easy. "You've already changed it. At least about one in particular. Jury's still out on the rest of them."

~

The last time Charley'd been this nervous, she'd been preparing for her first surgery. Since then, she'd learned to harness the emotion and turn it into energy. Training the butterflies in her stomach to fly in a disciplined pattern. Tonight, however, her trained butterflies had been replaced with moths. The kind that flung themselves head first into a bright lantern over and over again and accomplishing nothing but confusion and headaches.

Standing on her doorstep, eye level with Cooper who stood watching her, hands in his pockets, Charley had no blessed idea what to say. Her eyes traced his clean-shaven cheeks. She had never guessed such sculpted lines hid behind his beard. He wasn't in any danger of being called pretty, there was too much firmness in his face for that. But the lean lines fell in more-than-pleasant places, and paired with the rest of his tall, rugged frame, his appearance had her heart tripping all over itself. Her plans hadn't included falling for a man, but lately, her emotions had developed a mind of their own. Cooper Knight had invaded her life, her thoughts, and was now storming her heart.

He pushed his hat brim up, and in the dim evening light, she saw the skin between his eyebrows scrunch with worry. "I'm sorry I ruined our supper with my gloomy tale."

She lifted her hand but once more caught herself before it could test the smoothness of his cheek. His tale had provided welcome insight into his early reactions to her, but she wasn't so sure she welcomed it, given the intense urge she now had to hug away his hurt. "You didn't ruin it." She dropped her hand, but Cooper caught it before it settled at her side.

"I'm glad." His thumb smoothed over her knuckles.

The moths beat their frantic, powdery wings against her ribcage, and she couldn't concentrate on anything but the sensation of calloused skin caressing hers. She'd touched all kinds of people in her professional capacity of medical doctor, but never had a simple touch been so…well, *not* simple.

"Are you going with Ma Jankins on her visits tomorrow?"

Her tongue hopelessly tangled, all Charley could do was nod.

"If you visit the Whipples' place, you'll pass the turnoff to my ranch. I'd like to show you around. If you're interested." His thumb stopped its stroking, and his whole body stilled. waiting on her answer.

Her mouth finally formed words. "I'd like that."

His fingers tightened around hers in a gentle squeeze before he released them and retreated. "See you tomorrow?"

Her head bobbed again. "I'd like that. I mean, I'll see you. Tomorrow."

His soft smile wound around her like a hug, and she forgot to breathe until he disappeared into the evening shadows with a final glance over his shoulder and a wave. She floated inside and plopped onto the first seat she came to before her wobbly knees could betray her.

Before tomorrow arrived, she should study the most technical medical journal she owned. That way, perhaps she wouldn't sound like such a tongue-tied simpleton when she next saw him.

XV

Charley bounced out of bed the next morning at the memory of Cooper's invitation, and for the first time since she'd started accompanying Ma, the house calls dragged painfully slow. Charley had little to do except offer an occasional recommendation and listen while Ma chatted about everything from teething babies to laying hens. She should be adding the tidbits the women shared to her expanding knowledge about the resilient, self-sufficient people who'd settled the Dakotas, but her mind continually drifted to one resident in particular.

When they finally turned down a worn track that Ma said led to Cooper's place, Charley's heart pulsed into an offbeat rhythm. Which would be worse? Finding out last night's reaction had been nothing more than a sympathetic response to the pain Cooper had suffered in his past, or discovering that she was actually falling for him?

The buckboard bounced and rattled over a rise before they descended into a pretty valley dotted with wildflowers and surrounded by pine- and spruce-covered hills.

Ma pointed to the cattle grazing on the lush grass. "Those are some of Coop's herd."

A few of the animals lifted their heads to observe the interlopers, their jaws working from side to side. With the exception of the calves peeking around the safety of their mommas' bulk, they all sported horns and splashes of white across their black, red, or brown hides. Ma guided the buggy into a wooded section at the far end of the valley, and then into another clearing that had recently been enlarged—if the leftover stumps were any indication.

The sound of axe against timber rang out, and Ma pointed to the slope on their left. "There they are."

Charley leaned forward to peer around her. The man wielding the axe at the base of a tall, twisted tree looked like Cooper. High above his head, two taut ropes anchored the gnarled pine to nearby trees, and a couple of men Charley didn't recognize watched him. "What are the ropes for?"

Ma turned her docile roan gelding toward the three men. "Sometimes it's difficult to drop a tree where you need it. It could hang up in another tree and get stuck if it twists when it falls, or it might knock pieces off a nearby dead tree. The ropes help them control where it lands."

"It sounds dangerous." Charley's stomach tightened.

Her companion's gray head nodded. "Can be if you don't know what you're doing. But those boys have cleared a lot of land 'round here the last few years, and they're careful."

One of the men glanced around and saw them. He must have said something because Cooper paused and looked over his shoulder.

He waved his hand in a shooing motion. "Stay back 'til we get this down." The deep shout traveled easily through the clear air.

Ma tugged the reins. "I wasn't born yesterday, Coop."

Charley grinned at the woman's grumble. They were still fifty yards or so from the men, but she wasn't eager to get any closer until the tree was safely on the ground.

Cooper waited until their buggy came to a complete halt before returning to his task. Even from this distance, Charley could see the way the fabric of his shirt strained across his shoulders as he sunk the axe deep into the thick tree trunk with each powerful swing.

A splintering sound reached her ears when Cooper stepped back and eyed the top of the quivering tree. "Timber!"

The other two men edged farther away, and the tree shuddered hard before starting to fall. A split-second later, one of the ropes snapped, and the tree twisted, its clawing limbs snagging the branches of a nearby dead pine. Both trees lurched violently. With a sickening snap, the freshly cut tree broke loose and crashed to the ground, sending the spiky top of the dead tree hurtling through the air toward the two men like it had been released from a giant slingshot.

Ma gasped, but Charley's breath hung in her throat.

Cooper shouted, dropping the axe and sprinting around the shuddering branches of the green tree to get to the man who'd been unable to evade the chunk of flying debris.

Snagging her bag from beneath her seat, Charley started to jump from the buggy.

"Wait!" Ma grabbed Charley's arm. "This'll be quicker." She slapped the end of the reins against the rump of the horse.

The startled gelding jumped away from the unexpected sting, and broke into a run, the buckboard living up to its name, bucking and bouncing over the rough ground. They covered the remaining distance in seconds, and Ma hauled back on the reins.

Charley shot from her seat, running almost before her feet touched the ground.

Cooper and a younger man knelt on each side of their injured companion. Broken branches of the dead treetop littered the ground around them.

The injured man groaned and struggled to sit up. "I'm all right."

Cooper held him down. "Don't move 'til we make sure nothing's broken. If I know Dr. Charley, she'll be here in a second to check on you."

"I'm here." Charley touched his shoulder and sank to her knees beside him and the injured man. She nestled the confidence in Cooper's tone into her heart to be examined later and focused on examining her patient.

Worry creased Cooper's face. "I *knew* those two trees were trouble the first time I laid eyes on them." His voice hardened. "Should've let them be."

"It was an accident, boss. I've got a hard head. I ain't hurt." Despite his slight scowl and the blood running down the side of his face, the injured man's voice was strong, and his eyes were alert, unclouded.

Charley held up her hand in front of his face. "How many fingers am I holding up?"

The younger man kneeling on the other side grinned weakly. "That won't help, Doc. Martin's not much good at countin'."

"Four." Martin snapped. "And don't go buttin' your nose in my concerns, you young troublemaker. The lady was talkin' to me."

Charley swallowed an unprofessional grin and took a clean cloth from her bag. "Do you hurt anywhere else besides your head?" She gently pressed it to the wound to staunch the bleeding.

The prone man winced. "No, ma'am, uh, Doc. I just didn't get out of the way quick enough. One of the limbs caught me across the noggin and knocked me down, but I ain't hurt nowhere else."

"Do you mind if I check to be sure?" Sometimes pain in one area could mask injury elsewhere.

The older man's face flushed slightly. "Uh, no, ma'am. That is, Doc."

Grabbing Cooper's hand, Charley placed it over the cloth to keep it in place, ignoring his startled expression. "Keep pressure on that for me."

She ran her hands down each of the injured man's arms before pressing gently along the length of his ribcage, talking to distract him. "I don't believe we've met before. I'm Dr. Charlotte Adams."

"It's nice to meet you, ma'am. I'm Martin."

Reaching under him, she ran her hand along his spine, then passed probing fingers over each leg. "Well, Mr. Martin, at first examination, it appears you came out of this with nothing more serious than a cut on your head."

Cooper had practically hung over her shoulder, scrutinizing her every move, so she couldn't help but hear, and feel, the relieved breath that whispered past his lips at her statement. She moved his hand to reexamine the swelling abrasion midway between Mr. Martin's hairline and eyebrow. The bleeding had slowed but hadn't stopped.

"It's just Martin, ma'am. No 'mister' needed. Especially not from a pretty lady like yourself."

"I'm afraid the cut will need stitches." Charley ignored Martin's grin, the chuckle from the younger man, and the scowl from Cooper. "And it will probably leave a small scar." She carefully cleaned away the blood to examine the wound for splinters.

"A scar won't hurt this old cowboy." Martin's eyes fastened on

Charley's face while she worked, wincing a little at the sting of the liquid she used to clean it.

The younger man spoke again. "That's right. His wrinkles will hide it."

Martin grinned suddenly. "Lyle, you're just jealous the beautiful doc ain't leanin' over your sorry carcass."

Charley swallowed her laughter at the good-natured insults. Their antics lightened the mood, but they didn't need any additional encouragement from her. "Let's try sitting up now, Martin."

Cooper helped her ease the older man into an upright position. "I thought you were going to stitch that cut closed." He scowled at the bandage she wrapped around Martin's head.

"I will, but I need to wash my hands, and I want to clean that cut better. Is there any place nearby where I can do that?"

Cooper jerked his head. "My house. Around that hill."

"Good. You two help Martin to the buckboard." She picked up her bag, and Cooper and Lyle assisted Martin to his feet.

Ma kept the gelding and buggy still while they assisted Martin into it.

Charley climbed in beside him. "Take it slow, Ma. I don't want to jostle his head any more than necessary."

Ma clucked to the horse, and though he stepped off slowly enough, the vehicle bounced uncomfortably. Charley laid her arm around Martin's back to steady him.

"I'm all right, ma'am. Many's the time I've been hurt worse." His eyes twinkled. "It's kinda nice being fussed over by a pretty lady, though. Beggin' your pardon, ma'am."

Charley patted the work-gnarled hand that gripped his knee—the only visible sign of his discomfort. "No pardon needed. A doctor needs patients, and if all my patients were as nice as you, I'd be happier than a cat with a bowl of cream."

A hint of a flush returned to the man's weathered cheeks. "Then I'm pleased to be your patient a while longer. But not too long, mind you. Coop'll think I'm getting' too old and try to turn me out to pasture."

"With the exception of that goose egg on your forehead, I imagine you're tough enough to outlast us all."

"Thank you, ma'am. No wonder Coop's gotten over his dislike of doctors all of a sudden." He winked, flinching when the movement tugged against the cut on his forehead.

Charley felt a flush warm her own cheeks. "Why do you say that?"

The battered ranch hand gave her a disbelieving glance. "Have you never looked in a mirror? You're 'bout the purtiest little thing to ever land in these parts."

She laughed off the fulsome compliment. "Flattery won't save you from my needle and thread, Mr. Martin."

The older man grinned cheerfully. "Stich away, Doc. But do me a favor?"

They reached a neat white frame house, and before Charley could reply, Cooper stormed out the front door having raced his horse ahead and beaten them there. "Kitchen's in the back. I've got water heating on the stove." He tried to assist Martin out of the buckboard, but the spry gentleman shooed him away and stepped down under his own steam.

"Go help Mrs. Jankins or something. I prefer the lady doc's pretty face to your gloomy one. You'd have a man believin' he's dyin'."

Cooper's clean-shaven face made it easy for Charley to read the emotions that flicked across it. A wry smile replaced the tension in his jaw but didn't entirely erase the remnants of worry from his eyes. "I'm beginning to think that blow to the head didn't do anything but improve your looks, Martin."

"Now you're gettin' the picture, Coop." The grizzled-haired man chuckled and looped Charley's arm through his own. "Ain't nothin' wrong with me that this good-lookin' gal can't set to rights." He led her to the front door, and Cooper reluctantly watched them go.

Martin ushered Charley into the house ahead of him. "Dr. Adams? About that favor?"

"Yes?" She glanced over her shoulder at his whisper and caught Cooper eyeing them while he loosened the gelding's harness. Was he more worried about Martin or about what the *doctor* was going to do?

"I'd be obliged if you'd send Coop out of the room while you stitch up my head. He's fine in an emergency, but after the shoutin's over, he don't handle blood so good."

Charley chuckled. "I'll see what I can do."

~

Cooper unloaded the wagon Lyle had driven to the barn. They wouldn't be cutting any more trees today. Martin's accident had been too close to deadly for comfort, and it had been Cooper's fault. In anticipation of Charley's arrival, he'd let his caution lapse and allowed Martin to talk him into tackling that gnarled tree. It wouldn't happen again. They were steering clear of all snags and widow-makers after this. A storm, old age, or a combination of both would eventually bring them down anyway.

He sharpened all the axe blades before covering them with leather sheaths and hanging them on the wall. He'd been prepared to help Charley with anything she might need while patching up Martin, but to his immense relief—although he'd never admit it aloud—Ma had shooed him out of the kitchen before he could step across the threshold. The mere thought of a needle and thread piercing through Martin's scalp made Cooper's stomach feel like he'd swallowed a buckin' bronco. If he'd had to watch the operation, he'd have made a complete fool out of himself by passing out or losing his lunch or both.

The barn door creaked open to reveal Charley. She glanced around the interior of the spacious building before spotting him in the shadows and stepping inside.

"How's Martin?" He wiped his sweaty palms down the side of his britches.

"I believe he's going to be fine. From what I can tell, he only caught a glancing blow. Enough to split the skin and raise a lump. I want you to keep an eye on him for the next couple days, though. Don't let him do anything strenuous, and watch for any dizziness or confusion. If you notice either one, send for me immediately."

Cooper nodded. If he had to physically tie the man down, he'd keep him from anything more arduous than lifting a knife and fork for a week. "Where's Martin now?"

"Ma's feeding him. She says food will take his mind off his sore head, but I think he's eating up the attention instead."

Relief unknotted his stomach, and the tightness in his chest loosened. "Sounds like Martin." He shook his head. "A real ladies' man."

Charley's face lit up. "He does have a certain rough-edged charm. Reminds me of someone else I know."

Cooper's breath hitched at her beautiful smile.

A few weeks ago, the way she'd ignored Lyle and Martin's bickering would've made him think she was cold, hard hearted, and detached. But today, her calm, unshaken focus had inspired reluctant confidence in her ability, and he'd been able to see her compassion and painstaking attention to the patient under her care. There were so many sides to this woman, and he was finding himself fascinated with each new facet. Including the one that handled the messiness of doctoring with unruffled calm and practiced ease. Nevertheless, he was relieved the accident hadn't resulted in a more serious injury. For all their sakes.

Her eyes lowered before glancing around the barn again. "You have a…a nice place."

How long had he been staring at her without speaking? "Would you like to see more than this dusty barn, or do you have to leave right away?"

"No. I mean, I'd like to see more. If you have time, that is. We visited all the places Ma wanted to go before we arrived here."

Her sudden nervousness made him smile. She could be smooth and calm like a pasture pond one minute and ruffled and babbling like a mountain brook the next. Keeping up with her kept a man on his toes.

"It sounded like she and Martin were settling in for an extended discussion about…biscuit dough?"

Cooper chuckled and led the way into the afternoon sunshine. "Martin's determined to make biscuits that taste like Ma's, but each attempt fails, and mine aren't any better. He swears she's left an important step out of the recipe she wrote off for us. I've told him he just needs to marry the woman so he can have her biscuits whenever he wants. But he says he's been a bachelor too long to 'get hitched' now."

Charley laughed lightly and followed him up the hill that shielded the house and outbuildings from the worst of the winter winds. It was his favorite spot to view the layout of the ranch buildings.

"This is such gorgeous country." She spoke softly after a minute of simply looking. The light breeze played with the ends of the ribbon that held her silky hair away from her face.

The view had definitely improved. "I think so too."

She caught him watching her, and a pretty shade of pink infused her cheeks with added color. "I'd better head back. If we don't leave soon, it'll be dark before we reach town."

She was right. But he didn't want her to leave. "Did you see the rest of the house earlier?"

"No."

"Come on then. I'll walk you through it." Without giving her a chance to refuse, he grasped her hand and jogged down the hill, pulling her behind him.

They reached the house laughing and out of breath from their impromptu run, and Cooper could hardly keep his eyes off her. His boots hit the back porch with a thud, and he threw open the door.

"Good grief, where's the fire?"

He dropped Charley's hand but not before Ma's sharp eyes had spotted it in his grasp. "No fire. I want to show Charley the house before you leave."

"We do need to leave soon, but I ain't in *that* big a hurry. Slow down before you fall down." Ma admonished, her eyes twinkling at him as he led Charley through the kitchen.

Charley paused for a moment in front of a full bookshelf in the sitting room. "Have you read all of these?"

"Yep. Most of them more than once. Takes a few tries to make sense of some of them."

Her fingers ran along the titles of the leather-bound volumes. "*Last of the Mohicans, The Canterbury Tales, Plutarch's Lives, Paradise Lost...*" Her voice trailed off, and she turned to face him with something like respect in her eyes. "You're well read."

He shrugged off the compliment and pointed out the two bedrooms. He read for the sheer pleasure of it. Not to impress anyone. He wouldn't mind if the house he'd planned and built so carefully impressed her, but when he looked at it through her eyes, he realized how painfully bare and plain it was. It lacked the soft, refining touch of a woman.

But not just any woman...

"I built the house so it would be easy to add on to when children come along." The words hurtled past his lips before he could grab them. But once they were out, he couldn't quite regret them. The last few days had proven that while he wasn't fully comfortable with *what* Charley did, he was extremely attracted to *who* she was. And a man liked to know where he stood.

She turned from the window she'd paused to peer out. Her smile was thin, and her forehead puckered. "Oh, are you planning on marrying soon?"

Cooper stepped closer and shoved his hands in his pockets to keep from touching her. "Nothing definite yet. But I've got my eye on someone."

Her head tilted, and her voice cracked enchantingly. "You...you do?"

"Um hmm."

Green eyes fastened somewhere on his shirt front. "Anyone I know?"

"I reckon you know her better than anyone, and I'm wondering if you know what she thinks about stagecoach drivers." A trickle rolled down his spine. He'd faced Indian attacks that hadn't made him sweat this hard.

"Charley? You ready to head home?" Ma entered the front room carrying Charley's bag. Martin trailing behind her, the white bandage around his head the only evidence of his mishap. "It'll be dark before long."

"Uh. Yes." Charley's eyes darted between him and the iron-haired woman. "If you'll put my bag in the buggy, I'd like a drink of water before we leave."

Ma nodded. "All right, but hurry up. This old cowpuncher is about to talk my ear off."

Martin followed the woman out the front door. "Now see here, woman. Who you callin' old?"

Charley rushed to the kitchen, skirt fabric swishing in a purely feminine sight and sound. She splashed water into the tin cup by the pump, drained it, set it aside, and then without saying a word, returned to the front room.

Cooper followed, unsure whether to press her or take her silence for her answer.

Before she reached the door, she spun to face him. "To answer your question. If we're talking about the same person, she thinks knights of the ribbons..." She paused, glancing down at her hands.

Cooper grimaced. Where in the world had she heard that namby-pamby term for stagecoach drivers?

Charley peeped up through her lashes, pink tinting her cheeks.

"She thinks they're pretty special people." She whirled on her heel and trotted toward the waiting buggy before Cooper could say a word.

A grin stretched his cheeks, and he caught up to her, cradling her elbow to steady her while she stepped into the buggy. The warmth of her skin through her dress sleeve branded his hand. When she sat down, her emerald eyes found his, and she smiled, her eyes holding an openness and a vulnerability he'd never seen before.

Ma cleared her throat and laced the reins through her fingers. "You changed your mind about doctors yet, Coop?"

His eyes remained fastened on the beautiful physician who'd somehow managed to steal his heart when he wasn't looking. "Not about all of them. I'll never think much of doctors like Edmund Musgrove and his ilk." He grinned at Charley. "But Dr. Charlotte Adams is worth her weight in gold."

XVI

I'll never think much of doctors like Edmund Musgrove...

Cooper's statement had burned into Charley's brain and repeated all night long, making sleep impossible. She gave up trying an hour before daylight, lit a lamp, and went to her office desk to catch up on her recordkeeping and reading. But neither of those tasks could completely distract her. Finally, she slammed the thick medical text shut and forced herself to face the previous day's revelation head on. The doctor Cooper had named as responsible for killing his best friend was her Uncle Eddy. The man she'd looked up to and aspired to emulate.

She eyed the dull, scarred leather of the medical bag sitting on the corner of her desk, ready to be grabbed on her way out the door to the next house call or the next emergency. Uncle Eddy had sent it to her in congratulations for being accepted into medical school, and she'd always taken pride in carrying and using it. Because it not only represented successfully reaching her dream of becoming a doctor, it reminded her of the man who'd inspired and encouraged her to dream in the first place.

No!

It couldn't be the same man. There had to be more than one Dr. Edmund Musgrove. The compassionate man she'd called uncle would never do anything that might interfere with what he considered his sacred calling—to save lives, to heal, to provide comfort whenever humanly possible.

The man Cooper spoke of *could not* be her uncle.

Doctors like Edmund Musgrove... Edmund Musgrove.

The words pounded through her skull over and over, and she kneaded her temples with trembling fingers. It just couldn't be.

The massaging motion pulled a long-forgotten memory from the depths of her brain. One night, after her parents thought she'd gone to bed, she'd gotten up for a drink of water and overheard her father express concern to her mother that even after two years, Uncle Eddy didn't seem to be recovering from the death of his wife, and that he might be using opiates to compensate for his lack of sleep. She'd shrugged it off at the time, certain that in her sleepiness, she'd misunderstood or dreamed the conversation, and a few months later, Uncle Eddy had announced his plans to travel west. She had been heartbroken to lose her favorite uncle, but her parents had believed the change of scenery would lessen his grief. She'd soon forgotten about their worries because she used every spare moment to study and prepare for medical school, but she'd treasured each letter that arrived from him, imagining him helping the brave pioneers of the west. Even though they'd been infrequent, his short notes had fueled her determination to become a doctor like him.

Pockets loudly protested her abrupt removal from the warm lap under her body when Charley shoved away from her desk, set the cat aside, and rushed to her bedroom. Sitting the lamp on a nearby table, she knelt by the trunk at the end of her bed and raised the heavy, rounded lid. Her keepsake box sat in the top tray, and she lifted it out and sat it on her lap. After opening it, she eyed the small stack of letters sitting quietly inside. She'd forgotten how few times he'd actually written.

Charley slowly slid each letter free of the string binding them together and read them, one by one, the paper cool and smooth beneath her trembling fingers. As a girl, when she'd accompanied him on his house calls, his handwriting had been firm, strong, and neat—indicative of his character. But his last letters to her revealed a different story. How had she not remembered the way his writing had deteriorated into an unsteady and sometimes nearly illegible scrawl? If his penmanship had changed so much from her girlhood memories of him, what else had changed?

She reread each of his missives to her, searching for something—anything—to prove her beloved uncle hadn't been the same Dr. Musgrove of Cooper's acquaintance. Her heart stuttered to a stop when she read the scrawled postscript from the last letter she'd ever received from him.

Have taken a temporary assignment as a contracted civilian doctor for the Army. Direct correspondence to Fort Bowie, Arizona Territory.

Charley stared at the words, and the hopes she'd begun to entertain about her future shriveled and crumbled to ashes around her. When Cooper learned she was the niece of the man he'd wanted to kill, he would want nothing more to do with her.

If he learned.

No. Charley squelched the insidious thought before it could grow any further. She'd always faced things squarely, and she wouldn't stop now. She had to tell him. She *would* tell him. But she couldn't spring such news on him without warning. She needed to put some distance between them first, and once her heart accepted the fact it couldn't have Cooper Knight for anything more than a friendly acquaintance, she'd tell him. Maybe then it wouldn't rip her heart out of her chest when the inevitable revulsion filled his face upon learning the identity of her uncle.

Muffled shouts pulled her head up. The faint clatter of the stagecoach pulling up in front of the hotel to pick up passengers for its morning run filtered through her open window. A breeze parted her curtains, and the sudden shaft of sunlight made her blink. Rising stiffly, she blew out the lamp's feeble flame then sank onto the edge of her mattress. No matter how much her heart wanted a glimpse of Cooper, she wouldn't allow herself to stand at the front door and watch him leave on his stage run. When performing surgery, it was best to have a sharp scalpel and make a swift, decisive, and clean cut. Going slow wasn't merciful. It only prolonged the agony.

She closed her eyes to block out the sounds, but they only magnified in her ears. She might as well be standing right beside the stagecoach, watching his every move. Whether she actually heard Cooper speaking to his team before they thundered out of town or only imagined his voice in her head didn't matter. It hacked into her insides with all the finesse of a dull knife.

When she no longer caught even a hint of sound from the departing stagecoach, Charley forced herself to stand, pull a clean blouse over her head—instead of the beckoning bed covers—and fasten her skirt around her hips. At her dressing table, she ignored the bottle of her favorite crabapple blossom perfume and reached for her hairbrush. The cheery, floral scent she loved belonged to the past with its bright hopes for the future, and those hopes had died at the hand of her deceased uncle before they'd ever gotten a chance to fully live. Calling on all the grit that had seen her through medical school, Charley fought down the growing desire to curl into a ball and cry and instead coaxed a hint of life into her limp locks before heading to the kitchen to start a day she didn't want to face.

Pockets howled in wounded protest when Charley blindly trod across the tip of her tail while preparing breakfast and retreated to the windowsill to sulk, refusing to come down for her saucer of milk.

"Fine. I'm eating without you." Charley scraped butter over burnt toast and ignored her glowering kitten and the blackened edges of her fried egg. Pockets would live and a little charcoal never hurt anyone.

A frantic knock on her front door pulled her away from her tasteless breakfast, and she gratefully hurried after the anxious bank clerk to check on his sick wife. It was time to concentrate on what she'd come here to do. Treat sick people. Not fall in love with the first big, gray-eyed, well-read man who brought her kittens and flowers. She was a physician. And if that's all God wanted her to be, it would be enough.

It had to be enough.

~

Charley tucked her medical bag under her arm and transferred the basket of food she'd picked up at Ellie's kitchen to her other hand. Even her supper felt too heavy to carry this evening. The nasty outbreak of stomach illness that had ripped through the community came with two welcome benefits, though. For the first time since her days working with Dr. Tidd in St. Louis, she had almost more patients than she could handle, leaving her no time to think about anything else. And when she did actually have a moment or two to rest, her exhausted body forced her mind to sleep instead of dwelling on Cooper. But oh, was she ever tired.

A persistent, familiar sound broke through the weariness

fogging her mind and weighting her shoulders, and she followed the noise around the side of her house, groaning when she saw the small wooden crate sitting in the shade by her back door. The one with a note tied to the top and holding two perturbed, squawking hens.

There was also a *disadvantage* to having a lot of patients. And the proof was in her rapidly accumulating flock of feathered fowl. Puma Ridge's preferred method of payment for services rendered was a live chicken. Not cash.

"What am I supposed to do with all of you? I can't keep locking you all up in that old barn. And I definitely can't eat all of you, even if I wanted to."

"That wouldn't be makin' good use of your resources, ma'am."

The unexpected voice would have made her jump if her muscles weren't worn out from forty-eight hours straight of leaning over sickbeds. Her feet shuffled her around, and she squinted at the older gentleman standing a few feet away. It took a second to recognize him. "Mr. Beckenback?"

The man turned his shabby hat in his hands with a self-conscious smile. "Yes, ma'am. Me and a bar of soap got reacquainted, so I reckon I'm somewhat cleaner than the last time you saw me."

A lot cleaner actually. His worn clothes had been washed, and he'd shaved the scraggly whiskers from his chin.

Charley's exhaustion-muddled brain showed surprising agility when it leapt to the memory of another freshly-shaven face— Cooper had looked so handsome without the thick beard.

She lowered her supper basket to the porch stoop and struggled to corral the unwanted direction of her thoughts. "It's nice to see you again. How's your head?"

"It's fine." Mr. Beckenback played with the brim of his hat. "I came by to apologize for my rudeness when you tried to help me that day."

Charley pressed her hands to her aching spine. "I don't recall you saying anything that merits an apology, Mr. Beckenback."

The hat rotated through his fingers in a steady motion. "Nevertheless, I am sorry. I also wanted to thank you for your kindness and see if there was any way I could repay you."

She shook her head. "Mr. Beckenback, I don't expect…"

"No, ma'am." He interrupted her. "That's what made your actions so kind. It's been a long time since anyone looked past the dirt and treated me with dignity—not that I've given them much reason to. After my wife died, I, uh, made the saloon my second home until I lost my first. And that tends to stick in people's minds."

The defenseless hat was going to come apart if he didn't stop worrying it, but there was no self-pity in the man's voice. Only a simple matter-of-factness that tore at Charley's heart.

"If there's nothing you want me to do for you right now, I'll quit taking up your time. I just wanted to say thank you and let you know that if you ever need anything, I'm available." He plunked his hat on his head and turned to leave.

"Mr. Beckenback?"

He stopped and looked over his shoulder at her. "Yes?"

"What did you mean earlier when you said I wouldn't be making good use of my resources?"

He shoved his hands in his pockets and faced her again. "Well, if you give those chickens some room to roam and a secure place to roost at night, they'll start providing you with eggs. If you let the hens sit on 'em, you'll have pullets. Before long, you'll have a good flock that'll keep you in eggs and meat. And likely give you enough to sell to the mercantile."

"You have a good point. But the problem is," Charley softened her explanation with a smile, "I hardly have time to feed myself, much less care for a flock of chickens. There are about ten more in the barn back there." A piece of her tired brain clicked into place. "Ellie always fixes me enough food for two meals. Why don't you join me?" She gestured toward the cloth-covered basket.

The man blinked at the abrupt change of subject. "No, ma'am. I didn't come to impose on you."

"Mr. Beckenback, I am tired, hungry, and ready to sit down, but I also need to figure out what to do about these pesky chickens. Are you going to join me or not?" She was running out of energy and patience.

A hint of a smile twisted the man's mouth. "Yes, ma'am. I'll even carry that basket inside for you."

Charley puffed out a relieved breath. "Good." She forced herself to move again and slogged into her kitchen.

After they had divided the food and Charley had quieted the growling of her stomach, she addressed the issue again. "I haven't purchased a horse and buggy for house calls because I don't have time to tend to them, so I rent from the livery stable. And although that takes care of my need for transportation, if I keep having patients—and I sincerely hope I do—and they keep paying me in livestock, I'm going to need someone to take care of those animals. I simply don't have the time right now. Do you want the job?"

Hiram Beckenback choked on the last forkful of mashed potatoes from his plate. "The job?"

"Taking care of my current flock of chickens and any other livestock I acquire." The idea of hiring him had made perfect sense to her sleep-deprived brain. But now that she said it out loud, she was having second thoughts. "But I'll warn you right now, I will not abide drinking, and I'll expect you to attend church on Sundays. Because the only way you'll ever get over the need to dull your pain with alcohol is for someone bigger than yourself to help you conquer it."

Hiram eyed her thoughtfully. "I think I can handle those conditions. If I can't, I'll leave."

"All right. Good." In for a penny. In for a pound. "Come back in the morning, and we'll work out all the details."

He pushed from the table. "I'll put the hens in the barn before I go."

"You don't have to start tonight."

His shoulders firmed and an almost-confident smile softened his weathered features. "It's my job now. Remember?"

Charley smiled for the first time in days. It was faint, but she felt it pull at her mouth. "I remember. And thank you." She closed and locked the kitchen door behind him, and leaving the remains of supper on the table, she walked to her bed and collapsed on top of the quilt. Asleep before she could kick off her shoes.

XVII

One hundred and sixty-eight hours, give or take a couple minutes.
Seven days.
An entire week.
No matter which way he said it, the words didn't shorten the time that had elapsed since he'd seen Charley.
The first morning after Martin's injury, Cooper'd expected to see her in the front window or door of her office. But although he'd checked several times before setting the horses in motion, her face had not appeared between the ruffles of her fancy curtains. When he'd returned that evening, a note on her door had stated she was out on a call. He hadn't been able to return on Saturday due to a break in one of his fences and loose cattle, and on Sunday, Hannah had explained that Charley and Ma's absence from church was a result of an illness raging through many of the townsfolk. Charley *was* a doctor, and if he wanted her to stay in Puma Ridge, she needed patients. But this sudden abundance of them felt like a scheme specifically designed to keep them apart. He wanted to continue the promising conversation they'd started on the tour of his house, and the delay chafed him worse than a shirt full of sawdust and hay chaff.

A rut in the road jarred the coach, and the man riding beside him slammed into his shoulder, jostling the reins and causing the team to break stride. Cooper bit back the growl that sprang to his lips and spoke quietly to the horses. The shotgun rider flopped around the seat like a rag doll—no backbone at all. He'd much rather have Charley with him. He didn't mind when she bumped into him—not that she had more than twice, maybe three times. The eastern woman had handled the rough terrain like she'd been born to it.

Unlike a certain new guard who couldn't seem to stay on his side of the bench.

And it had nothing to do with Cooper's driving.

The shotgun rider bounced hard on the seat again and threw a glare at Cooper. "Do you have to hit *every* bump in the road?"

Cooper didn't bother to reply. He felt more like throwing his unwelcome seatmate off the coach than apologizing for the rutted condition of the road. There was nothing like suddenly assigning an armed guard to each run to advertise the fact they carried valuable cargo. Even a tenderfoot like Charley had recognized it. The company had added a line of explanation to their newspaper advertisements, claiming it was a simple precautionary measure to ensure their passengers' safety following the robbery of other stagecoaches in the territory in recent months. But anyone with an ounce of curiosity was bound to ask themselves why former Army scout Cooper Knight suddenly needed help protecting his stagecoach. And if they looked closely enough at the second mail pouch under his feet, they'd arrive at an answer all too close to the truth.

After having their payroll stolen one too many times, several mine owners had decided to vary the routes and stage lines they used in order to throw off the thieves. It had worked. The payment had gotten through three months in a row now with no trouble. And then the head of the stage line Cooper drove for had gotten nervous. Cooper had argued until he was blue in the face. The abrupt appearance of an extra guard would attract unwanted attention, and the thieves who'd lost their easy pickings were bound to notice or hear about the change. But Cooper's protests had been overruled. At least he only carried the actual payroll once a month rather than twice a month, and the mine owners had agreed to vary the shipping times so that it wasn't on a predictable schedule for either of the stage routes they used, but a guard accompanied Cooper on every run now. And today, the man's presence grated against Cooper like a hoof rasp across bare knuckles.

His mood improved slightly when they reached Puma Ridge

without a whisper of trouble, and he handed over the extra satchel to the station manager to be stored in the office safe overnight. It only had one more leg to go before it reached its final destination, but that was another driver's headache for tomorrow. Cooper had a doctor to find.

Her front door held no note this time, but his repeated knocks went unanswered, and the door was locked when he tried to open it. Where *was* that woman? When he hadn't wanted to see her, she'd turned up everywhere. But now that he did want her around, he couldn't find hide nor hair of her.

The sound of hammering reached his ears, and he jogged down the steps and around the corner. The banging came from inside the small barn that sat behind Charley's house. It sported a fresh coat of paint the same color as the house, the roof had been patched, and the sagging doors had been rehung.

He entered the open one, his eyes searching for a bright gold head and green eyes. "Charley?"

"Dr. Charley ain't around right now." Old Hiram poked his head up from behind a half-built partition in the front right corner of the building.

Cooper's brows lowered. "What are you doing here?"

"Building nesting boxes for the hens." The man's speech was clear, and his eyes bright.

"Hens?" What did a doctor need with chickens?

"Yep. People keep givin' 'em to her for payment. She wound up with a whole flock of chickens and no fit place to house 'em."

Cooper shook his head. The woman truly did need someone to take care of her if she didn't have enough sense to insist on cash for her services. Or at least some form of payment that didn't cause her more work.

Hiram propped his arms on top of the partition and continued affably. "She wasn't sure what she was going to do, since she's so busy with patients, but we worked out a deal. I'll take care of the place and the livestock, let people know where she's gone if they need to find her, and help with any unruly patients. I fixed up the outside of the barn yesterday, and today I'm working on the inside. In exchange, I get a place to live."

"What?" Cooper's shoulders tightened. The west might not be starchly civilized like the east, but things like this weren't tolerated.

He wouldn't tolerate it.

"I know I ain't fit company for a fine lady like Dr. Charley, but she's been awful nice to me, and I want to help her out."

"You can't live in her house!"

Hiram blinked at Cooper's explosion. "Who said anything about living in her house? My room's back there." He jabbed his finger over his shoulder.

Cooper's brows slammed together in confusion. "Huh?"

Hiram chuckled suddenly. "Come with me." He walked deeper into the building and opened a door Cooper hadn't noticed. "Have a look."

Poking his head inside the tiny space, Cooper saw a bed, a ladder-back chair, three wall hooks, and a small chest of drawers that held a washbowl and pitcher on top.

"Dr. Charley wanted to rent a room for me at the boarding house or build something bigger onto the barn, but I convinced her this space was a whole lot warmer and drier than an alleyway or a stall at the livery stable, so she gave in. And now I can return the favor and be close enough to keep an eye on her, the chickens, and the goat."

Cooper backed away from the door, fingers scouring the hair behind his ear while he tried to make sense of the man's words. The town drunk. Keeping an eye on the big-hearted, soft-headed petticoat doctor. To be fair, though, Hiram looked cleaner and neater than Cooper had ever seen him. Dust and sawdust clung to his clothing, but they weren't the tattered, grime-encrusted ones he usually wore, and the man smelled only of soap, wood, and honest labor. Could one woman's kindness and quiet compassion make this much difference in so short a time?

Wait a minute… "Goat? What goat?"

The man shut the door to his tiny closet of a room. "It's her most recent payment. I got a makeshift pen put up for it this morning. Cutest little kid I ever did see. Wanna see him?"

Cooper shook his head. "No, thanks." Chickens, a goat, and Hiram. The woman had collected a menagerie in a week's time. Was he guilty of starting the ball rolling by giving her that kitten? "Do you know when Miss Noah will be back?"

Hiram erupted into a gleeful chuckle. "Hee, hee! That's a good one. Miss Noah. 'Cause of all her new critters." He laughed again.

"Miss Noah drove out to check on a family still suffering from that stomach illness. She said if she wasn't back by dark, someone was worse and she'd had to stay overnight."

Cooper exhaled in disappointment. He'd missed her *again*, and unless he came up with a genuine excuse, he wouldn't have another chance to return to town until Sunday. He started to leave the barn-turned-chicken-coop-turned-living-quarters then stopped. "Will you tell her I dropped by?"

"Sure will, Mr. Knight." Hiram saluted Cooper with his hammer before returning to his work.

Cooper didn't like the arrangement Charley had put herself in, but other than marrying the woman—which was hard to do when he couldn't even track the lady down—all he could do was issue a warning. "Hiram?"

"Yes, sir?" The man straightened, eyeing him curiously.

"If I hear of you drinking again or if you do *anything* to hurt Miss Adams, we're going to have a long and uncomfortable discussion. Do I make myself clear?"

The man's Adam's apple bobbed up and down. "Clearer than glass, Mr. Knight." He cleared his throat. "I ain't takin' cash money from Miss Charley, so I won't be tempted to spend it at the saloon. I wasn't drunk the day Miss Charley met me, only three days without a solid meal. I've been dry since I lost my farm nine months ago, and I intend to stay that way."

Cooper eyed the man for a long second. "I'll be watching to make sure of that." To his surprise, the warning had the opposite effect of what he expected.

Hiram's eyes began to twinkle, and the corner of his mouth kicked up.

"You find something funny about what I said?"

The older man shrugged, undaunted. "Miss Charley said the only way I'd get over my need for alcohol was for someone bigger to help me. I assumed she meant God. Now I'm thinkin' she meant you." With a grin, Hiram picked up a nail and hammered it into the side of a nesting box.

The man's dry humor nearly made Cooper smile, but the urge lasted less time than it took to reach the street. Hiram Beckenback hadn't had a place to live before Charley offered him one? If so, why hadn't someone helped him before now? Or had they had tried and failed? Cooper couldn't recall hearing much about the man, but he had personally seen Hiram staggering out of the saloon twice.

His steps slowed.

Twice. In the entire time Cooper had lived in the area. Maybe the man didn't have a drinking problem so much as a pain problem.

Cooper knew that emotion all too well. He hadn't tried to mask the pain of his losses with drink, but he'd buried it in hard work and by closing his eyes to the problems of others. He was fiercely protective of his family and those closest to him, like Martin and Lyle and Ma, but he'd become blinded to anyone outside that select circle. If he'd reached out a hand to Hiram when he'd first noticed the man, could he have made a difference? Like it seemed a certain petticoat doctor had done?

Guilt burned his gut. *Lord, I'm beginning to think Hiram is a picture of what I look like on the inside. I feel more rotten than he looked and smelled like the other day. Forgive me for all the hurt and anger I've allowed to come between you and me. Help me to forgive and put it in the past.*

Cooper quickened his stride toward Hannah's house. The prayer was bare-bones simple, but a peace he hadn't felt in a long time brushed across his soul, and with it, a certainty that his petition had been heard. A reluctant smile tugged at his lips. God had sure used some unlikely messengers to get his attention. A sawbones. And a reformed drunk.

The walk to his sister's place worked the ache out of his spine from the pounding of the stagecoach, but an ache of a different sort replaced it. All day, he'd anticipated inviting Charley to supper and spending time with her. He shouldn't miss someone he'd known for such a short time, but he missed Charley. A lot. And not seeing her for a week made him realize how much she'd come to mean to him. It scared the stuffing out of him.

Benji and Digger met him at the door, and Benji pointed to the dog's shoulder. "Look. You can hardly see the scar now."

Cooper dutifully eyed the patch of short hair. The cut had healed until only a thin line showed through the fur that was rapidly growing back. Soon there would be no visible reminder of the dog's misadventure.

"Dr. Charley did a good job, didn't she?" Benji boasted.

Digger seemed to know he was the subject of the discussion and gave a wide doggy grin of approval.

"She sure did." In more ways than one. The woman had not only saved the dog's life, she'd also spared a boy from yet another loss in his young life.

Cooper had lived through the deaths of his parents, his best friend, and his brother-in-law and would do his best to shield his nephew from that kind of pain.

"Wash up, boys." Hannah plunked a dish onto the table with more force than necessary. Her tight mouth and lack of greeting signaled that all was not well under the Olson roof.

When Cooper pulled out Hannah's chair for her, cold radiated off her like a snow bank in January. He slid into his seat, and when Benji spoke a short blessing over the food, Cooper offered up a quick prayer of his own. It had been a while since he'd seen his sister so riled.

Benji chatted easily, not sensing the tension in the room—or maybe Cooper was the only one receiving the glares—and devoured two helpings of everything on the table before Hannah sent him outside to play with Digger.

Cooper waited until the door closed before facing his sister. "You going to tell me what's got your apron strings in a knot or make me guess?"

Her arms crossed across her apron bodice, and her fingers tapped against her upper arms. "Like you don't know."

Why did she always assume he could read her mind? "I *don't*, so why don't you just tell me?"

"What did you do to Charley?"

His mouth dropped open. He thought he'd been prepared for whatever had stirred her up, but that heated accusation had come out of nowhere. "What?"

"Even though I think it's *long* past time you put it behind you, I understand your dislike of doctors. I *do*. But I thought you were getting over that with Charley. I thought you'd finally realized that she's different."

"I was. I mean, I am. I mean, she is." His tongue was more tangled than his brain.

"Then why hasn't she come to see us since she was out at your place last week?" Hannah shoved out of her chair and grabbed dishes from the table, her movements choppy with irritation.

"She's been busy with a lot of new patients." Suspicion niggled at him. "Hasn't she?"

Her snapping eyes narrowed. "So, you didn't say anything unkind about what she does? Or try to scare her away or something?"

That arrow bit deep. "Is that what you think I'm capable of?"

"I don't know." She exhaled sharply and her shoulders sagged. "No. I'm sorry. It was the only thing I could think of that might explain…"

The muscles in Cooper's shoulders bunched painfully. "Explain what?"

Hannah recrossed her arms, but this time the move looked defensive rather than angry. "I've seen her a couple of times in passing, but she's always in a hurry and doesn't have time to chat. She's polite enough, but it feels distant. Cold, almost."

Cooper knew that sensation and Charley's remote smile all too personally. But he hadn't seen it in weeks. What had had happened to bring it back?

"And today when I saw her, she looked terrible. Like she hasn't been eating or sleeping. Her dress looked baggy, and there were dark circles under her eyes." Concern took the place of Hannah's previous ire.

"Ma Jankins said *she's* been so busy she's meeting herself coming and going." Cooper had passed the midwife on the road several times in the last week, but she'd been alone every time. "I'm guessing that it's been the same for Dr. Adams, too."

Hannah sucked in a big breath. "I suppose so. Still, call it my imagination or whatever you want, but I think something else is going on."

Cooper's gut agreed with his sister. But Hannah didn't need additional worries in her life. She'd lost her parents, then her husband, yet she stubbornly insisted on maintaining her own household instead of moving in with her big brother. The least he could do was distract her from this new concern.

He grabbed a cloth and started on the washtub of dishes, glibly explaining about Charley's recently acquired menagerie and blaming it for her distraction and fatigue. Benji popped in the door, and upon hearing the conversation, proceeded to regale them about his visit with Hiram and how the baby goat tried to butt Digger out of its pen. By the time Cooper hung up the dish cloth and took his leave, Hannah's smile had returned, and she hugged him goodbye, earlier concerns apparently forgotten. But his own smile faded when the door closed behind him.

Was Dr. Adams' absence from their lives a result of an outbreak of illness? Or was she using it as a convenient way to avoid them? To avoid *him*?

The question dogged him all the way home.

XVIII

The dull film on Charley's bureau silently proclaimed her love of open windows for fresh air and the consequences of living at the far end of the main street through town. However, the dust on the black leather book beside her bed accused her of avoiding more than just Cooper and dusting. Her reflection frowned back at her while she carefully pinned her hat atop her hair. It wasn't like she'd had spare time lately. There'd been a small epidemic after all.

Charley jerked away from the mirror and snatched up her dusty Bible. All right. So not quite an epidemic. But enough sick people to keep her on the run, and enough patients to fulfill her dream of helping people heal. Except, now she knew the whole foundation of that dream was rotten. The very man she'd wanted to emulate and honor by continuing his legacy had not practiced what he'd taught her. He'd harmed instead of healed. And now her motivation for entering medicine and fighting through all the obstacles lay in pieces, their jagged shards stabbing her every time she picked up her instrument bag.

The toll of the church bell startled her out of her woolgathering. She was almost late, but if she hurried, she could slip in the back before the opening hymn ended. She firmed her sagging spine and marched toward the door. It was time to quit delaying the inevitable.

She needed to face Cooper and move on. And a public meeting was more conducive to polite distance. She'd avoided him for over a week, but she couldn't hide forever unless she planned to move away from Puma Ridge.

Charley reached the steepled building as an older couple climbed the steps to the entrance, and she hurried to follow them in, relieved to have someone to hide behind. But her relief died a swift death when they squeezed into the last two spots on the back bench. She searched for a place to sit while the hymn came to a close. The church house was fuller than she'd ever seen it, and the only remaining seats were on the front two benches. She slid her foot backwards, her hand reaching for the door handle. No one was looking her direction, and when the next song started, she would slip out with no one the wiser.

"Dr. Adams. Welcome!" Pastor Schwartz's exuberant greeting cut off Charley's escape.

The entire congregation turned in their seats to stare at her, and she froze for half a second before muscle memory took over.

Lifting her chin, she ignored the multiple sets of eyes fastened to her and pinned her gaze on the preacher, a calm smile firmly in place. "Good morning, Pastor Schwartz. I apologize for my late arrival."

He stepped to the side of the pulpit, grinning widely. "No apologies necessary. We're glad to see you here today. We've all been praying for you while you've used your skills to minister to our friends and neighbors."

Charley caught the movement of heads nodding in agreement from her peripheral vision. A few weeks ago, the pastor's kind words and the congregation's show of support would've made her heart sing with triumph, but there was only one person's approval she wanted now. Unfortunately, the only thing she could expect from him was disgust and revulsion.

"Would you be willing to come up here and report on your patients?" The frock-coated man held out his hand to beckon her forward.

Charley strode to the front, the years of practice confronting disapproving professors and fellow students coming to her aid.

She faced the audience and kept her voice steady despite her churning stomach. "Thank you all for your prayers on behalf of myself and my patients. I am happy to report…"

Without permission, her eyes found Cooper, and her heart pounded like a runaway horse, robbing her lungs of air. He sat with Hannah and Benji on the third row, watching her with unblinking scrutiny—his gray eyes not quite ice cold but not warm, either. If only she could return to that moment right before he spoke her uncle's name and soak in the way he'd looked at her with so much warmth and promise. Sadness threatened to choke her. She would never again see that wonderful expression on his face.

Charley forced herself to look past him and focused on Ma Jankin's wide, approving smile while resurrecting the armor around her heart. She should never have lowered her defenses in the first place.

She cleared her throat and continued. "I'm happy to report that all of my patients are doing well, and I haven't seen a new case of the illness in three days. I know your prayers have played a part in that, so thank you again."

A smattering of applause greeted her statement, and Charley retreated to an open seat on the front row, sinking onto it as quickly and gracefully as possible.

"Thank you, Dr. Adams, for that encouraging report. Congregation, let's all stand and sing the Doxology. God deserves all our praise for the healing He's given to the sick in our community over the last few days."

Charley stood but only mouthed the words of the old song. Her front-row position demanded she at least appear to be participating and paying attention to the sermon, but when Pastor Schwartz closed his Bible and offered the closing prayer, she couldn't recall a single verse he'd read or point he'd made. The desires of her heart warred with the dictates of her head, leaving her caught in the crossfire.

She stood to leave with the rest of the congregation, and her gaze collided with the one she'd felt on the back of her head throughout the entire service. Unable to hold his probing gaze, she ducked her head. If she couldn't look him in the face now, how would she ever find the courage to tell him about Uncle Eddy? Maybe it was best to simply keep her distance until he'd lost interest in her. If it meant going miles out of her way to avoid crossing paths with him, so be it. It might be the coward's way out, but it would spare her heart a worse blow.

"Dr. Adams? I have someone I'd like you to meet." The pastor's wife touched Charley's arm, turning her toward a young woman with a fussy toddler on her hip.

Grateful for the interruption, Charley greeted the shy young mother, and when Mrs. Schwartz asked Charley's opinion about the best remedies for teething pain, Charley transitioned into the safe and comfortable role of physician. By the time she'd peeked at the toddler's gums, checked his general state of health, and given the weary mother some suggestions for pain relief, the building had emptied. She exited the church behind Mrs. Schwartz and the young mother, and her shoulders relaxed. The church yard was nearly empty, too, and the delay had been long enough for Cooper to be nowhere in sight. She had a reprieve.

Ma motioned for Charley to join her at her buggy. "Come to lunch with me. If you're as worn-out as you look, you need a rest."

Charley's stomach rumbled at the mention of food. When had she last eaten a decent meal? Or been hungry, for that matter?

"That sounds wonderful." She gathered her skirts and climbed aboard. "Your comment doesn't do much for my self-esteem, though."

Ma set the horse in motion with a cluck of her tongue. "I'm merely stating the obvious. You look like you've been pulled through a knothole and then shoved right back in. When's the last time you slept?"

"I'll have you know I had a full night's sleep last night." She'd been too exhausted to do anything else.

"Looks to me like you need a full *week* of sleep." The midwife guided the horse down a side street. "You won't do anybody any good if you take ill, too."

"You haven't exactly been lazy yourself, Ma. I might have provided the diagnosis and medicine, but you were right behind me with soup and scrub bucket."

The woman grinned and patted her stout middle. "Yes, but I have enough in the storehouse to see me through hard times." She pinched Charley's arm. "You, on the other hand, need fattening up."

Charley's stomach rumbled, and she grinned. "My belly agrees with you and wants to know where we're going. This isn't the way to the café or your house."

"Don't worry. We'll have a plate in front of that hungry beast in a few minutes. We've both been invited over to eat, and I promised to give you a ride while our hostess went on ahead to put the food on the table."

Charley caught sight of a small house at the end of the quiet side street, and her mouth slammed shut on her next question. All her previous hunger disappeared. She knew the identity of their hostess. She hadn't gotten a reprieve after all. She simply changed locations and was going to be served the last meal of a condemned prisoner.

The horse plodded to a stop beside Hannah's house, and Cooper stepped off the back porch. His eyes locked with hers, and Charley flinched at the contact that felt almost physical.

Benji and Digger bounded around the front. "Dr. Charley! Come see what Digger can do."

She clambered out of the buckboard and practically ran toward the boy and his dog, pretending to be appropriately awed by the terrier's energetic spins, rollovers, and jumps. However, she was aware of every movement Cooper made. He assisted Ma to the ground, led the horse and buggy to the shady spot where his own mount was tied, and offered it a bucket of water.

"I'd better see if your mom needs any help." Charley rubbed the dog's floppy ears before straightening.

"Okay. Come on, Digger. Let's go help Uncle Coop." With an enthusiastic bark, the happy dog trotted after his master.

Hannah left the stove when Charley entered the kitchen and greeted her with a quick, hard hug. "I'm *so* glad you could join us. I've missed seeing you around the last couple of weeks."

The embrace nearly unraveled Charley's control. It had been necessary to avoid Hannah and Benjamin to keep from accidentally running into Cooper, but it hadn't been easy, and it had hurt. "I've missed you, too."

Hannah gripped Charley's shoulders and pushed her away slightly. "You look terrible."

"I heard a similar version of that statement from someone else recently." Charley grimaced at Ma who'd entered the room. "Between the two of you, I don't have to worry about having an overly high opinion of myself."

The younger woman brushed away the teasing comment. "That's not what I meant. It just looks like you haven't been eating or sleeping enough lately. I know people get sick, but you can't help them if you're sick, too."

The genuine caring in Hannah's eyes warmed Charley's heart. "You and Ma should compare notes. I'm getting the same lecture from both of you. But thank you for caring. I *was* able to catch up on some sleep last night." She sniffed the air. "And whatever you're cooking will take care of the not-eating part. It smells delicious."

Cooper and Benji entered the back door, hands dripping from washing up at the outdoor pump.

"Since everyone's here, and the food is ready, let's eat." Hannah waved them toward the table.

Maneuvering quickly, Charley snagged the chair beside Ma. She wouldn't be able to swallow a bite if she had to brush elbows with Cooper. She smoothed her napkin over her lap, inhaled quietly to steady her nerves, then raised her head.

Her breathing hitched in her throat. She'd prevented Cooper from sitting next to her only to have him land directly across from her.

He stared at her through eyes the color of heavy storm clouds.

Charley re-smoothed the napkin across her lap with trembling fingers but forced a polite, acknowledging smile.

His eyes narrowed.

She quickly turned her attention to Hannah sitting at the head of the too-small table. It was going to be a long meal. To make Ma and Hannah happy, she would need to make a good show of eating, but her stomach ached like she'd eaten too many green apples.

Benji spoke a sweet blessing over the meal, and Charley did her best to contribute to Ma and Hannah's lively conversation while steadfastly avoiding the gaze of the man across the table. If the others noticed, they didn't show it, but Cooper's silent attention burned into her skin, slowly but surely sapping her ability to think straight.

Unable to swallow another mouthful of food, Charley pushed away from the table and walked her plate to the basin of soapy water. "Since you prepared the meal, Hannah, I'll do the dishes."

"No, you will not." Hannah jumped up and whisked the cloth from Charley's hand. "I didn't invite you and Ma here to work. I wanted a chance to visit with you while I fed you, but now, at the risk of sounding rude, the both of you should go home and rest before someone else needs you."

"You don't sound rude at all, Hannah." Ma spoke up. "Unfortunately, I have a visit to make this afternoon and I don't have time to take Charley home. Coop, will you take her?"

"No." The word squeaked through Charley's tight throat. "I can walk—"

"Yes, ma'am." Cooper ignored her protest. "I'll make sure she gets home safely."

"Thank you, Cooper. And thank you, Hannah and Benji, for the wonderful meal. Forgive me for leaving so abruptly, but I promised Mrs. Carter I'd run over this afternoon and help her with something." Ma whisked out of the kitchen, faster that someone her age should be able to.

"I'll hitch up Hannah's buggy and drive you home." Cooper lifted his hat off the peg by the kitchen door.

Charley dried her wet hands. "Please don't go to all that trouble. It's only a short distance home. I'll be fine."

"All right." He acquiesced easily. "We'll walk."

Charley's stomach churned around the few bites of lunch she'd managed to swallow. According to Hiram, Cooper had come looking for her more than once, and now that he'd cornered her, the man seemed determined not to let her out of his sight. But she wasn't ready for the conversation that would follow. "Hannah, are you sure I can't help you with the dishes?"

Hannah shook her head firmly. "I'll take you up on that offer when you don't look like you could fall asleep on your feet." She hugged Charley again then pointed her toward the door Cooper held open. "Now shoo! Go get some rest."

Charley obeyed, patting Digger's head and bidding Benji goodbye before she strode briskly past Cooper. It would be unladylike to run all the way home, but the temptation was nearly irresistible.

Cooper caught up with her and matched her stride but didn't speak until she turned down an alleyway she'd learned was a shorter route to her house. "What's your hurry?"

She resisted the urge to quicken her pace. That was a dangerous question if she'd ever heard one. "After all that food, I find I'm ready for that nap Hannah suggested."

"You didn't eat enough to keep a bird alive." His tone said he wasn't buying her blithe explanation.

She searched for a different topic of conversation. "The views out here are wonderful. It's one of the things I love most about this place."

"I'd agree with you if you weren't looking at the rear of the saloon."

Heat surged up Charley's throat. She'd been too distracted by the man beside her to actually see her surroundings. "I meant the scenery in general, not that building in particular."

She desperately wanted the safety of the façade of cheerful indifference she'd perfected at medical school, but when he studied her with those narrow gray eyes, her old defenses were about as substantial as a soap bubble.

The haven of her house beckoned from the distance, and her feet moved faster. "Thanks for walking me home. I'll be fine from here."

He didn't take the hint and matched her step for step until she reached her yard then he stopped her with a hand on her arm. "May I take you to supper tomorrow evening, Charley?"

Her nerve endings stood at attention, and all the moisture drained from her mouth. He'd spoken her name with a mixture of guarded hope that stabbed her through the heart. The longer she delayed the inevitable, the worse it would be. All she had to do was tell him the name of her uncle, and Cooper would rescind the offer instantly. Then she wouldn't have to avoid him anymore. He'd avoid her. Like the plague.

She opened her mouth, but words wouldn't come. Merely imagining the expression on Cooper's face when he found out her uncle's identity made her want to sob.

Maybe it would hurt her less if he thought she just didn't care. "I'm... I'm sorry. I can't. I have a full day tomorrow." Her voice sounded as stiff and wooden as her face felt. She edged away.

Cooper didn't release her arm. "The next day then."

"No. I'm sorry." Charley tugged at her arm.

He released it like it had burned him. "You *have* been avoiding me." The growl she'd heard the first day she'd met him had returned. In full force.

She lifted her chin and hardened her resolve. "Yes."

"Why?"

"I can't afford to be distracted. It's not fair to my patients, and it's not fair to you. You deserve someone who can give you her undivided attention." The explanation rolled off her tongue like if she'd rehearsed it for months, but every syllable punched a fresh hole through her heart.

His jawline tightened, and his chest rose with a huge intake of air. "So that's all I am? A distraction?"

The fury in his low question gave her a sickening hope. Maybe she'd only injured his pride, not his heart. Cooper hadn't known her all that long. He'd get over his attraction to her. The last man in her life had gotten over her quickly enough. In fact, he'd been engaged to her next-door neighbor within three months.

Charley forced her wooden lips into a semblance of a smile. "No. You've been exceptionally kind to a newcomer, and I'm grateful." The word was totally insufficient to describe what she truly felt, but it was all she could let him know.

The molten steel of his eyes blazed hot, and she turned and fled inside her house, expecting him to grab her and demand an explanation of her behavior. He let her go, though, and she collapsed against the inside of her door, struggling to draw air into her burning lungs. Had she done it? Had she managed to convince him she didn't want his company?

She turned the lock and tiptoed to the lace-covered window. The man she'd so foolishly allowed to steal her heart strode away from her house, his shoulders set, his fists clinched. His entire posture shouted that he didn't plan on returning anytime soon. If ever.

The sight shredded her already bleeding heart. She'd accomplished what she'd sat out to do. She'd run Cooper off.

Wouldn't her uncle be proud? Blood *was* thicker than water, and it ran true. They were both murderers and cowards. Charlotte Adams had followed right in her uncle's footsteps and killed something beautiful.

XIX

He'd *known* a female sawbones was bad news, but he'd allowed Charley's striking green eyes and pretty figure to blind him to the fact that she was as false as fool's gold. He'd seen an example of her hypocrisy when he'd first brought her to town. The nervous, chattering passenger beside him had descended from the stage and immediately transformed into a cool, composed, smooth-talking creature, and she'd proceeded to bamboozle the mayor and entire town council into overlooking that she was a female when they'd expected a male physician. Yet in spite of her strange behavior, Cooper had believed she was being genuine with him. But no. It was just another one of her many faces.

What an idiot he'd been. She'd played him easier than a schoolyard game. No doubt laughing up her sleeve at how quickly he'd fallen. Well, she deserved the laugh. She'd taught the lesson well. No matter whether they were male or female, doctors and their questionable remedies weren't worth a wagonload of fool's gold.

"How's that good-lookin' doc gettin' along up there in Puma Ridge?" The ticket agent tossed the last piece of baggage to Cooper.

Cooper slammed the bag into place, flipped the heavy leather cover down over the rear boot, and buckled it closed. Did he look like the local newspaper?

"I figured people wouldn't trust a female doc, but if what I hear is true, she's holding her own." The talkative agent followed Cooper around the stagecoach, seemingly unperturbed at the one-sided conversation.

Cooper climbed to his seat and unwrapped the reins from the brake handle. There were a few holdouts, but every day, more people succumbed to Miss Adams' bright smile, smooth tongue, and kind eyes.

He yanked his hat off and jammed his fingers through his hair before slamming it back on his head. "Load 'em up. I ain't got all day." His barked order spurred on the dawdling passengers.

Minutes later, the shotgun rider took his seat beside Cooper, and the ticket agent tapped the closed door to signal everyone was aboard. Cooper released the brake and flicked the reins. He wasn't in any rush to return to Puma Ridge, but the sooner he finished the run, the sooner he could hightail it to the solitude of his ranch. But even there he couldn't escape the green-eyed woman who invaded his thoughts. Why had he ever invited her to his home? A month had rolled by since she'd been there, yet her memory inhabited nearly every inch of the place. When he entered his barn, she smiled from the shadows. When he worked outside in the sunshine, he saw her on the hill behind the house admiring the view while the breeze teased the tendrils of hair against her neck. Or he felt again the brush of her fingers against his shoulder when she'd knelt to help Martin on the tree-lined slope.

It was worse inside his house. He'd stuffed her handkerchief into the back of a drawer to keep from seeing it and holding it to his nose to catch her scent. But putting the lacy scrap of fabric out of sight didn't stop him from remembering its owner standing at his bookcase and running her fingers over the titles. Or turning to face him in the front door and calling him that ridiculous term for a stage driver—knight of the ribbons. All the while looking like she belonged there. With him. Forever.

As dangerous as those memories were, they were safer than meeting her in person on the streets of Puma Ridge. Because it was impossible to reach out and pull a memory into his arms. Not that he wanted to pull the flesh-and-blood woman into his arms. Unless it was to shake her for playing him like a fool.

Maybe that's why she seemed to go out of her way to avoid him.

He'd only seen her one time since the Sunday she'd called him a distraction. It had been Lyle's turn to make the ranch's supply run, but he and Martin had mutinied, saying they *both* needed a break from Cooper's bad attitude, and as a result, Cooper'd come face to face with Charley in the entrance of the general store. The bruised smudges under her eyes when she'd glanced up in surprise had made his heart clench, but before he could say a word, she'd politely nodded and scooted around him, almost running in her attempt to get away.

She was going to kill herself trying to prove that females could be good doctors.

Cooper urged the team to pick up speed. Why was he worried about her? She'd made it quite clear she wasn't interested in his opinion or his help. Or in him.

"You trying to break a record or something?" The guard gripped the metal rail at the edge of the seat.

Cooper shook his head. "I don't aim to haul this load any longer than necessary." He dropped his gaze to the canvas pouch beneath his feet.

"Aww. You worry too much. Everybody knows this line don't carry nothin' but passengers and freight."

Ignorant pup! "Which would explain why we suddenly carry an armed guard now." Cooper failed to keep the sarcasm from his remark. Not that he tried too hard.

Alonzo shut his mouth, but his youthful arrogance soon resurfaced, and he patted his shotgun. "If anybody's foolish enough to attack us, we'll give 'em a fight they won't soon forget."

Cooper grimaced. A wet-behind-the-ears braggart eager to prove his mettle was all he needed. "If it's all the same to you, I'd prefer not to have a fight at all."

"If you're so scared, why do you tote all that hardware?" Alonzo jerked his chin to indicate the pistol strapped against Cooper's leg, the knife scabbard on his other hip, and the coach gun and rifle sheathed inside the compartment under their feet.

Cooper gave a humorless grunt. When the kid'd had a few bullets snap past his noggin, he'd learn fear wasn't a bad thing. A healthy dose kept a fella cautious and taught him to keep his head down. "I ain't itchin' for a fight, but if one comes looking for me, I don't plan to disappoint it."

Alonzo crossed his arms over his chest and patted his shotgun. "You just take care of the drivin'. I'll take care of the fightin'."

Cooper nearly gave in to the urge to kick the arrogant, young upstart off the coach and see if he could walk as well as he could run his mouth. Instead, he called to the team. "Hah! Git up!"

The horses stretched their long legs, eating up the flat stretch of road.

Alonzo fought for his balance when the front wheel hit a deep rut and opened his mouth to complain, but after a glance at Cooper, he shut it.

For a change.

Hank looked up when the stage thundered into the yard of his swing station. He laid aside the curry comb he'd been using and hurried to the head of the sweaty team. "You running *from* a fire or *to* one? You're more than ten minutes early."

Cooper jumped down and began unbuckling harness straps. "Neither, I hope. But I notice you weren't caught napping." He gestured toward the fresh team tied along the corral railing.

"No driver has ever caught me napping, and you won't be the first." Hank chuckled and led one of the horses over to replace the leader Cooper unharnessed. His voice dropped to a low murmur. "Carryin' a special delivery today?"

Cooper dipped his head in reply and hitched the new steed into place. Hank was as trustworthy as Martin, Ma, and Hannah. More than once, the man's sharp eyes and nose for danger had prevented trouble before it could occur.

Hank led the sweat-soaked leader away and returned with another fresh one.

When they swapped out the last horse, Hank spoke under his breath. "Keep your eyes peeled. I've had an itch on the back of my neck all day. Trouble's brewin'." He rubbed the spot emphatically.

"You, too?" Cooper shoved his hat off and scrubbed the pads of his fingers over his scalp. "I was hoping it was just me being twitchy."

"Nope. I reckon that's why we're both in a hurry today. If there *is* trouble down the road, maybe you can miss it by being ahead of schedule."

Cooper tried to shake the worry. His preoccupation with Miss Adams had him jumping and snarling at shadows. "We're getting more nervous than two old spinsters at a box social." He slapped Hank on the back, and a cloud of dust, horse hair, and hay chaff puffed into the air.

The hostler coughed and spat a mouthful of grit to the side. "Who you callin' old? I'm in the prime of my life." He swiped his hand over his bristly white beard then pulled a scarred timepiece out of his pocket. "You're still well ahead of schedule. If you ever wanted to set a record for this stretch of road, today would be a good day for it." He patted the rump of a heavy-boned wheeler and pocketed his watch.

Cooper eyed the horses in appreciation. "You put together a fast team. We'll flat outrun any trouble that comes our way."

Hank grinned and tapped his forehead beneath his battered hat brim. "That was the general idea, son."

After grabbing a quick drink and refilling his canteen, Cooper double-checked the horses, harnesses, coach wheels, and undercarriage before climbing to his perch.

"All aboard." He shouted the departure warning to the guard and two male passengers.

The coach rocked gently from the men's haste to board it, and Cooper lifted the reins and hissed through his teeth. Eager to move, the horses jumped into action and hit the trail at a brisk trot. If his hunch was right and trouble *was* waiting between him and Puma Ridge, it wouldn't have to wait long.

Less than an hour later, his skin began to prickle from the inside out, and his already alert senses sharpened to razor focus. The road ahead climbed and narrowed to a choke point, surrounded with enough rocky, brushy cover to conceal a small army. It was a spot Cooper usually slowed the horses to save their energy, and a perfect setup for an ambush. But this team was fit, spirited, and still moving easily. Hank had given him the pick of the corral. Not only did each horse love to run, each one had plenty of bottom and staying power. They had a lot of go left in them before they'd be ready to quit.

Cooper studied the terrain for anything out of place—for any hint they weren't alone. The trail wasn't blocked. If someone lay in wait, they were depending on the element of surprise and his habit of slowing the team.

Habits were made to be broken.

He one-handed the reins and slid the short-barreled coach gun from its scabbard. "Get ready." His quiet growl was barely audible over the noise of the coach and horses. "I think trouble's about to find us."

He shouted to the horses, and they responded instantly, haunches bunching and flexing to launch them from springy canter to surging gallop.

Lord, if you could spare a couple of angels and a fiery sword or two, I think we're gonna need 'em!

The horses hit the choke point at a run.

Masked riders boiled from behind the rocks like angry hornets, their stingers firing hot lead. Pain punched deep into Cooper's right thigh, but there was no time to dwell on it. He unloosed a blast from one of the shotgun's double barrels. The rider closest to Cooper fell, but a second one spurred his mount to the head of the team, grabbing for a bridle to force the horses to a standstill. Cooper fired the other barrel of the shotgun, and the misguided bandit slumped to the side of his saddle, his horse slowing and falling behind.

A pistol boomed at close range followed by a shotgun blast. Alonzo had finally gotten his gun into action.

Cooper dropped the coach gun into the boot beneath his feet and grabbed his little-used whip. He popped it over the backs of the running horses, but the sound disappeared under the noise of the gunfire crashing around them.

An explosion came from inside the coach.

"Got one!" The passenger with the hog-leg pistol strapped to his hip must have joined the fight.

Red-hot pain seared Cooper's right side.

The whip followed the shotgun into the coach boot, and Cooper shucked his pistol and snapped shots back along the side of the coach. It wasn't the most accurate way to shoot, but it would add to the daunting wall of lead Alonzo's and the passenger's guns were throwing out.

The bandits jerked their mounts behind the coach for cover but continued to shoot, hot and heavy.

Alonzo grunted suddenly and slumped into the seat. "I'm... I'm hit."

Cooper shoved his pistol into his holster and grabbed for the young man, his fingers curling into Alonzo's jacket collar to stop his sideways sprawl over the edge of the seat.

The kid's gun hand hung limply, and red seeped from the same shoulder.

Bullets scorched the air around them. The bandits had lost at least two of their gang, but the lure of a payroll pouch holding several thousand dollars was stronger than the danger of a well-armed stagecoach.

"Can you fire with the other hand?" Cooper flinched instinctively from the bullet that buzzed past his ear like an angry wasp.

Today was an especially good day to be carrying freight on top. The crates and boxes that wouldn't fit in the back provided a little extra protection.

"Don't know. Never tried." Alonzo gasped for breath like he'd been punched in the bread basket rather than the shoulder.

"Then hold the reins. Don't pull on 'em, and don't drop 'em!" Cooper made sure they were secure in Alonzo's hands before grabbing his own rifle.

He ignored the burning ache in his side and leg and twisted around to kneel on the narrow bench seat. Nestling the rifle on a sack of potatoes, he began firing. The pitching coach didn't allow for much accuracy, but his third shot dropped one of the remaining three bandits. His next shot winged another one, and the last uninjured bandit yanked his horse to an abrupt, rearing stop.

Cooper held his fire. If they were done, so was he.

The bandit he'd winged shouted something, and his unwounded companion jerked his rifle up for another shot.

He missed. Cooper didn't.

The bandit slumped over his horse's neck, and his rifle thudded to the ground. The wounded rider who'd ordered the shot wheeled his horse and sank spur, fleeing the scene at a gallop.

Cooper sent a couple bullets buzzing over the man's head to encourage his permanent retreat then leaned over the side of the coach to the nearest window. "Everybody all right in there?"

"Couple scratches but nothing serious." The passenger sounded unfazed by the running gun battle. "Did they give up?"

"Yep. Thanks to your help." Cooper twisted into his seat and returned his rifle to its sheath.

"Coop, you'd better take the reins." Alonzo's voice was faint, and his eyelids fluttered. The guard was fading but had retained a tight grip around the leather straps.

"I got 'em, you can let go." Cooper tried to ease the reins from Alonzo's hands. "I got 'em, partner. That's it. Let go."

When Alonzo's grip finally loosened and Cooper had control of the reins, the guard slumped sideways toward Cooper in a faint. Cooper shifted and pinned the smaller man against the coach with his shoulder and elbow and slowed the horses to a canter. He kept the team at that pace for another mile then gradually slowed them to a halt. If the last outlaw had continued riding in the opposite direction as fast as he had been when last seen, there should be enough distance between them to be relatively safe for a moment.

"Why're we stopping? Shouldn't we be getting to town to tell the sheriff what happened?" The owner of the hog-leg pistol stuck his head out the window.

"Yes, but the guard's been shot. Help me get him down and inside with you."

The two men sprang from the coach and caught Alonzo's limp form when Cooper slid him off the high seat.

"What about you? You're bleeding, too." The second passenger pointed to the stain on Cooper's side.

"Just a scratch. From the looks of it, we're all cut up some." Both passengers had scratches on their faces from flying splinters, and the man with the hog-leg pistol had a bloody notch across his upper arm. "Get him inside and try to slow the bleeding. I'll get us to town."

While the two men loaded Alonzo into the coach, Cooper scrutinized the team from the driver's seat. Miraculously, it didn't appear that any of the shots had hit the horses. They were breathing hard, but their heads were up, their ears were pricked, and they stomped impatiently, anxious to put the gun battle farther behind them. He should climb down and inspect them closer, but if he got down, he might not be able to get back up. Already, the blood running down his leg and pooling in his boot had him slightly light-headed.

One of the passengers tapped the side of the coach. "We're all set."

Cooper clucked to the horses but kept them at a walk and eyed each animal closely. When their sides weren't noticeably heaving, he asked them to trot then canter. They were no longer being chased, but Alonzo needed attention sooner rather than later.

"You fellas have earned your grain tonight." Equine ears swiveled toward him, listening while he called out soft encouragements. "That's it. Keep it up. We're almost there."

He pushed the team hard, but the road seemed to double in length, and minutes felt like hours. When the outlying buildings of Puma Ridge came into view, he had to squint to bring them into focus. Dr. Adams had better be in town and not off gallivanting around the countryside with Ma Jankins because he was bringing her some real business. And if his head didn't stop swimming, he was liable to be an unwilling part of it.

His movements were sluggish and jerky and even his grin felt sloppy.

God, thanks for the help back there. But don't think I've missed the irony of all this.

Miss Adams might not be interested in him for husband material, but sure as Digger loved a juicy bone, Dr. Charley Adams would relish having Cooper Knight enter her office as a patient.

XX

"Dr. Charley! Dr. Charley!"

"I'm back here." Charley exited the barn Hiram had so meticulously mended and painted, wiping her hands on her apron after feeding the chickens.

Benji and Digger pounded around the house and raced toward her. "Uncle Coop's hurt!" He skidded to a halt, gulping air and pointing over his shoulder. "The stage... There was a holdup."

Alarm jolted her. She'd heard the stage rumble into town but had stayed in the barn, resisting the urge to catch a glimpse of a certain driver. "How bad is he hurt?" She pushed the words past her tight throat.

Benji's eyes were dark with fear. "He had blood all over him. Alonzo's shot, too."

Charley's trembling fingers struggled to untie her soiled apron. "Go tell them I'm coming and not to move anybody until I get there. Then go find Ma Jankins and tell her I need her."

He nodded again, his chin quivering.

Charley gave up on her apron strings and gripped the boy's thin shoulders, hunching down to look him in the eyes. "Don't worry. Remember how I helped Digger? Well, I'm even better at doctoring people, and I'll take *special* care of your uncle."

His chin firmed. "Thanks." He took off at a run, Digger barking at his heels.

Charley wasted no time watching him leave. She flew into her kitchen, slowing only long enough to scrub her hands and don a crisp, clean work smock before snatching up her medical bag and charging out her front door. It was only a few yards down the street, but her heart pounded like she'd run for miles when she reached the crowd gathered around the coach.

She shoved through them, searching for Cooper. The sweat-lathered team stood with drooping heads, splintery gashes marred the body of the stagecoach, and a dark, sticky substance smeared the backrest of the driver's seat.

Blood. She'd seen enough to recognize it. And it stained both the side where the guard rode and the side where Cooper sat. But where was he?

"Excuse me. Let me through." Charley elbowed her way between the barber and the blacksmith.

The sheriff knelt with his back to her, blocking her view of the man who sat on the ground, resting against the front wheel. "You rest easy, Coop. You've done your job; we'll clean up the little you've left us to do. Those mine owners owe you a big debt." The lawman got to his feet and called for his deputy and two other men to get their horses and follow him.

Charley inhaled sharply when she saw him. "Cooper."

He wasn't dead. But the amount of blood soaking the right side of his shirt and pant leg spiked concern through her, and her heart ached in a most un-physician-like way.

"Hey, Doc." He smiled weakly up at her, his head resting against a spoke of the wheel. "Got a patient for you." He motioned a thumb up toward the coach door.

She dropped to her knees beside him, assessing him with one swift but thorough glance. The blood on his shirt looked dry and stuck to his side. Removing it from the wound would likely start it bleeding again. She'd leave it alone until she got him in her examination room.

She stuck her fingers through the hole in his pants, ripped the soppy material, and eyed the torn flesh of the entrance and exit wounds. They seeped blood, but it was slow, not spurting. She breathed a bit easier and dug in her bag for dressing material.

Cooper touched her arm. "Check on Alonzo first. He's worse than me." His voice was husky and low, and his eyelids blinked sluggishly. Almost like he had to force them open each time they fell shut. "I brought him to you quick as I could."

"You did?" Charley's hands stilled in the act of pressing folded bandages against the wounds in his leg.

His eyelids slid closed, and his hand dropped away. "Yep. You're the best doc I know around these parts."

A spurt of hope shot through Charley at his matter-of-fact statement, but she immediately squashed it. The only thing that had changed was his opinion—and only because he needed her help. The real problem still existed. Uncle Eddy.

"I'm the only doc around these parts." She firmed her face and voice and motioned for the barber to come closer. "Hold these pads tight against his leg while I check on the guard. We need to stop the bleeding."

"Sure, Doc."

Cooper grunted when the man took over and pressed hard.

The pained sound tightened Charley's jaw as she moved to the coach door. *He's just another patient. He's just another patient.*

Leaning in, she found the guard sprawled on the rear seat, another man holding a bloody handkerchief to the young man's shoulder. She crawled in the narrow space and knelt by the unconscious guard to check his wound.

"*You're* the doctor?"

She ignored the man's incredulous question and gently moved his hand aside to check under the blood-soaked cloth. "You did a good job getting the bleeding slowed." The guard's wound barely oozed. "How long since he was shot?" She felt for a pulse and eyed the slow rise and fall of the young man's chest. His breaths were shallow, but his pulse was steady.

"'Bout an hour or so, I'd say, since we put him in here with us. The driver told us to try and stop the bleeding so that's what we did." He gestured to someone behind Charley.

She glanced over her shoulder.

A man with shoulder-length, iron-gray hair, dressed in a fringe-leather jacket, eyed her through the coach door. "They going to be all right?"

"If I have anything to say about it, they will." She nodded toward the blood staining his sleeve. "You've been shot, too."

"Only a scrape, ma'am." He brushed off her concern. "It'll keep until you get the guard and driver patched up."

She crawled out of the cramped space and checked on Cooper again. His eyes were closed, and she felt under his jaw. His breathing was shallower than it had been minutes earlier, his pulse thready. How much blood had he lost while bouncing around on that seat?

With the barber's help, she wrapped a long strip of cloth around the folded bandages to hold them in place and keep pressure on them.

"You, you, you and you," She pointed to the barber, the blacksmith, and two other strong-looking men. "Help Cooper and Alonzo to my place. And do it gently!" Her sharp warning softened the rough hands that hoisted a limp Cooper to his feet.

Giving him one last look, she dashed up the street and flung her door wide. Cooper had been awake and fairly alert when she first saw him, but of the two, he appeared to have lost the most blood. She was going to have her hands full tending two seriously injured patients. Hopefully, Ma wasn't out of town visiting someone.

The front room shrank in size when Cooper and the stagecoach guard were carried through the door.

"Put Cooper in here." She led them to the bed in the small chamber off the examination room. The recovery room hadn't been needed up to now, but already she was a bed short. "Now move that long couch from the examination room in here for my other patient. That way I won't have to move either man again."

They followed her instructions, and in minutes, the injured men lay on either side of the narrow room.

"I'm here." Ma sailed through the door, Benji and Digger on her heels. "You fellas get on out of the way, and give the doctor room to work. Benjamin, your ma will want to know what's happened, but tell her not to worry. We'll take care of Cooper." The feisty woman efficiently cleared the room. "Where do we start, Dr. Adams?"

Charley straightened from examining both men again. "With Cooper. The other one is stable right now and not bleeding, but this big fellow is bleeding like a stuck pig." She kept her voice light, but it took effort.

"Is that any way for a lady to talk?" Cooper mumbled without opening his eyes.

Charley smoothed back the lock of hair that had fallen over his forehead. His hat had gone missing somewhere, and road grime marred his face.

He was the handsomest man she'd ever seen. "If you wouldn't get in the way of bullets, Mr. Knight, I wouldn't have to watch my language."

Slivers of gray appeared through his dark lashes, and he rolled his head to see Alonzo. "How's the kid?"

"He's hurt, but I promise to patch him up. And you, too." She squeezed his shoulder then stepped around the corner to scrub her hands and gather her wits. *He's only a patient.*

If *only* that's all he was.

Father God. Calm my heart. Guide my hands. Steady *my hands.*

After several deep breaths to quiet the tremor rattling her insides, Charley returned to Cooper's side with the tray of supplies she'd need.

She gently pressed a wet cloth against his ribcage where the shirt had stuck to his side, and his eyes cracked open again.

"Wait." He squinted, trying to focus on her. "Promise you won't cut anything you're not supposed to?" The faint whisper of teasing in his voice didn't quite eclipse the anxiety on his face.

Charley smiled reassuringly. "I promise." She held up her left hand. "See that? Steadier than a rock."

"Aren't you right-handed?"

"If you keep distracting me, Mr. Knight, you'll bleed to death all over my clean floor. Right-handed or left, I promise all I'll cut out is any bullets I find." She rewet the cloth and squeezed it onto his shirt, softening and loosening the dried blood so the material would come free without pulling against the wound. "And perhaps some of that grumpy attitude, while I'm at it." She dropped the cloth in the basin and reached to unbutton his shirt.

"I heard that." There was no bite in his sleepy growl, and it warmed her heart.

Until he continued speaking.

"Do your worst." His voice faded off to the merest breath of sound. "You can't hurt me any more than you already have."

~

After reassuring Hannah and Benji that she'd send for them if

Cooper showed any signs of waking or taking a turn for the worse, Charley saw them to the door, then sank into the kitchen chair across from Ma. Her lower back spasmed in protest, stealing her breath. She'd extracted two bullets, dug out splinters, and cleaned and stitched wounds on four different patients—Cooper, Alonzo, and the two passengers—and her muscles were loudly reminding her of that fact.

She rested the back of her head against the top of the chair. "We make a good team, Ma. That would have been much more difficult without your capable hands."

The woman slid a cup of coffee to Charley before taking a sip from her own. "Mmm. That hits the spot." After a few more sips, Ma lowered the mug. "I'll be your nurse anytime. That was as neat a job of bullet removal as I've ever seen, and those tiny, even stitches will make the women in the sewing circle jealous."

Charley smiled wearily. "Mother always made me work on my needlework every Sunday afternoon. I hated it until Uncle Eddy…"

"When your uncle what, dear?"

Charley took a big swig of coffee, pretending it was the reason for her long pause, and was rewarded with a scalded tongue. "He told me it was good practice for when I would need to stitch up a patient. Needlework was never a chore from then on." The memory had been a sweet one. Now it carried the bitterness of betrayal and disillusionment.

"Sounds like a wise man." A yawn cut off the woman's words. "Goodness, it's been a long day. Do you want to take the first shift or me?"

"Go on home. I need to keep a close eye on them tonight. If you'll come back in the morning, I'll catch a few winks then." Her body was exhausted, but her brain was too alert to be sleepy.

"No. I'll run home for a few things and come right back. It wouldn't give the right impression for you to be here overnight, alone, with two men."

Charley bristled, fatigue and worry putting a bite in her voice. "I'm a physician. Not a…a…whatever it is you're thinking. And those men have been shot."

Ma stood and patted her shoulder soothingly. "I know that, and you know that. But people are watching you closely. You don't want to damage the headway you've made in getting them to accept a woman doctor. Everybody noticed how well you and Coop were getting along a few weeks ago, so I'll play chaperone to ward off any gossip and be here when you need an extra hand."

People and their ever-ready tongues. If they could see what stood between her and Cooper, they'd know a chaperone was redundant. And the resulting gossip about *that* would start a forest fire.

All the more reason to keep them from talking about *anything* concerning her. "All right. I'm sorry. You can have my bed. I won't be using it tonight."

Ma plunked her bonnet on her head, leaving the cloth ties trailing. "I'll return shortly."

Charley swallowed the last of her coffee and went to check her patients. They'd both come through their surgeries well, but they weren't out of danger. Both men had lost a lot of blood and infection could set in. There would be no sleep for her. Unceasing prayer and a pot full of coffee would be her constant companion this night.

~

An oil lamp's dim glow lit the far corner of the room, but even that small amount of light hurt his eyes. Cooper let them drift close. He never drank anything stronger than Martin's coffee, so why did it feel like he was suffering from a hangover? His head throbbed like a drum, and his mouth felt like an old wool sock. Tasted like one, too.

The low murmur that had pulled him from sleep drifted past his ears again.

"Easy. Only a few sips at first."

Turning his head slowly to keep from jarring his brains out his ears, Cooper squinted against the light. He lay on a narrow bed against one wall of a small room. Against the other wall, Alonzo lay on a long leather couch and drank from a cup that Charley held to his mouth.

She eased Alonzo's head onto his pillow and set the glass aside.

"Thanks, Doc. That tasted fine." The kid smiled up at her like a besotted puppy.

Cooper focused on the water. It should be attainable even if the woman holding it wasn't. "Can I have some of that?" His hand flew up to hold his throbbing head. He shouldn't have spoken so loudly.

"Hey, Coop. Glad to see you awake. I wasn't sure we were

gonna make it out of that dustup alive."

Cooper's eyes slid shut. He wasn't sure he was glad to be awake or not.

A gentle hand slid under his head and lifted it, bringing the cup to his mouth. He drank eagerly, the cool water relieving his parched throat. Too soon, the cup was pulled away, and he groaned in protest but opened his eyes. The ache behind them had eased a fraction.

Charley was so pretty in the lamplight. It disguised the shadows under her eyes that had been so noticeable the last time he'd seen her.

She lowered his head to the pillow then laid her hand against his forehead. "You can have more in a minute. How do you feel?"

"Was I shot in the head?" The whisper didn't make his skull react so badly this time.

Alonzo snickered. "Nah. That's the chloroform. Had my head fit to bust, too, when I woke up. You'll get over it."

Cooper would've glared at the boy if he'd had any energy to spare.

Charley glanced over her shoulder. "You should try to sleep, Alonzo. Your body needs rest." She offered Cooper another sip of water. "The headache is a side effect of the chloroform, but it'll ease soon. How are you feeling otherwise?" Her eyes ran over him, evaluating him like he was nothing more than an interesting medical specimen.

He shifted, vainly trying for some much-needed distance. The dull aches in his ribcage and thigh roared to life at the movement. Breath hissed through his teeth, and he stiffened, arching his back against the red-hot pain spiking through his leg.

Firm hands pressed his shoulders. "Lie still. You'll undo all my hard work and start bleeding again."

Sparks danced in front of his eyes, and he dimly felt her lift the blanket to check his side and leg.

Her fingers wrapped around his wrist. "Breathe, Cooper. You need to breathe."

He released the lungful of air he'd been holding and sucked in another. The sparks slowly disappeared, but nausea roiled through his stomach and the pain remained. He wanted to move to escape it, but moving was what had ignited the fire that now chewed on him.

Charley retrieved a bottle and spoon from the small table beside his bed. When she brought the spoon to his mouth, Cooper didn't have the strength to do anything more than open it like an obedient baby bird. The medicine was bitter, but it gave him something to focus on besides the pain.

She laid a hand on his forehead again. "You don't have a fever. That's a good sign."

It was torture. Cooper wanted her to leave her hand where it was, but he needed her to take it away. He didn't want to be the patient she was dutybound to care for. He wanted to be the man she loved.

Rolling his head out from under her hand, he said the first thing that went through his muzzy brain. "Do I still have a leg?"

He hadn't realized she was on her knees until she popped to her feet, hands on her hips. "Yes, Mr. Knight. You still have a leg. I only removed the bullet stuck between your ribs. I couldn't find the bad attitude, though, or I would have removed that, too."

That statement sounded vaguely familiar to his fuzzy brain. "Sorry. Thass not what I meant…ezzatly." The pain was losing some of its edge, and his head felt like it was off the pillow.

"I think it's exactly what you meant, Mr. Knight." Her eyes flashed green fire.

Or maybe he simply imagined it in the dim room.

He fought to keep his eyelids open. The conversation seemed terribly important. But he didn't know why anymore. He sighed, too tired to fight the pull of oblivion.

Her stance and gaze softened. "But that's neither here nor there. You need sleep." She reached to tug the edge of the blanket over his chest.

Somehow his hand managed to find hers. "Thank you, Charley." He held tight to her fingers, fighting the darkness that sucked him into a dizzying whirlpool.

Before he could figure out if he was actually feeling Charley's hand against his cheek or only imagining it, the darkness claimed him.

XXI

Cooper slept the majority of the next two days, rousing only long enough to drink some water or clear broth and grumble about his forced inactivity before succumbing to heavy sleep once more. Charley gave scrupulous attention and care to his wounds, breathing a silent prayer of gratitude each time she checked them and found them free of redness, heat, and swelling. She gave the same level of care to Alonzo, but her insides didn't tremble when she touched him, and apprehension didn't grip her each time she unwrapped his shoulder bandage—Alonzo was simply her patient. However, no matter how many lectures she gave herself, she could not distance her heart from Cooper and view him as only a patient. She loved him. And she felt the pain of his wounds like they were her own.

When she'd finally given herself permission to admit that she did, in fact, love him, the magnitude and depth of it shocked her. Terrified her. What she'd thought she felt for Leonard and what she now felt for Cooper was like comparing a seedling to a hundred-year-old oak, and yet Leonard's rejection had left her scarred and bleeding. How would she ever recover from this bone-deep love for Cooper? All the walls she'd built to protect herself from being hurt again couldn't keep out an attack that came from inside her own rebellious heart. But they were all she had left, and she would stay behind them—crumbling though they were—until she regained control of her wayward emotions.

She *wouldn't* let her guard down again like she'd done that first night after he'd been shot. Although tears for what would never be had blurred her eyes, she'd yielded to the temptation to kiss his cheek while he'd clutched her hand and drifted into unconsciousness. She had come to regret that action each time she had to stop herself from checking for a fever with her lips.

Charley nibbled on her lunch and reminded herself for the thousandth time why a future with Cooper wasn't possible. Her resolution to get over him would be easier to do if he wasn't under the same roof and only a few feet away.

A crash shattered the silence.

She slammed her chair away from the table and sprinted toward his room.

Cooper sat on the edge of the bed, scowling at the overturned table, his blanket tangled around his legs.

"Are you hurt?" Water trailed across the floor from the broken pitcher, and Charley grabbed a towel to mop it up.

"Sorry 'bout the mess. I tried to stand but got dizzy, and that flimsy little table wouldn't hold me up." Sweat beaded his pale face, and he looked mad.

"Why were you trying to get up?" She righted the table and swiped the moisture off it.

"I was looking for my pants. I'm sick to death of this night shirt."

He was mad all right. And growling like a grizzly with a bee-stung nose.

"You don't need pants because you're not getting out of that bed." Scooping up the broken shards of pottery in the wet towel, Charley stood and deposited the whole wad on the tabletop.

"I've slept on rocks that were softer than this bed. I'm getting up."

"No. You're not. If you walk on that leg too soon, you'll start bleeding again." She reached to unsnarl the bed covers, but he caught her wrist.

"Alonzo's gone. Why do *I* have to stay in bed?" He gestured to the empty couch on the opposite side of the narrow room.

"Because *he* wasn't shot twice and didn't lose nearly the amount of blood you did, Mr. Knight. You had one bullet tear through the muscle of your leg and another bullet bury itself in your ribs." Using his last name didn't bring the hoped-for detachment when tingles were dancing up her arm from his touch.

She needed a better distraction. And fast. "Are you hungry?" Pulling away, she lifted his legs and gently twisted him around until he was back on the bed.

He held his injured side and slumped against the headboard. "I could eat an entire cow."

She tugged him forward a few inches and stuffed a pillow behind his back, noting the perspiration that dampened his brow and steeling herself against the gaze that never wavered from her face. "How about some nice beef broth?"

He grimaced. "I'd prefer steak."

"Let's see how you handle liquids and soft foods first. I'll be right back." He appeared groggy enough that she wouldn't be surprised if he were asleep before she returned.

He wasn't. If anything, he was more alert and sitting up straighter.

Charley straddled the feet of the bed tray across his lap, careful not to bump his bandaged leg. "Think you can feed yourself?"

He eyed the bowl of broth and piece of toast with an expression of resigned disgust. "I'm not so weak I can't pick up a spoon."

"Good." Charley wasn't sure she could handle being close enough to feed him. She scooped up the towel holding the pottery shards and headed for the door. "Call me if you need anything. I'll return for the tray in a little while."

She heard the spoon thump against the wooden tray. "If you leave me to stare at these walls alone, I'm going to climb out of this bed and go find my clothes and some real food."

She whirled around, her free hand on her hip. "Are you *trying* to be difficult?"

He stuffed a spoonful of broth in his mouth, swallowed, and almost grinned. "No ma'am. Ask Hannah. It comes natural."

"*That* I can believe."

"So, are you going to keep me company while I suffer through this dishwater soup? Or am I going to have to get up and find my clothes?"

"It is *not* dishwater. It's good, hearty beef stock, and frankly, you wouldn't make it to the door on that leg. But since I don't want to have to pick your bloody carcass off the floor, I suppose I'm keeping you company." Sparring with him was excruciating and wonderful all at the same time. "I'll return after I dispose of this mess you made."

Charley scurried from the room. If she was going to face those penetrating gray eyes without letting her emotions betray her, she needed a chance to catch her breath and tighten the armor around her foolish heart.

She dumped the soggy dishcloth and pottery shards into an empty pail to deal with later and dried her shaking hands. How had she wound up in this situation? Doctoring the man who had learned to despise physicians because of her uncle's actions.

"Charley." Cooper's tone warned her he would make good on his threat to get up if she didn't return, but it also betrayed the weakness he was trying hide.

She returned to his room because it was impossible to stay away. She loved him and wanted to be near him despite the secret that set in her stomach like a sack of bricks.

"All right, I'm back." Trying with all her might to pretend it was an ordinary day with an ordinary patient, she perched on the edge of the leather couch and eyed the almost-empty bowl. "Would you like more?"

"No. Either I wasn't as hungry as I thought, or you laced the soup with some kind of potion. I'm getting sleepy." Cooper laid the spoon on the tray and wiped his mouth with a hand that shook slightly.

"I didn't lace the broth with anything. You lost a lot of blood, and it takes a while to refill a big man like you." She stood and retrieved the tray.

"Don't go. I want to say something before I forget it." Food, sleepiness, or a combination of the two had soothed the ill humor out of his voice.

She kept her face passive, but it took effort. "Yes?"

Earnest gray eyes focused on her face. "I want to apologize."

Her fingers tightened around the edges of the tray.

"I let a couple of bad apples sour the whole barrel, but you're not like them. I think I realized that even before Alonzo was shot. But afterwards, I *knew* if I could get him here, you would help him."

His words robbed her knees of their starch, and she sank to the edge of the couch again. "But what if I hadn't been able to? What if Alonzo had died?"

Cooper's gaze held hers in its grip. "I would know you'd done everything within your power, and I wouldn't have blamed you." A worry line suddenly creased his forehead. "Alonzo is alive, right?"

She blinked then bristled. "Yes. He's fine." Her teeth bit off each word. "He left this morning. Upright and on his own two feet."

A cocky grin parted his lips. "Relax, Doc. I was only teasin' you."

Her unstable emotions were powerless to resist his good humor. "Keep it up, Mr. Knight, and I *will* put something in your food to make you sleep."

His face softened. "You were born to be a physician. I can see that now. But if you ever change your mind about…well, about me…us…" He studied the blanket over his legs. "All you have to do is say so."

The words hit her square in the stomach, robbing her of breath. Thankfully, he didn't see her impression of a stranded fish on a sandbar. "I…" She gulped and tried again. "I…" The stutter brought his eyes back to her.

She drew in another fortifying breath, but the slight movement breached her already shaky defenses and words spilled out before she could contain them. "The last several weeks, I've thought and rethought about why I went into this profession and whether or not I was going to stay in it."

Cooper watched her, all visible signs of his previous drowsiness gone.

It was unnerving, but since she'd started, she'd better finish. "The night you were shot, I finally realized that no matter what my reasons were for initially choosing to become a doctor—whether they were right or wrong—it's work I feel in my soul that God has called me to do. And He hasn't rescinded that calling. So, if the choice is between you and being a doctor…" She shook her head and willed the burning behind her eyes not to melt into tears. "I'm sorry."

During that first long sleepless night of keeping vigil over her two gun-shot patients, she'd dumped everything at God's feet and gave Him control to sort it all out without her interference. And when Ma had taken over the next morning, Charley had gotten her first peaceful, unbroken sleep since finding out what Uncle Eddy had done. Unfortunately, she'd picked the problem up later that afternoon and started wrestling it all over again.

Cooper's brows knotted. "Who said anything about a choice?"

It was her turn to frown in confusion. He *hadn't* said it in so many words, but she'd assumed he'd get around to it sooner or later. Leonard certainly had.

Cooper shook his head deliberately. "I might have been uncomfortable with your profession, but I never said anything about you giving it up if we started...well, courting."

~

Sleep tickled the edges of his brain, but the surprise widening Charley's eyes pushed it aside and made the pain in his side and leg a mere annoyance.

"You mean you weren't expecting me to give up being a doctor for marr..." She swallowed hard. "I mean, you?"

"No." The thought had crossed his mind, but he'd abandoned it. Charley was a doctor. He wouldn't change that now if he could. "Why would you think that?"

The question had been rather rhetorical, but the expression that flicked across her face before she glanced down at her hands said there was an answer to it. And something told him it was an answer he needed to hear. And an answer she needed to explain. "Why *did* you think that, Charley?"

He watched her struggle with whether or not to answer and ached for whatever caused her turmoil. Yet, at the same time, he was pleased she wasn't hiding it behind that hated mask of composure.

Finally, she spoke. "Because...Leonard expected me to give up doctoring for him."

Jealousy roared through him hotter than the pain in his ribs and leg. "Who is Leonard?"

"A physician. Back in St. Louis. He was nice, and I thought we had a lot in common. But when he asked me to marry him, he made it clear there was room for only one physician in the family." Charley studied the floor. "And it wasn't me."

That Leonard-skunk had added another black mark against the whole race of medicine men, present company excluded. So, it was ridiculous to be jealous of the scoundrel. He should be thanking the man for his stupidity. Without which, Cooper would've never met

Charley. "Did you love him?"

She shrugged without raising her head. "At the time I thought I did. Just like I thought he loved me."

"A man who truly loved you would not ask you to give up what you loved." Not even if he wasn't entirely comfortable with it.

The vulnerability he'd seen on her face that day at his house after Martin was injured returned in full force. "He wouldn't?"

"He most certainly would not." Cooper held out his hand, pleased when she slid off the brown settee to land on her knees at the side of his bed.

Instead of taking her hand, though, which had been his original intent, his fingers cupped her cheek. How was it possible to feel ten feet tall when he was sitting in bed in a nightshirt with bullet holes through his hide and a blanket lying across his lap like an elderly invalid?

Charley looked slightly dazed, and her hand crept up to curl around his wrist.

His eyes fastened on her lips, and the desire to taste them demanded satisfaction. He leaned forward, anticipating the moment.

A streak of fire shot through his ribs. "Ouch!" He grabbed at the crease in his side that he'd almost forgotten about.

Charley shot to her feet. "Are you trying to make yourself bleed again?" Her hands flew to the buttons on his nightshirt.

Her imperious bluster didn't quite disguise a tremor in her voice, so Cooper didn't let it or the pain in his side and leg deter him from his objective. "No. I'm trying to kiss you." He couldn't be sure if it was his words or his hand on her waist that put an end to her fussing, but he took advantage of it and gently tugged until she perched on the edge of the bed, her eyes wide and unblinking.

Cooper's hand slid past the curve of her cheek and guided her face to his, but he paused a hairsbreadth away from her lips, asking permission. When her lashes shuttered her pretty green eyes, he closed the distance. His body protested the movement, but he was too busy to care. The kiss was everything he'd dreamed it would be and more. Her lips were exquisitely soft, and she smelled of flowers and soap and medical potions.

He smiled against her mouth. Her fragrance was as complicated as the lady herself. And he needed to stop kissing her while he could. Even if he didn't want to. *Especially* because he didn't want to.

Her eyes drifted open when he pulled away, and for several heartbeats, they stared at each other. The self-possessed physician who'd coolly shut the door in his face after saying she couldn't be distracted by him was gone. In her place trembled a butterfly-fragile woman clearly uncertain whether to take flight or lean in for another kiss.

Words left Cooper's throat before he had time to think them through. "I can't get down on one knee because a certain sawbones we both know would have a conniption fit. But Charley?" He gathered both her hands in his. "Would you marry me?"

Maybe it was too quick to ask such a question, but since it had finally made it through his thick head that he loved her, and since he'd come uncomfortably close to dying, why should he wait?

Another second passed without a sign that she'd heard him, then her face went white. "I can't."

The gash on his side was barely noticeable when he wasn't breathing. "What do you mean you can't?"

She yanked her hands free and retreated until the back of her knees hit the leather couch. "I have to tell you something. Something that will make you change your mind about me." Her hands twisted together in an uncharacteristically nervous action and contrasted sharply with the stillness of her pale face.

His heart winced with every twisting, wringing movement. "I won't change my mind."

"You haven't heard what I have to say yet."

"Then spit it out and get it over with. Whatever it is can't be that bad." The throbbing in his leg flared, unintentionally roughening his tone.

What had caused this abrupt about-face? One second, she was kissing him back. The next? She looked like she was about to deliver a fatal diagnosis to an ill patient.

If he weren't already in pain, he'd kick himself for jumping the gun. Whatever was in that medicine bottle had muddled his brain. He should have waited until he was on his feet to have this conversation. Something was wrong, but he couldn't think clearly enough to figure it out.

The burn in his thigh intensified.

Cooper sucked air, but even in the rising flood of agony, he couldn't miss the transformation from fickle female to probing physician.

"I shouldn't have let you stay up so long. You're in pain." Charley briskly poured another spoonful of bitter medicine and efficiently poured it down his gullet, ignoring his weak protest. "Here. Let me help you lie down so you can rest." Her hands were gently relentless, and she eased him onto his back.

Cooper struggled against the sleep that offered blissful oblivion to the gnawing pain. "Wait. You can't leave me hanging."

"While you're under my care, I'd prefer you at least tolerated me." Her smile was sad. "When you can stand on your own two feet again, I'll tell you whatever you want to know."

The first half of her statement made no sense, so he hung on to the last part. "Promise?" He couldn't keep his eyes open. "Promise?" He forced himself to stay awake until he heard her reply.

"I promise, Cooper."

He slid into the black relief of oblivion, unsure if she'd answered or if he'd only dreamed it.

XXII

Cooper unfolded the weekly newspaper, and its crisp sheets rustled softly. The six pages wouldn't distract him for long, but he was grateful Benji had been willing to fetch him a copy before he and Hannah went shopping. The house was too quiet without his sister's cheerful bustle and Benji and Digger's rambunctious energy, but they'd played nursemaid to him long enough. He loved his sister and nephew with all his heart, but they'd all needed a break from each other. He was sick of being corralled in their tiny house and tired of being nagged if he took more than two steps without that bothersome crutch under his arm.

In the weeks since he'd been shot, he'd learned that recuperating was worse than the initial injury. In fact, the resulting boredom might well be fatal if he didn't escape soon. Charley had all but promised to give him permission to lose the crutch when she dropped by later, but if she didn't, he was going to bust it in two like he'd done with that rotten ladder and ride back to his own place, permission or no permission. His leg was almost healed and only twinged a little when he put his weight on it. He had a ranch to run, and he couldn't keep doing it long distance. He was leaving town after he took care of one last thing—Charley.

It was long past time the stubborn woman explained why she'd said she couldn't marry him. And long past time he kissed her again. Ever since their first kiss and his proposal of marriage, he hadn't managed two minutes alone with her. Ma, or Hannah, or Benji, or even Martin and Lyle were somehow always underfoot when Charley was anywhere in the vicinity. Trying to get a private word with her lately was like trying to lasso a butterfly. She was avoiding him again, but he didn't know why. And the not knowing was worse than his forced inactivity. If Charley hadn't shown up by the time Hannah returned from the general store, he'd march himself over to the doc's house and settle the matter once and for all. Even if he had to kidnap her to do so.

Cooper skimmed the first page of the newspaper and turned it when nothing caught his attention. He was halfway down the second page when a name leapt off the sheet and slammed into his chest. His entire frame stiffened, and he read the editorial from the beginning—the stark, black print burning into his brain.

We at the Puma Ridge Gazette consider it our solemn duty to inform our readers on the issues that affect our fair town, however, we withheld our opinion on the rather startling turn of events that happened here this spring. Like the majority of Puma Ridge's citizens, our initial reaction to the arrival of the new doctor was one of anger and disapproval, but then we remembered that haste and fools are irrevocably linked in the writings of wise old Solomon. Thus, we held our pen and kept our own counsel.

Our forbearance was not in vain. With each week that passed, we witnessed the skilled care and concern with which our new physician treated all her patients, from the lowliest hound to Puma Ridge's highest official. Despite the remarkable detail that our pretty physician wore skirts rather than trousers, a circumstance that continues to unduly influence the remaining doubters, this writer soon came to the conclusion that Heaven was smiling on Puma Ridge the day Doctor Charlotte Adams replied to Mayor Hennessey's advertisement.

The absence of fresh graves behind the church house in the aftermath of the recent illness that plagued our town, and the speedy recovery of the men wounded in the violent stage holdup should be ample testimony to Dr. Adams' skill. If further proof of her experience and training is needed, however, call on our office. We will be happy to share the correspondence we received from the physicians Dr. Adams trained and worked under and the patients she served in St. Louis. Without fail, they all praised her kindness, compassion, and competence and expressed their unhappiness at losing her to the west.

Through this correspondence, we also learned that Dr. Adams has followed in the steps of her maternal uncle. Dr. Edmond Musgrove was a highly respected physician in eastern Missouri, and beneath his tutelage, Charlotte Adams bravely set her feet on the course that led her to us. Dr. Musgrove has since gone to his eternal reward, but Dr. Adams is a credit to his memory. We are happy to be able to announce that we heartily endorse Puma Ridge's newest physician. Dr. Charley, welcome to town.

The edges of the paper crumpled beneath Cooper's grip. No matter how many times he reread the paragraph, the name remained unchanged.

Dr. Edmund Musgrove.

He closed his eyes, but the insidious, incriminating words would not be blocked out. *Dr. Adams' uncle. A highly respected physician. A credit to his memory.* Cooper smashed the news sheets between his hands and flung them to the floor. He had no such respect for the villain whose ineptitude had led to the death of his best friend.

Images of Van's smile and the echo of his laughter filled Cooper's mind. After the death of his parents and the struggle to provide for Hannah and himself, Cooper had nearly become too serious for his own good, but Captain Vandever had shown Cooper how to relax and have fun despite their hard and dangerous jobs. He'd also demonstrated to Cooper and the rest of his men that Christianity wasn't merely a title or a one-time experience but something to live out joyously every day. The man could have more fun than anyone Cooper had ever met, yet he was the most respected and dedicated soldier in the entire fort.

Anger and renewed grief tightened their iron bands around Cooper's chest until he couldn't breathe. The life of Captain Vandever, one of the best men he'd ever known, cut short by one of the worst men he'd ever met.

Dr. Edmund Musgrove. Charley's *uncle.*

~

"Charley!" Hannah hurried out of the general store, a cloth-covered basket swinging from her arm. "If you care anything for my sanity, you'll send Cooper home to his ranch. I love my brother, but he's wearing out my floors with his pacing and my ears with his grumbling."

Charley summoned a grin. "I apologize for the delay. I had to stitch up a nasty cut this morning, but I'm on my way to your place now. If his wounds look as good as they did yesterday, I'll send our recalcitrant patient home to torment Martin and Lyle."

"Thank you! I am in your debt." Hannah laughed and hugged her.

Charley returned the squeeze then quickly pulled away. "I'd best get over there. I'll see you later." She hurried off before the sweet woman could witness the collapse of her smile.

The day Cooper had been given a crutch, he'd moved to Hannah's house, allowing Ma to return to her own bed at night while staying close enough for Charley to keep daily progress of his healing. She'd had a fight on her hands to keep him from doing too much too soon, but his injuries had healed rapidly, and his leg grew stronger each day. She could have released him yesterday, but she'd delayed the inevitable like the coward she was.

Dread pooled in her stomach with each step that carried her closer to Cooper. He'd focused his attention on getting well with such single-minded determination, she was convinced if he ever decided to fly, he would accomplish it one way or another. But he didn't want something that simple. His sights were firmly focused on something far more difficult—the explanation for her refusal that she'd promised him in a moment of stupid, unthinking emotion.

She paused on Hannah's doorstep and sucked in a fortifying breath. It was futile and wrong to hope that Cooper had experienced an overnight setback to his healing. Which meant it was time to give him permission to return to a moderated version of his regular activities. And time to give him the explanation he deserved. Unfortunately, she couldn't come up with a single, coherent beginning. How did a woman go about telling the man she loved that his best friend had died at the hands of her uncle? There was no way to soften that kind of blow and little hope of ever recovering from it. All she could do was just get it over with.

Gathering the remnants of her tattered courage, Charley tapped lightly on Hannah's front door. When Cooper didn't answer, she slipped inside and found him dozing in the front room's cushioned easy chair. The hardheaded man had argued daily that he was better, but he still tired easily. If there was the least possibility of him cooperating, Charley would keep him confined to Hannah's house for another week. But if she tried, she'd have a mutiny on her hands. She would simply have to trust Martin to keep his boss from overdoing it when he returned to the ranch.

It made her heart ache to look at him and know he would hate her before long, but she looked anyway. Sunshine streamed through the window pane, highlighting the reddish tint in his hair. He was so handsome. Even when his features were tight and lined with a scowl.

Her medical training elbowed aside her foolish longings. Why was he scowling so fiercely in his sleep? Had he been lying about how much pain he still experienced? Or had she not been careful enough and infection had finally set in? Charley lowered her bag to the rug and dropped to her knees beside him to unpin the split trouser leg that allowed her access to the bandage wrapped around his thigh.

"What are you doing?" Cooper jerked upright, his voice rough from sleep.

Charley shot him a frown but continued unwrapping the bandage. "Sit still. You are *the most* difficult patient." She examined the fresh, puckered scar, feeling for heat that would indicate infection.

Some of her tension eased when she found none, and she rewrapped it in a fresh bandage, refusing to acknowledge the tingle in her hands each time her fingers brushed his skin. As often as she'd treated and bandaged his healing wounds, she should be immune to the sensation by now.

"Well?" He watched her, his scowl firmly in place. "I can see for myself that it's better."

"I don't know *how*, given the way you refuse to stay off of it, but it's healing almost as fast as your side has." Charley stood, nervous energy making it impossible to remain immobile. "I'll send you home with some clean bandages. Keep it wrapped for a few more days to protect the wound and to give it some support for walking and riding. Both injuries will remain tender for a few more weeks, so please remember to take things easy until they're fully healed."

Cooper brushed aside her advice. "Am I done with the crutch?"

He sounded odd, but maybe that was simply because she was

hearing him through the roar of her own guilty conscience. "Yes—not that you've been all that diligent about using it anyway."

The storm clouds in his gray eyes weren't easing her anxiety one bit. She could almost imagine he already knew what she needed to confess.

Cooper rose from the chair with an ease that denied he was still recovering from two gunshot wounds. "What do I owe you?"

She flinched at the hard edge in the question. "You don't owe me anything, Cooper."

"That's not how you run a business, Doctor Adams." He dug in his pocket and pulled out several coins. "Will ten dollars cover my bill?"

It would more than cover her normal fee, but she'd rather have a barn full of noisy chickens than the hard cash that was being offered to her so coldly. "You don't owe me anything, Mr. Knight."

His jaw tightened, and he held out the coins. The mulish set to his face said he would wait all day if need be.

Charley reluctantly stretched out her hand, and the coins clinked into her palm.

He withdrew without his fingers brushing against hers. "Now that I've paid you, I'm no longer your patient." His icy gaze froze her in place. "You owe me an explanation, Doctor Adams."

"A...about what?" Charley's heart stuttered worse than her tongue.

Heat melted the ice and nearly singed her. Cooper snatched something off the floor and thrust it at her. "Stop it! I know who you are."

Her flailing, numb fingers managed to grasp the wrinkled page before it fell to the floor again. "What do you mean?" How could he possibly know?

"You could have at least had the decency to tell me the truth before I had to read it in the paper." He spat the accusation at her.

"I don't know what you're talking about." She glanced at the newspaper in confusion.

And couldn't wrench her horrified gaze away from the awful words that marched across the page.

Her knees buckled. She sagged into the chair Cooper had abandoned and read the betraying editorial. If Mr. Farnsworth hadn't named her uncle, she would've been pleased at the endorsement. But now… Now, the flattering editorial might well destroy her entire practice in Puma Ridge like it had just destroyed any chance of a future with Cooper.

"It's true, isn't it? I can see it on your face."

She looked up and immediately wished she hadn't. The hard set of Cooper's features, his inflexible tone, and the ice in his gray eyes pierced her like a dozen scalpels. "I didn't know, Cooper. I didn't know my Uncle Eddy was the one who…" Even now she couldn't speak the ugly truth. "Not until you said his name the day Martin was injured."

Cooper glowered at her, unmoving, unblinking, his expression harder than the granite that jutted out of the Black Hills.

She opened her mouth then shut it. What was there to explain? The facts were all too clearly piled up between them. She rose from the chair and reached trembling fingers to touch his arm, a mute plea all she could manage.

He recoiled at her touch.

Charley hunched her shoulders at the pain that ripped through her.

Cooper whipped his hat off the peg by the door and strode out of the house with barely a limp—the silent closing of the door ten times worse than an impassioned slam.

She stared at the motionless door, willing him to walk back through it. But he was gone.

What remained of her heart shattered, and she curled around the aching hole it had left behind. Cooper was gone. She'd lost him. She'd known she would. She just hadn't realized how excruciating it would be. Her eyes burned but remained dry. Not even tears could reach this pain.

Charley pushed herself upright. She had to get home before Hannah found her like this and began to ask questions. In a dazed panic, she grabbed her bag and hurried home, slipping through alleys and side streets to avoid meeting anyone. When she reached her own parlor, she collapsed into a chair. Medicine had given her such fulfillment, but today it had robbed her of something so infinitely precious she hadn't fully grasped its immense value until it was gone.

The light had faded from the sky before she blindly made her way to her bed and crumpled onto it, turning her back on the golden feline who brought a fresh wave of grief when she jumped up to curl at Charley's feet. Each dark hour crept past while she stared at the ceiling and tried to pray, but the words remained incoherent until daylight filtered through the thin curtains once more.

"Father God. Help me." The sob rasped past Charley's tight, dry throat, startling Pockets awake.

Thirty more minutes ticked by. No special cure appeared out of the blue. The pain didn't disappear. But a single ounce of strength seeped into her weary soul, and Charley stiffly slid off the bed. She would rather endure a week in a rat-filled closet than suffer another night of such anguish, reliving every second spent in Cooper's company, and realizing afresh what she'd lost.

Dry eyed and listless, she changed into a clean dress, washed her face, and brushed her hair before feeding Pockets and wandering outside.

Hiram came out of the barn with the feed bucket but stopped when he saw her petting the small goat. "You don't look so good, Dr. Charley."

Even her pretend smiles were broken, and she only managed a half-hearted lift of her shoulders.

"Mr. Knight's not doing worse, is he?"

She shook her head. "No. He won't be needing me anymore." Her voice cracked.

"Ah." Hiram leaned his back against the fence but didn't say anything further.

A curious hen scurried over, and Hiram dug a handful of cracked corn out of the bucket and tossed it on the ground. The rest of the flock rushed over, and he tossed out more. Then in silence, he and Charley watched the chickens eat.

The man's quiet company was a drop of balm on Charley's sore heart. "Thanks for being a friend, Hiram."

"It's easy to be a friend to you, Doc. You gave me a reason to get up in the mornings, again. I don't know what's wrong with Mr. Knight now, but he'll come around. You wait and see."

She swallowed her emotions back into her chest and shook her head. "I'm afraid not. There's a person in my past he can't get over."

Hiram scattered another handful of corn for the clucking, hungry fowl at their feet. "You were right about me needing someone bigger than myself to deal with my problems. My feeble attempts to deal with them only landed me flat on my face. I've got a long way to go, but I'm not doing it alone anymore. God is walking with me this time—or maybe it's me walking with Him now—and He's given me people like you and Mr. Knight to encourage me."

Charley leaned over and stroked the soft-looking feathers of a particularly brave hen investigating the ground between Charley's feet for stray kernels. "Mr. Knight encouraged you?"

Hiram laughed. A rusty but happy sound. "Yes. In his own way, he encouraged me to stay on the straight and narrow this time." The older man's demeanor hinted there was more to the story, but he continued without telling it. "Anyway, I'd like to return the favor in some small way." His voice turned tentative. "Would you mind if I talk to Him," he jabbed a crooked thumb toward the cloud-studded expanse of blue above their heads, "About you and Mr. Knight?"

Charley patted Hiram's arm. "I would greatly appreciate it. Thank you." Her eyes prickled, and she hurried toward the house to hide the tears she couldn't stop. Who would've ever thought that the grimy man she'd pitied would be the one to reach her hurting heart with his simple kindness?

XXIII

Somewhere between the time Charley had ridden into town on his stagecoach and his waking up with two bullet holes in his sorry hide, Cooper had downright lost his mind. In his pain-confused state, he'd proposed to a *doctor*. And not just any doctor, but the niece of the man he hated most in this world and a murderer.

Whosoever hateth his brother is a murderer.

Cooper swung his axe, splitting the log down the center. A jolt of pain radiated through his side and down his leg, dulling the satisfaction he should have felt at the clean, even split of the wood. He refused to rub his sore leg, though. Every time it ached, he thought of the woman who'd patched him up. Why hadn't she admitted who her uncle was before he'd made a fool of himself?

Two more swift blows turned the halved log into four uniform chunks of wood, ready for the woodstove come wintertime. He tossed them on top of the growing pile before setting up another log. Sweat dripped into his eyes, but he swiped it away with his sleeve and continued to swing the axe with deadly accurate blows. The stack of split wood grew with each quartered wedge he flung atop it.

"Hey, Boss. Don't you think you ought to give yourself a rest?"

The log split cleanly. "I'm *fine*." He'd sure like to find out who'd given Martin permission to act like an old mother hen.

"You keep workin' like that and you're gonna wind up bustin' somethin' wide open." Martin paused and cocked his head, a sly grin creasing his face. "Or are you're huntin' an excuse to visit the good doctor?"

"Why don't you mind your own business." Cooper sank the axe blade into the top of a log before stomping toward the barn to escape his tormentor.

"Um hmm. I thought that was the wasp in your britches. What'd she do? Have the good sense to refuse to marry up with a cantankerous ol' bachelor?"

Cooper spun on his heel, right into the path of his nosy friend. "How did you know I asked—" He slammed his betraying mouth shut.

Martin smirked. "I ain't blind. You been stormin' around worse than a cyclone since you got back. I naturally concluded it was heart trouble."

Cooper clenched his fists and glared at his old friend. "If she'd been honest with me about who her family was, I'd never have thought about asking her in the first place."

Martin's knowing grin flattened. "What's her family got to do with anything?"

The urge to hit something returned. Cooped stomped back to the wood pile, picked up the axe again, and cracked another log wide open, letting the words spill out of his festering hurt. "I mentioned once about an Army sawbones who killed a friend of mine."

Martin nodded, standing well out of range of the swinging blade.

"He happens to have been Miss Adams' uncle." The sharp blade bounced off a knot in the center of the log.

"So?"

Cooper frowned and aimed the axe to the side of the knot but only succeeded in splintering a small uneven piece off the side of the log.

He kicked the remainder of the log over and rolled it out of his way. The knot was too hard to crack with an axe. He'd have to use a wedge and splitting maul on it. "*So*, I hated that man. He's a murderer. I'm not about to marry his niece."

The outburst didn't seem to faze Martin. "The Good Book says if you hate someone, *you're* a murderer. How are you better than him?"

The question bit into Cooper's soul far more effectively than his axe blade had on the knotty piece of wood. "It's not the same."

"In God's eyes it is. Was Miss Adams there when your friend died?" Martin raised one bushy, salt-and-pepper eyebrow.

Cooper's jaw clenched. "No, but—"

"You're more knotheaded than that stump you're whackin' on. You're blaming Miss Adams for the sin of a dead man. A sin that, in God's eyes, you're guilty of, too."

The truth punched Cooper in the chest again. And it hurt. His jaw loosened, and he exhaled roughly. "You don't pull any punches, old man."

"I call things like I see 'em. And I ain't old. I can outwork you any day of the week. It'd sure be nice if you got over your past and on with your future, though. You were a whole lot easier to be around when you allowed Dr. Charley to sweeten your disposition."

Martin's convicting wisdom was as impossible to ignore as the expression on Charley's face before Cooper had stormed out of Hannah's that awful day. There'd been no mask to hide her feelings then. He'd read the stark pain and shattered hope in her eyes as easily as he'd read that wretched newspaper. But he'd been more concerned with his own wounded, snarling heart and had utterly ignored her hurt.

He sank onto another upturned log and dropped his head into his hands. "I'm a fool."

A snort greeted his mumbled statement. "You won't get any argument from me, but that's beside the point. What are you going to *do* about it?"

Cooper raised his head, his forearms resting against his knees. "I don't know yet. I guess I need to straighten a few things out with God first."

"That'd be a good place to start." All teasing humor vanished from Martin's voice. "I'm heading out with Lyle to check on the cattle in the south pasture." The older man gripped Cooper's shoulder hard before striding away.

Cooper remained where he was until the two men rode away from the barn and out of sight. His leg complained when he rose and walked toward the house, but it didn't hurt anywhere near like his heart did. He sat in his chair in the dusty front room, picked up his

Bible, and flipped through the pages. Seconds later, he found the verse that had crossed his mind earlier. The truth stared up at him in black and white from First John 3:15.

Whosoever hateth his brother is a murderer.

Cooper leaned forward, elbows on his knees, head bowed. "Father, I claim to be your child, yet I've allowed hate to fester in my heart and drive me away from you and others. Your word says I'm as guilty of murder as Dr. Musgrove." The confession cleared the soot from his soul, allowing him to see clearly for the first time in ages. "What Dr. Musgrove did was wrong, but he didn't realize what he was doing that day." He swallowed hard, tears burning his throat. "Help me to forgive him, and forgive me for hating him."

A weight he hadn't realized he'd been carrying, lifted away on the wings of his prayer.

He inhaled deeply. "Father, if it's not too late, if I haven't destroyed my last bridge with Charley, would you please give her the grace to forgive me and give me a second chance?"

A sweet peace and sense of coming home spread through Cooper's soul. He settled back into the chair and turned to the first of the short epistle and read all five chapters, stopping often to pray over what he read. When he laid his Bible aside and stood, he felt lighter than he had in years. The most important relationship in his life was repaired, and it was time to work on the second most important.

Unfortunately, his meeting Charley came with no guarantee of a warm or welcoming reception. In fact, he wouldn't be at all surprised if she tossed him out on his ear. Or more precisely, greeted him with an unbreachable wall of polite, cold indifference. But he had to try.

He glanced at the clock on the mantle over the fireplace. If he left in the next five minutes, he could reach her house before sundown and find out for sure. And if he had to lay siege to her defenses, he would.

But when he dismounted at the neat little blue house, Hiram walked around the side of it and coolly informed him that Dr. Charley had gone.

"What do you mean she's gone?"

"What do you think it means?" Hiram's old eyes were shrewd and assessing.

"Is she coming back?" Cooper sidestepped the overall-clad man with dirt-stained knees, intending to enter the house and check for himself.

Hiram was surprisingly quick for his age, however, and blocked him, arms crossed tightly. "You once told me that if I did anything to hurt Miss Adams, we were going to have an uncomfortable discussion." Accusing eyes pinned him in place. "You remember?"

Cooper nodded cautiously. "I do."

"But you're the one that hurt her, aren't you?"

Cooper grimaced. Humble pie was bitter and didn't go down easy.

He swallowed it anyway. "Yes."

Hiram's scowl was fierce. "What are you going to do to fix it?"

Cooper had the sudden urge to grin. Since when had Puma Ridge's former vagrant become Dr. Charley's avenging guardian? "I'm going to find her, tell her I was wrong, beg her forgiveness, pray she does, and ask her to marry me. Again."

Hiram's arms uncrossed. "You mean you already asked her once?"

Cooper scratched behind his ear. "Yep."

"Well, don't that beat all?" Hiram rubbed his chin and studied Cooper for a long minute. He must have found what he was looking for because he suddenly grinned. "What are you standing around here for? Go get her."

"I would, but I don't know where she is."

Twinkles danced in Hiram's clear eyes. "She rode the stage to Buffalo Gap a few days ago." He dug in his pocket, "But I got a telegram this afternoon saying she's returning tomorrow."

Cooper slapped Hiram on the shoulder. "I think my leg has had plenty of time to heal, and tomorrow sounds like a good time to return to my route."

Hiram laughed. "I kind of thought that might be your answer."

Cooper ignored the twinges in his leg and hustled to the stage station to speak to the manager about scheduling him for the next day's route. When that stage left tomorrow morning, he'd be holding the reins, or his name wasn't Cooper Knight.

~

Charley's temporary withdrawal to the railroad town of Buffalo Gap nearly turned into a full-fledged retreat all the way back to St.

Louis. But when she stepped inside the train depot to buy a ticket home, a cold, harsh truth halted her in her tracks. She was running away. Just like Uncle Eddy had done. Rather than stay and deal with the loss of his wife, he'd abandoned his friends, family, and the patients that depended on him and fled. But the consequences of that rash decision had been disastrous.

Charley stuffed her ticket money into her reticule and returned to her hotel room to take a long, hard look at herself. She might have temporarily fooled herself and successfully bluffed her way through disapproving medical students, professors, and wary patients, but she was a coward, too. One who ran and hid at the first sign of trouble. One who had, in fact, been running and hiding for a long time.

The unwelcome insight burned through her, and she sank to the edge of the thin hotel mattress with a groan. Building internal defenses had helped her survive medical school, but she'd remained firmly behind them ever since. When had she become so afraid of being hurt that she stopped forming real connections with people and held them at arm's length? How long had it been since she'd had an honest-to-goodness friend?

Ma had come close to breaking through that barrier, but Charley had subconsciously resisted letting that relationship progress past that of colleague. And Hannah…

Remorse bit deep. That sweet friendship was all due to Hannah's efforts, but Charley had held part of herself back and then ultimately pushed it away, too, fearing that it wouldn't last if things didn't work out with Cooper.

Cooper.

No matter when or how he'd found out about Uncle Eddy, he would have been hurt. But if she hadn't been such a coward maybe she could have softened the sting of reading it in the newspaper.

She dropped her face into her hands. "Father, I'm so sorry. Like Hiram, I tried to handle my troubles with my own strength, and it is nowhere near sufficient. I've made a complete mess of everything, and I don't know how to fix it. Please help me!" Tears flowed down her cheeks while she poured her hurting heart out to God. When the words and the tears dried up, she curled onto her side, succumbing to the sleep that had eluded her for too many nights.

It took two days of much-needed rest, a little shopping, and plenty of quiet time with the Lord before she gained the courage to do what she needed to do. After she'd mailed a long letter to her parents, she sent a telegram to Hiram. It was time to go home. But home was no longer St. Louis. For good or ill, a little Black Hills' town had sunk its roots deep into her heart, and it was calling her to return. In spite of what had happened, or maybe because of it, God still wanted her in Puma Ridge.

Living and working so near Cooper would be difficult, but she would trust God to give her the strength to handle it. Regardless of the pain of Cooper's rejection, she'd discovered that it wasn't her uncle that had called her to this job. Uncle Eddy was simply the impetus God had used to show her what He'd created her to do. She, Charlotte Adams, was an extension of God's hands to help hurting people.

Girding on her courage and begging her stomach to cooperate, she dressed in her traveling outfit, purchased a ticket to Puma Ridge, and boarded the stagecoach out of Buffalo Gap.

The summer day was stifling when she arrived in the small town where she would change coaches. Declining the offered noon meal, she carried a cup of water to a chair by an open window inside the station's waiting room. The shade and breeze made it a fraction cooler, and after draining the cup, she leaned her head against the wall and closed her eyes to wait for the last leg of her trip to begin. She wasn't looking forward to the hot, stuffy ride, but at least Cooper hadn't returned to his driving job. She wasn't ready to face him yet.

It was strange not to see him behind the reins, though. She missed hearing him call encouragement to the horses, missed seeing him handle the six-hitch team with effortless ease. However, his absence had made it easier to sneak away. Had he even realized she was gone?

"Stage leaves in five minutes." The station agent's warning jolted her out of the dangerous and depressing line of thought.

The young man she'd seen helping with the horses earlier poked his head through the door. "Can I load your bags for you, ma'am?"

"Yes, thank you, but I'll keep this one with me." Charley patted the leather satchel on the chair beside her.

Since losing her almost-chance with Cooper, she could begin to sympathize with the pain that Uncle Eddy must have experienced with the loss of his wife. The way her uncle had chosen to handle his grief was wrong, but she was going to remember the man he had been when he was young, fresh, happy, and idealistic. But from now on, she would be following in God's footsteps, not her uncle's.

The young man grabbed the larger bag at her feet. "They'll be loadin' passengers in a minute or two. Better hurry."

"I'll be there." She stood and shook her skirts out before following the young man into the hot sunshine. *Lord, whatever the future holds, give me the strength to face it with grace.*

Charley squinted in the bright afternoon light and angled for the open coach door. There weren't many passengers—she peered inside—and there was an opening on the back seat.

Thank you, Lord.

"Lady, you gonna get on my coach or not?"

XXIV

Every nerve and muscle in Charley's body froze.

The emotions she'd thought were under control *weren't*. Instead, they were playing tricks on her ears. Cooper had barked the same words at her the first time she'd met him. Only this time, instead of being gruff and impatient, his voice was warm, soft, and oh, so dear.

She tightened her grip on her bag and her unsteady emotions and attempted a pleasant but impassive expression when she turned to face the man who'd claimed her heart. With unerring accuracy, her eyes locked on Cooper, and her heart clenched so hard she flinched. She feared her raw feelings were on display for everyone who glanced her direction.

Cooper stepped off the boardwalk and stopped beside the front wheel. Beneath a thin layer of trail dust, he wore a white shirt and string tie with his dark brown trousers. He pushed the brim of his Sunday hat up, leaving his cleanshaven face free of shadow. He held her gaze for several excruciating seconds, then he stretched out his hand and wordlessly invited her to climb up to the driver's seat.

She hesitated, desperately trying to read his face.

"Well?" Cooper's smile was all the more beguiling for its slight tentativeness. "Make up your mind. I've got a schedule to keep."

Charley blinked. "I... You..." Her medical bag was a leaden

weight in her hand, reminding her of the obstacle between them. "Is it all right if I keep this with me?" She held it up, hating herself for reminding him of it yet needing to know where she stood with him.

But his expression told her nothing. He simply nodded. "I wouldn't expect you to go anywhere without it." Taking the bag from her unresisting hold, he set it up on the seat then lightly grasped her hand and guided her aboard.

Her ascent was more graceful than that first awkward time, and when he climbed up beside her, he gave her time to get settled and put her bag in the compartment beneath their feet before tipping his hat to the station agent and setting the horses in motion.

She'd forgotten how little room there was on the driver's seat, and Cooper's proximity wasn't helping what little composure she had left.

She pinned her focus to the horses below her. "I didn't know you'd returned to driving. Are you sure you're ready?"

"When I heard who the passenger was going to be on the return trip today, I came back to work early."

It took effort, but Charley kept her attention squarely on the team. She would not assume he was talking about her—there was no way he could've known when she was returning. *She* hadn't even known until right before she'd sent Hiram the telegram. Cooper had to be talking about someone else. She tried to recall the other passengers but failed. She'd been too involved in her own thoughts to notice who had boarded. Twisting around, she leaned over the side to look down at the coach windows.

Cooper grasped her arm. "Hey. Don't fall off and break your neck. What would we do without a doctor?"

His touch turned Charley's stomach into a frantic swarm of trapped moths.

She straightened and smoothed her skirt, distracting herself before she could blurt out her feelings. "Find another one I suppose?" Her attempted drollness fell pitifully flat.

"Impossible." Cooper's statement held no bite. In fact, it sounded almost caressing.

If she didn't look at him, she could almost imagine this was their first ride together and forget that crushing, icy anger when he'd confronted her with that betraying editorial. His current attitude might be confusing, but it was better than sullen silence or outright anger, so she would go along with it. "Who's your special passenger?"

"Don't you know?" The gentleness in Cooper's question, the brush of his arm against hers—she *really* didn't remember the seat being this narrow.

She'd changed her mind. Sullen silence or outright anger would be easier to handle. She'd prepared herself for that. But this... She didn't know how to handle it, and she didn't dare hope. Her heart was already miserable.

"It's you, Charley. I came to bring *you* home."

Charley couldn't have stopped herself from looking at him even if a bandit had been holding a gun to her head. The way he'd said her name...

Cooper's intense, gray gaze held hers, and unruly hope surged through her veins and into her pounding heart.

Remorse creased his face. "I accused your uncle of killing my friend, but I'm guilty of the same thing. I murdered your uncle in my heart over and over. Then when a merciful God offered me the opportunity of an exciting future with the man's wonderful niece if only I would forgive, I slammed the door in God's face and yours. I am so sorry I refused to forgive him, and even sorrier that I hurt you. Can you forgive me?"

Charley blinked away the prickle in her eyes. Cooper's humble apology added a level of attractiveness that had nothing to do with his physical looks and everything to do with his character. Her hand itched to take one of his, but they held the reins for six horses who steadily cantered down the road despite their driver's inattention. "Cooper, I understand. I should have told you the minute, the *second* I realized the connection between you and Uncle Eddy, but I delayed telling you because I was scared." Her voice fell to a whisper. "I knew I would lose you. That you would hate me."

"I don't hate you. Please forgive me." Gray eyes pleaded with hers.

"I already did." There had never been any other option. She loved him too much to do otherwise.

Cooper searched her eyes. "Thank you." He faced the road again, but he didn't relax or appear satisfied. His jaw muscles clenched, unclenched, and clenched again. "Was your trip to Buffalo Gap for medical reasons?"

"Um...no." She didn't want to admit she'd simply tucked tail and run.

"But you took your medical bag with you." His hands tensed around the reins.

She would have missed it if she hadn't been watching him so closely. The horses noticed it, too. They slowed then cocked their ears in confusion when Cooper clucked to them, urging them on.

She exhaled the stubborn hope that had bloomed inside her. "I never know when someone might need my services, so I keep it with me, even on a shopping trip."

Apology notwithstanding, Cooper apparently still had trouble with her profession. She would have to be content with clearing the air between them, and maybe she would be able to work in the same town with him—if she could ignore how terrible it felt to have him so close and yet so far.

"So, you weren't leaving?" His eyes were on her again.

Her breath snagged. "I, uh, thought about leaving—almost bought a train ticket, to be honest—but then I remembered that this is where God wants me to be. And here I'll stay until He says otherwise. So, I guess you'll have to put up with me a while longer."

He shook his head. "I don't want to put up with you. I want to start over."

Charley stopped breathing. There went that unruly hope again. Seizing any excuse to spring out of control.

"I don't want to start all the way over, though." Cooper's slow smile did wonderful things for his eyes. "Just from a certain part."

"What part?" Charley's voice squeaked.

Cooper set his foot against the brake and brought the team to a standstill.

"Hey, what's going on?" A passenger hollered out a coach window.

Charley wanted to know the answer to that same question. Preferably before her heart managed to beat through her ribcage.

"Keep your seats, folks. There's no trouble. I have a quick piece of business I need to take care of." Cooper wrapped the reins tightly around the brake handle and shifted to face Charley full on. "My leg is healed, thanks to your excellent doctoring, but I'm still not in a good position to get down on one knee. Nevertheless, I'd like to repeat a certain question."

He scooped Charley's clenched hands off her lap, and she quit breathing altogether.

Disregarding his orders, the passengers clambered out of the coach to stare up at them while Charley struggled to wake up from the dream.

Because it had to be a dream.

Cooper's fingers tightened around hers. "Dr. Charlotte Adams, I'm a hard-headed, stubborn old stagecoach driver, but I love you with all my heart. Will you marry me?"

Charley discovered she *did* have some air left in her lungs. Because it suddenly left in a rush. "You love me?"

"Well, of course I do." He suddenly squeezed his eyes shut then quickly reopened them. "I forgot to tell you that the first time I asked, didn't I?" He growled under his breath. "I should never have tackled such an important subject right after being shot." The tenderness in his eyes melted her heart. "Forgive me for not saying it in the first place. I love you. More than I can put into words—although I will spend the rest of my life trying. I would be honored if you would be my doctor-wife and spend the rest of *your* life loving me, putting up with me, and patching me up when I need it."

If this was a dream, Charley's heart was going to break all over again when she woke up. But the large, calloused hands holding hers didn't feel like a dream. They felt like heaven. "Do you mean it? Are you sure?"

"He'd better mean it, lady. He's holding up a whole stagecoach to ask you." An amused passenger piped up below them.

"The man has a point, 'lady.'" Warm gray eyes held her captive, and Charley never wanted to be free. "And at the risk of my reputation for being a driver who's never late, I'm willing to sit here until *you're* sure, because I've never been surer of anything in my life."

"Lady." She repeated the title softly.

Cooper's brow wrinkled, silently questioning her.

The corners of her mouth kicked up, and unrestrained happiness flooded her. "I like it when *you* call me Lady. I don't when he says it." She spoke softly and tilted her head to indicate the nosy passenger.

His grin was immediate, huge, and irresistible. "It's a good thing I'm the one asking you to marry me, then. And in case you've forgotten, you haven't answered my question, yet." His voice dropped and shook slightly. "Will you marry me?"

Hot moisture flooded her eyes, and she nodded. "Yes. My answer is yes. Because I love you with all my heart."

Cooper's solid arms surrounded her, and his lips descended to meet hers. His touch sent delicious sensations bursting through her, and something that sounded like applause filled her ears.

She sighed and melted against him. Real life was so much better than her dreams had prepared her for.

~

Cooper's cheek muscles were starting to ache by the time he guided the team into the yard of the swing station, but each time he glanced down at Charley tucked under his arm, his grin popped back into place.

Hank jogged over to open the coach door and direct the passengers where to go to refresh themselves. When he'd finished, he looked up at Charley and Cooper, and his eyes began to twinkle. "Well, now. I was gonna ask if you'd run into trouble that made you late, but from that 'possum grin, I'm thinkin' you've been doin' some sparkin' on company time."

Cooper wrapped the reins around the brake and dismounted the coach. "I'm not late, Hank." He turned and held his hands up to assist Charley to the ground.

Her cheeks were pinker than he'd ever seen them.

She rested her hands on his shoulders, and he grasped her around the waist, easily lifting her to the ground in front of him. What wasn't so easy was letting her go. The woman had said *yes*! She was going to be his.

"It's late when we're talking about *your* runs, Coop, but if you don't dawdle *too* much, you might make up a few minutes on the next stretch of road." Hank grinned widely and eyed the possessive arm Cooper slipped around Charley's waist.

"Hank, let me be the first to introduce you to the future Mrs. Knight." Cooper watched Charley's cheeks blush a shade deeper. But her green eyes glowed with such a sweet smile, he had to lean down and kiss her again.

Hank cut the kiss short with a hearty smack between Cooper's shoulder blades. "Congratulations! Can't say I'm surprised, and I'm sure happy for you, Coop." He reached for Charley's hand. "Ma'am,

I've worked with this fellow a long time, now." The hostler shook his head in mock sadness. "You have my deepest sympathies."

Charley giggled, and Hank cackled, dodging Cooper's irritated swipe.

"Tell you what, Coop. I've a new boy working for me, and he needs practice changing out a team, so why don't you take Miss Adams to the barn and show her that new foal of mine. I'll holler when we have the horses ready to go."

Cooper didn't miss Hank's sly wink. "That's a good idea."

He quickly led Charley through the barn doors and into a shadowy corner. Looping both arms around her waist, he pulled her close. "I didn't dream that you agreed to marry me, did I?"

Charley shyly slid her hands around his neck. "Not if I didn't dream you *asking* me."

His nose was nearly touching hers anyway, so it was the matter of a mere tilt of the head to kiss her. How was it possible that she tasted even better than the first time? A man could get used to this real fast.

An insistent thought made him lift his head. But not far. "When?"

Her eyes slid open, and he had to smile at the dazed blink she gave him. "When what?"

"When will you marry me?"

"Oh." Her lips curved in an irresistible smile that he couldn't help but return. "How about two months from now?"

His grin faded. "Two months? I was thinking next week."

She stood on tiptoe and pressed a too-quick kiss on his lips. "My parents' last letter said they want to come for a visit next month. If we scheduled the wedding for the end of their visit, it would give the three of you a chance to get to know each other before we married."

"Two months, huh?" How could he argue when she looked at him like that?

"Two short months." She punctuated the demand with another kiss. "It would also give me time to make a dress."

A man would be daft not to agree with the woman who looked at him with such love in her eyes. "Two months, then. And I'll be counting the days."

"So will I." She hugged him hard.

Yep. He was definitely going to enjoy getting used to this.

"Horses are ready, and the passengers are boarding, Coop. Better hurry or you're gonna be late." Hank stomped noisily into the barn.

Charley pulled away from Cooper with a jerk, but he caught her hand, preventing her from going too far. "Those horses better be ready to run, Hank, because I don't aim to be late. Hannah's planning a big supper for us."

His bride-to-be glanced up at him in surprise. "Hannah knows?"

Cooper chuckled. "Yep. She informed me that I'd be in serious hot water if I didn't bring you back with me."

A sweet smile curved her lips, tempting him to taste them again, Hank's throat clearing made him settle for tightening his arm around her waist while he led her from the barn. They hurried to the stagecoach, and Cooper lifted Charley to the seat and climbed up beside her.

"It was sure nice to see you again, Dr. Charley. I'm sorry you spent all that time in the barn looking for that new foal. Old age must be catchin' up with me." Hank scratched his head but didn't bother to hide his mischievous grin. "I turned that filly and her momma out to pasture yesterday."

Charley's cheeks flamed, and a laugh started in Cooper's belly and rumbled up his throat. "Thanks, Hank. I owe you one."

"You can return the favor by invitin' me to the wedding." The old troublemaker crossed his arms with a satisfied smirk.

"Done. See you next trip." Cooper threaded the reins between his fingers.

His wife-to-be wrapped her arm securely around his and smiled up at him. "Take me home, Coop."

A heady mix of relief, happiness, excitement, and anticipation swelled Cooper's chest and erupted in an ear-piercing whoop that set the horses in motion.

Dr. Charley Adams-soon-to-be-Knight was in for the ride of her life.

Epilogue

"If you don't stop woolgathering, you'll never finish." Forcing her thoughts back to the business at hand, Charley carefully inventoried and replenished the contents of her medical bag. The buggy accident at the edge of town earlier in the afternoon had caused a lot of excitement, but thankfully the injuries of all three people involved had proven superficial and everyone would heal fine.

She closed her bag, finally satisfied that everything was in order and ready for the next time she was called out—hopefully not this evening. The surprise she'd been planning for Cooper was ready, and she couldn't wait to see his face when she presented the gift.

A firm tap on her front door made her grimace in disappointment. It didn't sound frantic, but it meant her plans might have to change.

She hurried to open it. Unlike a banker, a doctor's hours were anytime of the day and night.

"Good evening, ma'am. You know of a good doc in this town?" The handsome man who was never far from her thoughts leaned against the doorjamb, eyeing her lazily.

Charley's grin was instant and huge, but she folded her hands across her work smock to keep from sliding them around his neck. "I know of *two* good doctors in Puma Ridge."

Cooper's frown didn't hide the twinkle that flashed in the smoky depths of his eyes. He took off his hat and plopped it on Charley's head. "In my opinion, there's only *one* good doctor in town, and that's you."

Charley smiled and tossed the hat on a nearby chair. How she loved this man—even if he *did* occasionally still struggle with trusting the medical profession as a whole. "He came highly recommended by Dr. Tidd, and so far, he's working out fine. There is plenty of business to keep both us *and* Ma busy, what with the new mine opening up and new settlers moving in nearly every week. And with the three of us working, we're not running ourselves to death. The townsfolk have certainly accepted him." A whole lot faster than they did her, but that was the way of the world, and she wasn't complaining. Out loud.

Cooper folded his arms over his chest. "It's not the townsfolk I'm concerned about. It's Hannah. Every time I go over there, that shyster's either coming or going from her place, and Benji's mentioned the man has eaten more than one meal with them. Can he not eat at the café like everybody else?"

Charley hadn't heard Cooper growl in months, but it was back in full force this evening.

She laid a hand on his crossed arms. "Dr. Richards is not a shyster. He's a very nice man, and I've never seen Hannah's eyes sparkle like they do when she talks about him."

"I don't think I can handle two sawbones in my family." The growl was closer to a whine now.

"That's Hannah's call to make. Not yours."

"All the same, the next time I see that shys…" He swallowed the word at Charley's warning glance, "*Dr. Richards*, I'm going to let him know in no uncertain terms that if he even *thinks* about hurting Hannah or Benjamin, he'll have to deal with me."

She chuckled wryly. "I think he already knows that. He winces a little every time your name is mentioned."

Cooper's mouth turned up in a pleased smirk. "Good. A little fear never hurt anyone."

She laughed then changed the subject. "Was there a particular reason you needed to see the doctor?" She loved Hannah and Benjamin, but she wanted to talk about what interested her most lately. Namely, the man standing a breath away.

Her slow, inquiring smile did the trick. Muscular arms uncrossed and firm hands circled her waist in one swift move, tugging her close.

Cooper lowered his head until his nose touched hers. "Mmm hmm. I needed to see the doc for this..." Angling his head, he caressed her lips in a delicious, leisurely kiss.

Friendly, familiar butterflies took flight inside her ribcage, and she wholeheartedly kissed him back.

When he lifted his head, it took her a second to regain her breath. "I," Charley cleared her throat, "I certainly hope you don't do that to any other doctor."

He rested his forehead against hers. "Nope. Only ones named Dr. Charlotte Knight. Have I mentioned what a nice name that is?"

Her big grin matched his. "You might have mentioned it once or twice. I'm growing rather partial to it myself."

"Good." He kissed her again.

Charley grinned a little smugly when it ended. This time, she wasn't the only one who was breathless.

A sharp, approving whistle recalled her attention to the fact they stood in full view of passersby. Jonesy didn't bother to hide the teasing smile on his face, but he did tip his hat respectfully before continuing down the street.

Charley hid her face in Cooper's shoulder. "I don't really want the public displays of affection from the petticoat physician to become fresh fodder for the barroom gossips."

Cooper walked her inside and toed the door shut behind him before taking her in his arms again. "I don't think Jonesy will talk about you in anything but the most respectful and polite way. Not after you saved his life by pulling that bad tooth."

"I wouldn't go so far as to say I saved his life..." She squinted, searching his face. "Did you threaten him like you threatened Oscar?"

"I didn't threaten anybody." His affronted air wasn't convincing. "We simply had a chat about not appearing at a lady's house in a drunken state after dark."

"Cooooop..." Charley's half-hearted protest choked off in a laugh at her husband's calm explanation and smug expression. "He was sick and in pain that night. And I *can* take care of myself, you know."

"Yep. But now you don't have to." Cooper's reply was matter-of-fact.

She wrapped her arms around his middle and hugged him hard enough to make him grunt a little. The man took his responsibility to protect his loved ones seriously, and she'd already figured out he had no intention of abandoning it. "I'm ready to head home, but first, I want to show you something." She grasped his hand to lead him toward the kitchen.

"Before we go…" He tightened his grip around her fingers and stopped her.

"Is something wrong?"

Cooper scratched behind his ear. "Not to speak of, but while we're in here, you'll probably want to take a look at this." He released her and pushed up his shirt sleeve to reveal a handkerchief wrapped around his forearm.

"Cooper Knight!" Dried blood darkened the haphazard bandage and smeared the skin on either end of it. "What did you do?" She tugged him over to the pump and basin and carefully soaked the handkerchief in cool water to soften the dried blood before attempting to unwrap it.

"I was working on a section of fence when the wire broke and snapped back at me." His explanation was calm, but Charley noticed he watched her face and avoided looking at his arm.

She unwound the wet cloth to reveal a deep gash across the top of his arm, halfway between elbow and wrist. "Why didn't you say something when you first showed up?"

Married a little over a month, and the man was already giving her gray hairs. He couldn't handle seeing other people's blood, but he ignored injuries to himself, considering them no more serious than a splinter.

"Because I had more important business to tend to. I hadn't been kissed all day."

If she weren't rather busy trying to clean the long laceration that would undoubtedly leave a scar, she'd be tempted to smack him. "I kissed you before I left the house this morning."

"That was hours ago." Cooper leaned in to steal another one, but she sluiced disinfectant over the wound. "Ouch! That burns." He hissed and jerked back.

"Remind me later that I'm supposed to feel sympathy for a man who wraps a dirty rag around a nasty cut and waits for hours to get it tended to. Now hold still. This cut is not going to get infected if I can help it." She wiped fresh blood away. "Once I get it thoroughly cleaned, it's going to need stitches."

"I was afraid you were gonna say that." He groaned and made the mistake of taking his eyes off her to glance at his arm.

He wobbled on his feet.

Charley grabbed him around the waist. "Whoa. Don't faint on me yet." She guided him to the long leather settee along the wall of her examination room.

Cooper sank onto the edge. "I'll be all right."

"Yes, you will, and I'm going to make sure of it." She lifted his legs onto the couch. "Lie down. This won't take but a minute, but it *will* sting."

"Somehow, I knew you'd say that, too, Doc." The grin didn't disguise the way his suntanned cheeks had paled by several shades.

Charley quickly gathered up the items she would need and pulled a stool up beside him. "Why didn't Martin drive you in? You could have passed out on the way here."

"He didn't know about it, and I was fine until a second ago. I was too busy thinking about you to worry about a little scratch."

"This is not a *scratch*, Cooper."

He didn't respond to her reprimand. One glimpse of the needle between her fingers, and his lashes fluttered shut.

She shook her head, worry dousing the twinge of amusement. "At least you won't feel this now." She set to work, and in short order, she'd sutured the wound and bandaged it.

Cooper stirred and sat up while she cleaned her instruments. "I'm ready as I'll ever be, Charley. Better get on with it."

She laughed at the grim determination on his face. "I'm already done, you big fraud." She dried her hands and crossed the room to him.

Cooper lifted his arm and studied the white bandage. "You're good, Doc. I didn't feel a thing." He reached to tug her down for another kiss.

Charley grinned but resisted his charming wink. "Be careful. You'll mess up my pretty stitching."

He stood and wrapped his arms around her waist—remarkably steady for a man who'd fainted less than fifteen minutes earlier. "If

I do, my clever, talented wife can stitch it up again."

"Brave words for a man who once claimed he'd never let a sawbones get close to him with anything sharp." She shook her head in mock disapproval.

He grinned and kissed her forehead. "Whoever said that was a fool. Are you ready to go home?"

She kept her arm around his waist. "Maybe we should stay here tonight." The other rooms in the house were systematically being turned into additional patient rooms, but none of them were currently in use.

"Nope. Now that I'm not leaking all over the place, I'm fine. Besides, I've got a surprise for you." His eyes sparkled, and he looked eager—like Benji and Digger on their way to stir up mischief. "Come on."

"Speaking of Digger... I almost forgot. Stay here, I'll be right back." Charley scurried to the kitchen and scooped a sleepy bundle from a blanket in the corner. Hiram had worn the poor thing out this afternoon while she'd been busy with the buggy accident. "Close your eyes, Cooper." She peered into the room to see if he'd followed her instructions. "Now hold out your arms..."

His eyes flew open, and he carefully cradled the soft, squirmy weight against his chest. The yellow fluffball of a puppy yawned, its long, pink tongue curling before reaching out to swipe Cooper across the chin.

He laughed. "What's this?"

"You gave Benji a dog and me a cat, yet you didn't have a pet of your own. It's time we remedied that."

"I have a ranch full of cows, horses, and chickens. I don't need another critter to look after." Cooper settled the puppy more comfortably against his chest and scratched behind the animal's velvety ears.

The dog wriggled, trying to get closer to Cooper's face by climbing his chest. Cooper dodged an exuberant tongue, a reluctant smile forming. "Where did you get this thing?"

Charley smiled, satisfied. Cooper was falling for the brown-eyed charmer as fast as she and Hiram had. "One of my patients has a sweetheart of a dog that recently had puppies. I traded my medical services for the pick of the litter."

Cooper wrestled the playful pup and tried to frown. "If you keep taking animals in payment, I'm going to have to buy more land, Doc. What's Pocket going to think about this intruder?"

"She didn't mind Digger after she got to know him, and she already rules everything in your barn, so I think these two will get along fine. Eventually." Charley rubbed the puppy's silky fur. "He's going to grow large enough to follow you around the ranch even if you're riding." The puppy had been weaned for barely a couple of weeks yet it was already bigger than Benji's dog. "Do you like him? Is it all right that I got him for you?"

Charley shivered at the heat in her husband's eyes and the warm, full smile that lit up his face.

"Yeah. I like him." He leaned over to drop a kiss on her lips. "I like him a lot. But not as much as I like you."

He kissed her again, longer this time, but then she felt him grin against her mouth. When he drew back, his smile was mischievous. "And now it's time for my surprise."

Shifting the dog into the crook of his uninjured arm, Cooper gestured for her to lead the way out the front door.

She grabbed her bag on her way. Outside, two horses waited patiently at the hitching post.

"What do you think?" Cooper stopped behind her, close enough that her shoulder brushed his chest.

His big horse nickered a soft welcome.

"About what?" If she'd known he wasn't picking her up in the wagon, she'd have waited on the puppy. Carrying the dog home on horseback would be a pain. Literally—thanks to his injured arm.

"Of your new mount. The wife of a rancher should have her own horse, especially a wife who wanders all over the countryside."

She blinked and focused on the smaller horse. "Oh. Coop." Charley sat her bag on the ground and held out her hand to the velvety soft muzzle that stretched to investigate it. "She's beautiful." The coal-black mare tickled Charley's palm with her lips. Charley ran her fingers up the horse's delicate face and brushed aside the thick forelock. "She has a white star."

"When your parents were here, I mentioned that I was looking for a suitable mount for you, and your father said that when you were a little girl you always thought black horses with white stars were the prettiest. It took longer than I thought it would, but I finally found a good one that fit the description."

"I can't believe he remembered that. I didn't until I saw her." Charley walked around the elegant equine. "She's gorgeous. I love her. What's her name?"

Cooper set the puppy down so it could investigate both horses, and he laid his good arm over Charley's shoulders. "She's doesn't have one yet, but I kind of thought she looked like a little lady."

Charley shook her head and kissed her husband's jaw while still stroking the silky black coat of the mare. "No. That's what you call *me* sometimes, and although she's pretty, she can't have that name."

He curled Charley into his chest, his fingers slid into her chignon, and he lowered his head.

She halted him with her hands on his chest. "Coop! Everyone can see us."

"If anybody has a problem with the doc kissing her husband, they can take it up with me." He stole a quick peck before retrieving her bag and tying it to her saddle. "So, what are you going to name her?"

Charley circled the mare again. "She's so elegant… I think I'll call her Duchess."

Cooper chuckled and picked up his puppy without debating her choice. He lifted the flap of a saddlebag and carefully stuffed the wiggling puppy inside.

She giggled when the little fellow immediately poked his head out and sniffed his new surroundings. "I wondered how we were going to get him home on horseback, but I should have guessed. You brought my kitten by way of your pocket… Hey, why don't you name him—"

"Uh uh." Cooper cut her off with a firm shake of his head. "You can name your critters Pockets and Duchess if you like, but I am *not* naming that poor hound Saddlebags. Other dogs will laugh at him."

"They will not." Charley giggled as Cooper helped her into her saddle. "What *do* you want to name him?"

Cooper looked over at the puppy and back at her. "I think I'll call him Buck."

The dog yipped twice.

Charley giggled. "That's not very imaginative."

He smiled up at her, squeezed her knee, and moved to pat the impatient pup's head. "He likes it. I like it." Shifting the saddlebags to ride in front of him where he could keep an eye and hand on the yellow puppy, he swung up onto his own horse. "Majority wins. His name's Buck. Now, are you ready to head home, Lady? Where I can kiss you as often as I want, for as long as I want, without having to worry about who's watching?"

Another delighted shiver raced up Charley's spine. Although they'd had a rocky beginning to their relationship, God had known what He was doing when He'd brought them together. And whatever the future held they would face it stronger together than they ever could have separately. Spending the evening alone with this wonderful man—even if he *was* terrible at naming pets—was just what the doctor ordered.

"Absolutely. Let's go home."

THE END

Author's Note:

Although Dr. Charlotte Adams and her story is a product of my imagination, her character is a composite of the pioneering women who braved ridicule and scorn to enter the male-dominated world of medicine and pave the way for others to follow. Believing that need would outweigh prejudice, many of these tough-minded women took their education and skills to the frontier towns and mining camps of the West.

Dr. Flora Hayward Stanford was the first female doctor in Deadwood, South Dakota. Flora was born in 1839 and educated at the Boston University School of Medicine. She opened her practice in Deadwood in 1888 and became well-respected there. She charged $2 - $3 for an office visit, and $3 - $6 for a house call.

Dr. Georgia Arbuckle Fix was born in Missouri around 1850 and graduated from the University of Omaha in 1883. She settled on her own forty acres of homestead land along the North Platte River in western Nebraska and offered her medical services to those in her community. By May 1889, it was reported of her in the *Gerring Courier* that "Under the care of Doctor Arbuckle Fix any person can be expected to be nearly raised from the dead." (Dr. Fix's experience of removing a spurred-cowhand's bad tooth sparked the idea for a similar situation for Charley.)

Dr. Susan Anderson was born in Indiana in 1870, and graduated from the University of Michigan in 1897. Although she suffered from tuberculosis, she established her medical practice in Cripple Creek, Colorado, and later Fraser, Colorado, saving many lives with her skill as a surgeon and general practitioner. In spite of her lifelong battle with tuberculosis, Dr. Susan lived to be 90 years old and was recognized by the staff of Denver's Colorado General Hospital as an "exceptional healer and the best diagnostician west of the divide." (Dr. Susan's experience with a one-year-old girl suffering from an advanced case of scurvy is another of the true-life stories I drew from while writing Charley's story.)

The remarkable lives of these and many other "Petticoat Physicians" can be found in the book, *The Doctor Who Wore Petticoats: Women Physicians of the Old West* by Chris Enss. It is a fascinating read.

Do you like contemporary inspirational romances?
Then check out Clari's Men of KWESTT series:
Some Enchanted Evening - Book 1
Heart and Soul - Book 2
Secret Love - Book 3
You're Nobody 'til Somebody Loves You - Book 4
Catch a Falling Star - Book 5
How Sweet It Is - Book 6

An avid reader by age seven, Clari loved to hang out at the public library, and the local bookstore staff knew her by name. Her favorite books ranged from Marguerite Henry's horse stories to Louis L'Amour's westerns and Grace Livingston Hill's romances. Her fascination with books and libraries continues, and Clari now works as a public librarian by day and a writer by night. You can visit Clari on her Facebook page or drop her an email at cdeesbooks@gmail.com.

CPSIA information can be obtained
at www.ICGtesting.com
Printed in the USA
BVHW061134140123
656278BV00013B/2304